Fiery young "Nell" Belden went to Thorndene Castle to escape a lover, not to find one...

She was bound by the strict conventions of England's Regency to a man she could never love; then bound by the ties of passion to a man she could never marry! For at Thorndene, she discovered a new and startling love, a love that was as intense as it was doomed...

THE PHANTOM LOVER

Also by Elizabeth Mansfield

MY LORD MURDERER
A VERY DUTIFUL DAUGHTER
REGENCY STING
A REGENCY MATCH
HER MAN OF AFFAIRS
DUEL OF HEARTS
A REGENCY CHARADE
THE FIFTH KISS
THE RELUCTANT FLIRT
THE FROST FAIR
THE COUNTERFEIT HUSBAND
HER HEART'S CAPTAIN
LOVE LESSONS
PASSING FANCIES
THE MAGNIFICENT MASQUERADE
A MARRIAGE OF INCONVENIENCE
A SPLENDID INDESCRETION
THE GRAND PASSION
A GRAND DECEPTION
THE ACCIDENTAL ROMANCE
THE BARTERED BRIDE
A PRIOR ENGAGEMENT
A CHRISTMAS KISS
A BRILLIANT MISMATCH
A REGENCY HOLIDAY
(with Monette Cummings, Sarah Eagle,
Judith Nelson, Martha Powers)

Elizabeth Mansfield

The Phantom Lover

JOVE BOOKS, NEW YORK

THE PHANTOM LOVER

A Jove Book / published by arrangement with
the author

PRINTING HISTORY
Berkley edition / March 1979
Third printing / September 1981
Jove edition / August 1986

ISBN: 0-515-08742-4

Jove Books are published by The Berkley Publishing Group,
200 Madison Avenue, New York, N.Y. 10016.
The name "JOVE" and the "J" logo
are trademarks belonging to Jove Publications, Inc.

PRINTED IN THE UNITED STATES OF AMERICA

10 9 8 7 6 5 4 3 2

Prologue

IF HE KEPT his gaze on the river and didn't look at the devastation on the banks at either side, he might almost believe it was a peaceful day. The cracking reports of thousands of guns and the boom of the cannon had momentarily ceased, and the smoke of battle was beginning to dissipate into a thin haze, not very different from what one would expect on any July afternoon in Spain. Captain Henry Thorne shifted in the saddle and let his eye roam over the valley of the Tagus stretched out before him. The Spanish valley had probably been lovely before the battle had ravaged the countryside, before the thousands of boots, the horses' hooves, the wheels and the cannon shells had uprooted the shrubs, burnt the grass and rutted the ground beyond recognition. There was not much left to cool the eye. Through the haze he could see splashes of red and blue dotting the ground. The sight caused him to groan. The losses in this battle were staggering. Sir Arthur had expressed to him the fear that the English would lose more than five thousand before the day had ended.

He turned away and urged his horse forward, trying to erase from his mind the sight of the battlefield. He tried to think of something else. The letter from England came into his mind. It was dated April 13, 1809, but it had not found its way into his hands until the day they had arrived here at Talavera, July 27th. It was from his aunt, Lady Sybil Thorne, telling him that his grandfather was quite ill—possibly dying—and that he was wanted urgently at home. He yearned to comply, to forget his duties, to return to that green and pleasant land that was his home, to hold his grandfather's hand in his. But he had not had a moment to think, or even to reread the letter that rested at this very moment in an inner pocket of his coat. He had not had time in which to decide whether his duty lay in sticking to his post on Sir Arthur's staff or in obeying the summons from his family. And he had no notion of what Sir Arthur's reaction would be should he ask for leave.

Since the moment the British had joined forces with the Spanish troops, Sir Arthur had kept his staff working night and day, trying to overcome the difficulties thrust on him by that obstinate fool, La Cuesta. The Spanish General, old, infirm and incompetent, had been wrangling and quarreling with Sir Arthur throughout the ten days of the march to Talavera. Then, when they'd faced the French Marshal, Claude Victor, and his troops (numbering over fifty thousand), the Spaniards had retreated in panic. Sir Arthur, although outnumbered two to one, had rallied his troops, and the thin red line had held against the massed French columns. For two days now, the line was holding. And at last there were signs that the French were beginning to withdraw. Sir Arthur had done it! Perhaps now, Parliament would recognize what Sir Arthur's staff had always known—that Sir

Arthur Wellesley was the military genius who would some day defeat Napoleon.

Sighing, Captain Thorne nudged his horse, and they continued to climb up the mountainside. Sir Arthur had sent him to reconnoiter. If the French withdrew, the British commander intended to advance on Madrid. But he knew that somewhere on the Peninsula Marshals Soult and Ney waited with perhaps as many as 200,000 men. The British position here was vulnerable, especially through the pass at Baños. And La Cuesta had already indicated that he would not defend the pass. Captain Thorne was on his way to assess the situation.

A burst of gunfire from somewhere behind him made him turn in his saddle. The action had begun again. But not before he made out the movement of a blue line moving, as hurriedly as armies can, to the southwest. The French retreat had begun.

Directly below him, a British platoon seemed to be in difficulty. They had just been hit with heavy cannon-fire, and the line had broken. The officer seemed to be trying to rally his men. As Captain Thorne watched, the officer reared in his saddle and toppled to the ground. Another volley of cannonfire obscured his view.

He could not bring himself to ride on. Without another thought, he wheeled his horse around and galloped swiftly down the slope. The line must not break. He would take over and quickly bring the men to order. The noise around him became deafening. Volleys of shots, explosions of cannonballs, shouts and cries of the men all became indistinguishable to him. He spurred his horse faster, but to his surprise the horse seemed suddenly to disappear from beneath him. He felt a searing pain as his body flew through the air. Then, nothing...

There was music, and suddenly he could see, through a sort of mist, the ballroom at the Mannings' town house. He was crossing the room toward Edwina, who was sitting beside her mother under a shimmering chandelier and smiling up at him beckoningly. But he couldn't seem to reach her. A pain in his leg slowed him considerably. But he smiled and made his way to her steadily, ignoring the pain as best he could. Lovely Edwina—he must reach her! He held out his arms, and she ran toward him, her eyes warm and welcoming. She lifted her arm and put her hand on his shoulder ...

A hand touched his shoulder. He opened his eyes. He found himself looking up at a darkened sky. A red-cheeked soldier with a mud-smeared nose was smiling down at him. "That's the way, sir," the man said. "You'll be all right, won't you?"

Captain Thorne tried to nod.

"No need to move. Easy does it. Anything you want? Water?"

Captain Thorne tried again to nod his head. A cool metal cup was placed against his parched lips, and he attempted to drink. Most of it ran down his cheek, but some of it found its way into his mouth. He tried to swallow but choked. The movement stirred an agonizing pain which seemed to start in his left leg and spread to all of his body. He winced and bit his lip. The soldier's hand patted his shoulder. "Best not to move," he said again. Captain Thorne heard no more.

The breeze was stirring the white window-curtains, but the room was hot. He looked around him. What room was this? It looked like the corner bedroom at Thorndene, in Cornwall, the bedroom they'd given him that first summer he'd stayed there—the summer his father had died. He was lying in the fourposter he hadn't seen since he was twelve. Grandfather had taken him to Cornwall, hoping the sun and the sea and the Cornwall air would help soothe the pain that had settled in both their chests. But the pain was not in his chest. It seemed to be in his leg! The curtains lifted higher as the door opened. He raised his head and saw through the haze that his grandfather was coming toward him. His spirit rose as he saw the old man smile at him, his eyes full of love. Grandfather drew up a chair at the side of the bed and set up the chessboard.

Henry lifted his hand to make the first move, but the effort seemed too great. Grandfather opened his mouth to speak, but he couldn't make out the words. The birds outside were singing loudly... too loudly...

He opened his eyes. It was bright daylight. He was still lying on the ground. The birds were singing somewhere above him. In the distance he could hear the rumble of an army on the move. He tried to lift his head, but the movement caused the pain again, and he lay back and stared at the sky. The blue was almost clear; only a thin haze remained. The battle must have ended long ago. Was he still lying where he'd fallen, he wondered? He turned his head to the side. Some distance from him, another red-clad soldier lay on the ground unmoving. Was he alive or dead?

Soon they'd come with a stretcher. The soldier who'd bent over him (was it last night?) must have left a marker. He'd be taken to hospital and then be sent back to England. He'd have leave. He hoped they'd send him home in time to see his grandfather once more. The old Earl was the only family he had left. Oh, there were aunts and uncles and all sorts of cousins, close and distant, but it was Grandfather who had been his family after his father had died. He closed his eyes, remembering his dream. Yes, he would very much like to take Grandfather's hand in his once more.

He tried to recapture the dream, to see his grandfather's face. The only one left in the world he loved—except Edwina, of course. But her face eluded him, too. Beautiful Edwina Manning. It was unbelievable that she still waited for him. Perhaps he was lucky to have been wounded. On this leave he would marry her. She was old enough now to be able to cope with life as a soldier's wife.

The hours passed unbearably slowly. The rumble seemed to grow farther and farther away. Could he have been overlooked? Could the soldier who had found him have forgotten to leave a marker? He opened his mouth to shout, but his throat was so parched that he could only croak. The effort left him weak and trembling, and he lay unmoving, in quiet despair. Then a new sound reached his ears. Men were marching somewhere above him, from the *north*. Slowly, wincing with pain, he raised himself on his elbow and looked up the mountainside. In the distance he could see a blue-clad army on the move. It couldn't be Marshal Victor's defeated army—they had moved away in the opposite direction. It was either Soult or Ney—or both—coming through the pass at Baños!

At last he understood. Sir Arthur, learning of the movement of some or all of Napoleon's army in Spain, must have realized the danger of advancing on Madrid, or even remaining here at Talavera, and had been forced to fall back to the south. The British army would have had to cross the river in haste. They had had to leave the wounded behind!

Captain Thorne had been an officer long enough to know that such occurrences were not uncommon. Despite the gloom which enveloped him, he felt no resentment at Sir Arthur's action. Every soldier knows that, at certain times, he must be on his own. That time had come to *him* now. What he had to do was to examine his wounds and determine how he could move on his own. Move he must, if he were ever to find help and eventually to make his way back to London, to his grandfather, to Edwina, to love, to friends, to peace.

Painfully, he lifted himself on both elbows and looked down at his left leg which seemed to be the source of the most painful of the sensations his body had suffered. What he saw caused the blood to drain from his cheeks and a black cloud to settle over him. But before he fell back to unconsciousness, he realized that he could never go back to London. His life in London, his career in the army, his marriage to Edwina—all that was over ...irrevocably over.

Chapter One

NELL HAD BEEN betrothed to Sir Nigel Lewis for three months and had been regretting it for two. Sir Nigel was undeniably distinguished-looking, tall and very, very rich, but Nell knew she must cry off. Life with Nigel would be impossible. Tonight had been the last straw. They had dined with his family—a small dinner party for twenty— and it had turned out to be the greatest bore imaginable. The conversation had been tedious, Nigel's mother, a tall, forbidding dowager with steely eyes, had shown intense disapproval of every remark Nell had made (even the most innocuous references to the inclement October weather), his uncle had stared at Nell's décolletage with disconcerting attention, and his aunt had insisted that Nigel's young sister play the piano for them. The girl had played for what seemed like hours, and anyone with the slightest feeling for music would have agreed that the girl had not a spark of talent.

All this could have been forgiven if Nigel himself had *once* said something witty, had *once* come to Nell's defense against his mother or had *once* responded to her grin when his sister had struck a particularly horrendous wrong note. But he had done none of those things. He had endured the evening with the most irritating complacency, had applauded his sister's performance with perfect sincerity, had kissed his mother goodnight with uncritical affection and was now sitting beside Nell in the carriage in self-satisfied contentment. "Nigel," Nell ventured, turning to him and fixing her usually laughing eyes on his face, "did you enjoy yourself this evening?"

He looked down at her in surprise. "Of course," he answered promptly. "I thought the ragout of veal was superb, didn't you?"

Nell frowned in impatience. "I'm not referring to *food*! I mean the rest of the evening."

"I found it very pleasant," Nigel pronounced firmly. "Are you suggesting that you did *not* find it so?"

"That's *just* what I'm suggesting. Truthfully, I found the entire evening unbearable."

Nigel raised an aristocratic eyebrow and looked at her in disapproval. "I don't see why," he said coldly. "Mother's little dinners are always said to be bang up to the mark. I can name dozens of people—undisputed leaders of the *ton*—who vie with each other to receive her invitations."

"To hear the music, no doubt," Nell muttered drily, unable to stop herself.

"I beg your pardon," Nigel responded quellingly, "but I think that remark would better have been left unsaid. If the musical entertainment this evening was somewhat...er...modest, it is because Mother would not have wanted to offend you by having anything but a quiet evening. You *are* still in mourning, after all."

"I've told you repeatedly that I'm *not* in mourning. It's

been more than five months since the Earl died. And although I was most sincerely attached to him and miss him most dreadfully, he expressly forbade us to go into deep mourning. Furthermore, as you know perfectly well, *I* was not directly related to him. Even Charles has taken off his black gloves, and *he* is the Earl's oldest living son. So I see no reason why your mother should worry about *my* sensibilities."

"Well, Mama feels that the mourning period should last at least a year," Nigel said in a repressive, rather critical tone.

"Does she indeed!" Nell snapped. "I'd like to point out, my dear, that I would not take it upon myself to tell your mother (or anyone else, for that matter) how to express *her* grief, and I'd be obliged if she would grant me the privilege of expressing *mine* in *my* own way!" She concluded her outburst by favoring her intended husband with an I-dare-you-to-differ-with-me glare and turning her back on him.

Nigel was not in the least unsettled by her display of irritability. He felt no inclination to argue with her. Her words struck him as merely a typical exhibition of the odd humors of volatile females, and he had only to ride out the storm which he was sure would be of short duration and quickly forgotten. Lady Imogen Lewis, Nigel's mother, had warned him that Helen Belden was a wild, unpredictable, capricious girl, brought up since her parents' death (when she was barely ten) by her guardians, Lord Charles Thorne and Lady Sybil, who were themselves so disreputable as to be completely incapable of setting an impressionable girl a good example. Sir Nigel, however, did not share his mother's concern. He was perfectly capable of handling a girl like Nell. She would prove to be no more difficult than a skittish colt. Once he and Nell were buckled, he had no doubt that he could break her to the bridle.

He looked at her averted head with possessive satisfaction. A beautiful colt she was, to be sure. Her shiny chestnut hair curled in enticing little ringlets at the nape of her neck. Her shoulders and back, bare because of the rather-too-daring cut of her gown, gleamed whitely in the dim light of the carriage. His eyes traveled down to her tiny waist, now partially hidden by the shawl which had slipped from her shoulders, to the beautifully molded thigh whose outline he could discern through the thin silk of her dress, and finally to the shapely ankle peeping out from beneath the hem. To possess that loveliness would be well worth the trouble of taming her willfulness. He put his arm around her shoulders and made her face him. "I'm sure you can't blame Mama for feeling that your standards of behavior would benefit from a bit of guidance," he said indulgently, "although I assure you that no one blames you for your indiscretions, since you're known to have lost your mother at so young an age. Nevertheless, being brought up by Lady Sybil, who everyone knows is a bit rackety herself, cannot have been good for you. You'll have to admit that your behavior has been, at times, quite scandalous."

Nell drew back from him and raised her eyebrows haughtily. "Scandalous? In what way has my behavior been scandalous?"

"Come now, my dear, there's no need to set up your bristles. I *did* offer for you, knowing full well that you need a strong hand. Neither I nor my mother places any blame at your doorstep. It isn't your fault that you were orphaned, after all—"

"So I need a strong hand, do I?" Nell demanded, her eyes glinting dangerously. "You place no blame on me? How very kind! Pray be specific, sir. What have I done for which you and your Mama find it necessary to make these allowances?"

"Well, you must admit, if you are to be at all honest with yourself, that racing Tubby Reynolds through Hyde Park on that shocking blue phaeton of Lady Sybil's, or telling Lady Sheldrake to her face that her perpetual diet has done her no good at all, or wearing that shockingly revealing gown to Almack's, or jilting two perfectly respectable suitors in three months—not that I blame you for that, for neither one of those fellows would have suited you at all—are indisputable examples of scandalous behavior."

"Are they indeed? Well, you are certainly at liberty to think so, but for one thing, my race with Tubby was held in the *morning*, when Hyde Park is very thin of crowds. For another thing, Lady Sheldrake brought the incident on herself by asking everybody within earshot if she looked any thinner—we could all see that she was fatter than ever, poor thing, and no one could think of anything to say that wouldn't be an out-and-out lie. And as for my gown, which you say was so revealing, it was only your Mama who found fault with it. Lady Jersey herself told me that I was in very fine looks that evening. There is only one act for which I may be brought to task, and that is jilting Lord Keith. And poor Neddy Overton, too, I suppose. Perhaps I was hasty in crying off from those entanglements, for neither one of *them* ever told me I was scandalous!"

"They were both afraid of you. I am not," Nigel said with a condescending smile.

Nell clenched her hands in her lap. "I think, Nigel," she said, fighting to keep her temper in check, "that it is becoming quite clear that you and I don't suit."

"Nonsense!" Nigel declared, unperturbed. "A mere difference of opinion about a family dinner—"

"It's much more than a small difference about dinner. I believe our differences to be fundamental. I've quite made up my mind. Our betrothal was a mistake, and I must ask you to release me."

Nigel stared at her, his mouth gaping. "You can't be serious," he managed at last.

"But I am."

He shook his head in disbelief, but the firmness of her chin convinced him that she'd meant what she'd said. "I should have expected this," he remarked bitterly. "You

are well known to be volatile. Mama has remarked on it
frequently. You cried off from your promise to Overton
after only two weeks, did you not? And when you jilted
Lord Keith so soon afterwards, all of London gossiped
about you. But, as I told Mama when I determined to
offer for you, I scarcely consider myself in the same class
as Overton—or Lord Keith, for that matter. A girl might
be excused for dismissing *them*. But now it becomes clear
that Mama was right."

Nell suppressed a smile. In Nigel's view, any girl who
could give up a chance to marry *him* must be sadly
shatterbrained. Any misgivings she might have felt at
crying off were dispelled by his smug self-consequence.
She supposed that there was some justification for
society's view that, in capturing Sir Nigel Lewis, she had
made a brilliant coup, but she was both repelled and
amused to learn that Nigel himself was in whole-hearted
agreement with them.

Oh, well, she thought, she could not really blame him.
She was an impoverished orphan with very little to
recommend her on the Marriage Mart. Helen "Nell"
Belden had lost both her parents by the time she was ten.
She had been taken in by her godmother, Lady Sybil
Thorne. Sybil's busband, Lord Charles, had become her
guardian. But while the Thorne family moved in the very
highest circles of London society, everyone knew that
Charles Thorne was only a second son to the wealthy Earl
of Thornbury and had long ago dissipated his portion.
He'd lived most of his life on the largesse of his father and
his now-deceased elder brother, Edgar. Any man who
chose Helen Belden for his bride could expect nothing in
the way of settlements from her guardian.

Fortunately for Nell, her lineage was impeccable, and
she was endowed with considerable charm and attractive-
ness. Nell was not unaware that her laughing, green-
flecked eyes, her chestnut curls, her impish face and the
slender curves of her figure stood her in good stead. She
had never lacked for suitors, even without a fortune to

offer them. Of course, she knew that her behavior was not always proper. She had strong enthusiasms and was too often tempted to indulge them. Racing a phaeton was one of them, and the race with Tubby was not the only incident which had caused malicious gossip. Her taste in clothes, too (although she would not admit this to Nigel), tended to be somewhat impetuous. She enjoyed turning heads when she walked into a room and didn't hesitate even to damp her dresses if that trick would insure that her figure would be seen to advantage. Lady Sybil had taught her that a dress was to be despised if it went unnoticed, and she had followed Sybil's advice and chosen gowns that were remarkable either for their color, their flattering lines or their up-to-the-minute modishness.

Her two previous betrothals were also to be blamed on enthusiasm. Both Neddy and Keith had seemed quite adorable on early acquaintance, and each in his own way had made his offer so charmingly that Nell had accepted without much serious thought. It was only after deeper acquaintance that she'd realized that Neddy often behaved like a child, indulging in the most exhausting temper tantrums whenever he imagined that Nell had smiled at another man. And Keith, she soon learned, would never offer a wife half the affection he lavished on the dozens of dogs who shared his home.

Her betrothal to Nigel had been different. She had never felt any enthusiasm for him. It had been her guardians who had urged her to accept him. Perhaps she had been vain, but she had not dreamed that Nigel felt that he'd "condescended" when he'd offered for her. She suddenly realized that, even though she had hesitated for several days before accepting him, he had taken her eventual acceptance for granted. And now it was obvious that her rejection of his suit was completely incomprehensible to him.

She lifted her eyes to his face. He was looking down at her in cold vexation, but there was no pain in his eyes as there had been in Neddy's eyes when she had broken with him. "Don't be angry, Nigel," she said placatingly. "You won't suffer for this. You'll be *glad* in a day or two. Everyone will tell what a complete ninnyhammer I am for letting you slip through my fingers. You'll find a replacement for me in no time at all. And," she added irrepressibly, "your mother will be overjoyed. I'm sure Lady Imogen will be delighted to help you choose someone more suitable than I. Why, just think of it—you might have Juliana Holcombe, or Gussie Glendenning or even Edwina Manning."

Nigel turned away wordlessly. He didn't trust himself to speak. He was furious with her. He was well aware that she could be easily replaced—he didn't need her to tell him that! He drummed his fingers angrily on his knees and stared out the carriage window at the darkened streets. The girl was behaving foolishly and would no doubt regret this in the morning. The thought soothed him. She would be sure to reconsider after a good night's sleep. She couldn't persist in this idiotic obstinacy in the cold light of day. Besides, the Thornes would have something to say to her. They were not likely to let Nigel Lewis out of their clutches so easily. His lips twitched in a cold smile. He need not even bother to persuade her to change her mind—the Thornes would do it for him. And when they all came round to tell him she'd reconsidered, he'd not take her back so soon. He'd make them all stew for a while.

His smile broadened and he turned back to her. "I don't envy you the ordeal of telling your guardians what you've done tonight," he said maliciously. "What do you think they're going to do when they learn that you've broken a betrothal for the third time?"

Nell had been basking in the blessed relief of being freed from the most oppressive entanglement of her life, but the feeling evaporated at his words. Nigel was right—it would not be easy to break the news. Charles and Sybil had been urgently persistent in their support of

Nigel's suit. And now, with the late Earl's fortune all tangled up in legalities, their need for money was great. They had not spoken of this to her, but she knew that they had counted on her marriage to give them some measure of financial relief. How could she possibly break the news to them that, for the third time in less than a year, she'd whistled a fortune down the wind?

Chapter Two

THE SOUND OF voices raised in argument greeted Nell when she was admitted into Thorne House a few minutes later. Beckwith, the butler who admitted her, grinned widely and nodded toward the library door from which the noise emanated. "They're still at it," he said with a disparaging cackle.

"Haven't they finished with Mr. Prickett?" Nell asked in surprise.

"Not yet they haven't," the butler snorted. Beckwith did not have the dignity in manner and appearance which was usually required of the head of the domestic staff of an imposing household. He was short, stocky, cheerful and garrulous—characteristics which were considered by most of the gentry to be completely inappropriate for a man in his position. Lady Sybil found his presence a

17

source of great embarrassment and irritation, but the old Earl had willed that Beckwith was to be kept on as butler as long as he should want the position. Beckwith seemed to take perverse delight in upsetting his mistress by making comments on her orders, speaking too freely to her guests, or appearing at times without the coat of his livery.

These solecisms enraged Lady Sybil, but Beckwith merely chortled at her displeasure. Poor Lady Sybil received little help or sympathy from the other members of the household in this matter, for Lord Charles tended to ignore Beckwith (the domestic details of the household having no interest for him); his elderly aunt, Lady Amelia Thorne, had lived in the house for too long to take any notice of Beckwith's eccentricities; and Nell was convinced that Lady Sybil's standards for proper behavior in the domestic staff were excessively formal. Nell had a strong liking for the old butler and was often accused by her godmother of encouraging him in his annoying ways.

Perhaps Lady Sybil was right, for Nell now grinned at Beckwith conspiratorially. "How long do you suppose they can keep this up?"

"Wouldn't surprise me none if they was to be at it all night," he replied, chuckling.

Nell restrained her answering smile. "I suppose we shouldn't laugh," she murmured. "The length of the discussion means that Mr. Prickett has not brought good news. I'll peep inside and see what's causing the to-do." She handed the butler her bonnet and shawl and walked swiftly to the library door. With great care, she turned the handle and tiptoed in.

The library was an impressive room, its walls lined with leather-bound books, its windows reaching to the high ceiling, the carpets and draperies glowing in rich tones of dark red and gold, and the paneling of the walls elegantly carved and lustrously polished. This room had been a favorite of the old Earl, and the housekeeper still kept it as spotless and gleaming as it had been when he was alive.

The family's man of business, Mr. Prickett, was seated at a long oak table, a number of documents and papers spread out before him, his elbow resting on the table, and his hand supporting his forehead as he stared at the three people sitting before him, two of whom were glaring at him with expressions of decided antagonism. As Nell moved quietly to the nearest vacant chair, she saw Mr. Prickett remove his pince-nez and rub the bridge of his nose. She knew that gesture well. It indicated that the lawyer was exercising all his self-control to maintain the cool and dispassionate demeanor he considered proper for a man of his profession. He was not as adept at dealing with hostility from his clients as he was from his adversaries. Therefore, this had been a long, difficult evening for him.

Before Nell could sit down, she heard a grunt from her guardian. It was Lord Charles' way of acknowledging her presence. She nodded to him and slipped into the chair. Lady Sybil merely favored her with a flick of the eye, but the third member of the family, the elderly Lady Amelia, the late Earl's only surviving sister, gave her a welcoming smile. Nell smiled back at Lady Amelia brightly, hoping that an air of cheerfulness would alleviate somewhat the tension in the room.

After a brief bow in Nell's direction, Mr. Prickett spoke. "I can add nothing more, I'm afraid, to what I've already said a dozen times this evening," he said with strained patience, replacing his pince-nez and looking firmly at Lord Charles and Lady Sybil. "I assure you again that there is nothing anyone can do at this time. The Earl's wishes were quite explicitly detailed in the will."

"But the Earl could not possibly have known that Captain Thorne would be missing in action!" Lady Sybil objected. "There *must* be some provision for the unexpected."

Mr. Prickett almost sighed, reached for his pince-nez again, removed it and rubbed the bridge of his nose with twitching fingers. "But, as I've said—"

"We know what you've said," Lord Charles muttered in disgust.

Lady Amelia leaned forward in her chair. "Would anyone like some more tea?" she asked in her high, fluttery voice. "I believe it is still quite warm."

"Will you please refrain from offering us tea every five minutes?" Lady Sybil hissed in annoyance. "We've all told you we don't want any."

"But perhaps Nell...?" Lady Amelia suggested timidly.

"I'm sure Nell doesn't want any tea at this hour either," Lady Sybil snapped.

"But I *do*," Nell said with a warm smile for the old lady. "Please let me have a cup, Amelia dear."

Lady Sybil frowned at Nell in disgust. "You are interrupting the proceedings, you wretch. All that clinking of teacups will give me the headache."

"Sorry, my dear," Nell said with a contrite smile. "I promise I shall drink very, very quietly."

"In any case," added Mr. Prickett, packing up the papers on the table in front of him, "I believe the 'proceedings' are over, are they not?"

"They most certainly are *not*," Lord Charles declared. "You haven't told me how long I must wait to put my hands on the money."

This time Mr. Prickett actually permitted himself a small sigh. In his many years as legal and business advisor to the fifth Earl of Thornbury, he'd never had to deal with the Earl's willful, spoiled, rather dim-witted second son. All the legal and financial dealings had been strictly controlled by the Earl or by Edgar Thorne, the Earl's eldest son. Edgar Thorne had been the Earl's pride and joy, and the only member of the family whom the Earl had respected. But a hunting accident had taken Edgar's life fifteen years before, leaving the old Earl embittered and lonely. Only Henry Thorne, Edgar's son, had been any comfort to him, and *he* had left long ago for the army.

After Edgar Thorne's fatal accident, his son became

the heir to the title and lands, the Earl's grandson's claim
having precedence over that of the second son. The old
Earl had often confided to Prickett that this arrangement
was not only legally, but rationally and morally
justifiable. His grandson, Captain Henry Thorne, was the
only member of his family whom the Earl believed
capable of controlling the family pursestrings. The Earl
had been given ample evidence for concluding that Lord
Charles and Lady Sybil could, between them, easily fritter
away every penny brought in by the Earl's very large
estates.

Mr. Prickett was in wholehearted agreement, but of
course, he could not expect Lord Charles to be happy
about the arrangement. Slow in understanding, Charles
had only one interest in life—he was addicted to
gambling. He was, therefore, always deeply in debt. Now,
with Captain Thorne's disappearance, Charles had, not
surprisingly, begun to hope that he might come into
control of the inheritance.

"You are not answering," Charles repeated, shaking
Mr. Prickett from his reverie. "Didn't you hear me? How
long must I wait?"

"I simply cannot give you an answer. We must allow
time for the Captain to be located," Mr. Prickett said with
forced patience.

"He must be dead," Lady Sybil said funereally. "I feel
sure he must be dead. No one has heard of him in
months!"

"We've had a letter from Sir Arthur, you know,"
Charles added. "It doesn't offer a word of hope. Very kind
letter it was, praising Henry to the skies and all that, but
he admits that the poor fellow hasn't been seen since
Talavera."

"Nevertheless, we must keep looking. The law is quite
clear on that point. Does the letter say anything else?"

"No, nothing of any significance. Would you like to see
it? I believe I tossed it into the drawer there to your right."

Mr. Prickett found the letter and scanned it quickly.

"Well, my lord, you seem to be right. It gives us no new information about Captain Thorne's possible whereabouts." There was a moment of glum silence while Mr. Prickett perused the letter more carefully. "Interesting," he remarked, half to himself. "His lordship signs himself Arthur Wellesley. I suppose he wrote this before he learned of his being named Lord Wellington."

"I suppose so," Charles said uninterestedly, too involved in his own concerns to trouble his mind about the war. "The letter is dated two months past. The mails between us and the Peninsula are nothing short of shocking."

"Well," Mr. Prickett said in mild reproof, "there *is* a war going on over there." He folded the letter and replaced it in the drawer. Then, gathering up his papers, he said more decisively, "But let me assure you that, war or no war, we shall leave no stone unturned to locate the Captain."

"But what are we to do in the meantime?" Lady Sybil asked urgently.

"Your usual allowances will continue, of course," Mr. Prickett reminded her.

"Allowances? But they are a mere *pittance*!" Charles complained.

"Indeed they are. I can't even pay my *milliner* with mine!" Lady Sybil agreed. "I'm sure that if Henry were here he'd at least authorize the payment of our bills. He would surely do *that*, Mr. Prickett. Ask Charles, if you don't believe me. Ask Nell!"

Nell held up her hands in a gesture that emphasized her intention not to become involved in this discussion. "Don't ask me anything of the sort," she pleaded laughingly. "Never having laid eyes on the celebrated Captain, I am completely unqualified to comment on what he would or would not do."

"Of course you've laid eyes on him. It was when you first came to live with us, remember? He came home from school, I remember—"

"Really, Sybil! I was not eleven years old!" Nell laughed.

"I have no reason to doubt your word, Lady Sybil," Mr. Prickett intervened. "In fact, I quite agree with you. Captain Thorne is, as I remember, a most considerate and generous young man."

"Then why can't you authorize the payment of our bills? You admit that Henry would have not the least objection—!" Lady Sybil urged.

"I have no authority to take such action, my lady. My powers of attorney do not extend so far. I'm sorry." And he snapped his paper-case shut with a sharp click of finality.

"But suppose he *is* dead. And suppose we never find his body? Shall we have to wait *forever* in this impoverished state?" Charles asked irritably.

Lady Amelia shuddered. "Please, Charles, don't talk so," she pleaded. "It positively chills my bones. The poor, poor boy . . ." She put a trembling hand to her eyes to shut out the thought of such a tragedy.

Charles tossed his aunt a look of disgust. The sentimental old lady had more concern for the whereabouts of her grandnephew than she had for the disposition of the inheritance. Henry was dead—there was almost no doubt about that. *Now* the real and pressing problem was to be able to get their hands on the money. Charles had been fond of Henry Thorne, too—*very* fond of him. The boy had been a very pleasant fellow and a capital rider. Charles wished him no ill at all. Why, he could come home this very minute and take his place as the sixth Earl, for all Charles cared, *so long as the bills could be paid.* But Amelia's tears could not help anything at all.

Nell leaned forward in her chair and patted the old lady's hand comfortingly. Mr. Prickett coughed and rose from his chair, seizing the opportunity to take his leave. "Don't upset yourself, Lady Amelia," he said briskly, moving to the door. "There is every reason to hope that

Captain Thorne may yet be found alive." And bidding them all a firm goodnight, he hastily left the room.

For a moment, all four sat just as Mr. Prickett had left them—Lady Amelia dabbing her eyes with her handkerchief, Nell patting her shoulder, Lady Sybil and Lord Charles staring furiously at the door. "Hmmmph!" grunted Charles at last. "That was certainly a waste of time. I might as well have spent the evening at Brooks's."

Lady Sybil glared at him in disdain. "Not at all," she said cuttingly, "for you'd have probably lost a monkey by this time, and we'd be even deeper in the suds than we are now."

"Dash it, Sybil," he husband growled, "take a damper! If we are in the suds, its cause can more readily be laid at your door than at mine."

"At *my* door! Of all the unfair—!"

"Would anyone *now* like a cup of tea?" Lady Amelia interjected quickly, the frightening possibility of a quarrel between her nephew and his wife causing her to abandon the tears she'd been shedding for poor Captain Henry.

"I'm not a bit unfair," Charles went on, ignoring his aunt completely. "Your bills for ballgowns and gloves and other female fripperies are what has put us in the suds."

"*My* bills? Mine? When I have been scrimping and contriving for months to make do with these old rags?" Lady Sybil cried, holding out the skirt of the purple jaconet gown she wore. The soft, silky fabric had a decidedly fresh, just-purchased sheen, and the deep flounce at the bottom was so resplendent with intricate embroidery that the rich quality of the dress was unmistakable. Nell could not prevent a little laugh from escaping her lips.

"There! Even Nell is laughing," Charles declared with satisfaction. "Old rags, indeed!"

"Really, Nell, you are becoming quite impossible," Sybil said, wheeling about and facing Nell accusingly. "Have you so little gratitude? Didn't that gown *you* are wearing cost me a pretty penny?"

Nell bit her lip. "I'm sorry, Sybil dear," she said meekly.

"Let the girl be," Charles ordered. "If it weren't for her, we'd have no prospects at all."

Lady Sybil subsided reluctantly. "What prospects? She has not yet set the wedding date, although I've been urging her for weeks."

"You're right there, my dear," Charles concurred. "Nell, you must stop this procrastination. Sir Nigel can be no help to us until you have him firmly rivetted. What are you waiting for?"

Nell looked at her guardians in alarm. "I hope you've not been counting too seriously on *Sir Nigel* for financial assistance," she said uncomfortably.

"But of *course* we are, you goose," her godmother replied. "Why else would we have urged you to accept him?"

"You need have no scruples, my dear," Charles explained kindly. "Sir Nigel quite understands the situation. We had a completely frank conversation on the matter the day before we announced your betrothal. He has agreed to give us a very generous settlement. We shall contrive to manage on it very well until the matter of the estate is settled."

"But... but... *Charles*," Nell gasped, her face pale, "is *that* the only...? I mean, you certainly are not counting on Nigel's settlement as your primary source of support, are you? Mr. Prickett told me that your allowances are very generous and could keep us quite comfortably, if only we practiced a few economies..."

"Don't be ridiculous," Sybil said scornfully. "The economies that Mr. Prickett suggests are out of the question. He wants us to limit our entertaining to one or two small dinners a season, for example. And he told me to postpone the redecoration of the drawing room even after I clearly told him that I'd already ordered several chairs."

"The man has no understanding of our way of life,"

Charles added. "He as much as told me I should quit my *clubs*!"

"But... would it be so very bad to... to...?"

Charles and Sybil both turned and stared at Nell closely. "*To quit my clubs*?" Charles asked in a choked voice. "You must be *mad*!"

"And you'd be mad indeed if you failed to realize that one's social standing depends on the ability to entertain in the proper style," her godmother added, watching Nell through narrowed eyes. "But why are you suggesting such things?"

Nell sank back in her chair and lowered her eyes. "Well, I..." she began. Then her courage failed her and she remained silent.

Sybil and Charles exchanged puzzled glances, while Lady Amelia, sensing that an explosion was about to occur, jumped into the breach with the only defenses she had available. "Let us all have some tea to calm ourselves," she urged. "I've managed to keep it quite warm—"

"Will you tell your aunt to cease and desist?" Sybil muttered to her husband between clenched teeth. "I don't want to hear another word about *tea*!"

Charles rose and confronted his aunt. "Please, Aunt Amelia, you are driving us all to apoplexy! *We do not want tea!*"

"Very well, Charles," Amelia said in a voice that trembled in offended dignity, "you needn't shout. I heard your wife quite clearly. I shall not bring up the subject again."

"Perhaps you'd best go to bed, Amelia. All this commotion must have tired you," Lady Sybil suggested pointedly.

The old lady put her chin up defiantly. "Not at all," she said proudly. "I am quite well and intend to remain as long as I please. I would be much obliged if you'd take no notice of me. I shall simply sit here quietly and... and drink my tea."

Lady Sybil sighed in defeat. Lady Amelia had as much right in this house as she herself—more, if one took into account the fact that she had lived with her brother, the Earl, all of his lifetime and had been well provided for in the will. In addition, the Earl had stipulated that his estates must always be made available for her use whenever she should desire to occupy them for as long as she lived. There was nothing Sybil could do but put up with her. "Very well. Stay if you like. But don't interrupt us, please. Well, Nell, what were you about to say?"

"I was about to say that...that...we may *have* to institute the economies Mr. Prickett suggested," Nell said in a small voice.

"Why?" Sybil asked tensely. "What have you done, girl?"

Charles looked from his wife's tightly compressed lips to Nell's bent head. "Sybil? What is it? What's amiss?"

Sybil did not turn her eyes from her ward. "Nell? Not *again*! You didn't do it *again*, did you?"

Nell nodded sheepishly, not daring to raise her eyes.

Sybil let out a piercing scream. "No! N-No!" She clutched her breast and tottered to a chair. "I shall have a seizure! My God, I shall have a seizure and die right here this minute!" And she pulled a handkerchief from her dress and waved it weakly before her reddened face.

Charles gaped at his wife in confusion. "What is it, my dear? What has she done?"

Sybil glared at her husband impatiently. "Really, Charles, can't you *guess*? She's *cried off*!"

"Cried off?" Charles blinked his eyes slowly, but as the enormity of the situation dawned on him, his face reddened in fury. "You little *ninny*," he shouted, "did you *dare* to play that trick again?"

"Charles!" Amelia gasped, shocked by his rudeness.

"Stay out of this, Amelia," Charles told her curtly.

"Please!" Nell urged a little breathlessly. "I know I've shocked you both, but wouldn't it be best to discuss this matter a bit more calmly?"

Sybil turned to her ward with a desperate suggestion. "It was a lover's quarrel, wasn't it? Nothing but a lover's quarrel. Tell me that I've hit on the truth of it! It can be mended, can't it? It *must* be mended. I will go to see Nigel tomorrow and explain that you cried all night. He'll come rushing round to take you in his arms, and all will be well."

Nell shook her head. "It was not a lover's quarrel."

Sybil's face puckered and tears filled her eyes. "Of *course* it was a lover's quarrel. What else could it have been? Nell, my dear girl, don't you know I want the best for you? How can you *do* this to me? I've given you a home, a family, all my *love!*" Tears rolled down her cheeks and she held out a trembling hand. "Please, my dear, tell me it was only a little quarrel!"

Nell shook her head firmly and took her aunt's hand. "Please, dear, don't cry. We shall brush through somehow. But I *cannot* marry Nigel. He is the greatest bore, the most insufferable prig and the most conceited dolt. You cannot wish me to spend my life with such a man."

"But most women learn—as you must—to compromise their standards when they marry. We none of us find the man of our dreams! Why can't *you* make that compromise—like the rest of us?" Sybil asked urgently.

"I've tried, truly," Nell said, getting to her feet and speaking strongly. "I compromised with my heart when I first agreed to accept him. I did it to please you. But I didn't realize, because I didn't know him well enough, that wedded life with Nigel would be beyond compromise—it would be a prison sentence."

"You are overdramatizing," Charles said flatly. "You women have too much sensibility."

"Charles is right," Sybil agreed. "Something has happened to disturb you, and now you refine on it too much."

"How can you say that after I've told you what I think of him?" Nell cried.

"But, my dear," her godmother answered, "it doesn't matter what sort of man he is. Perhaps I shouldn't say this, but it is something you are bound to discover for yourself once you are married. Marriage is primarily for convenience. Before marriage, society's eyes are always upon you, but once you are wedded, you will find that you can contrive to go your own way. It is not an uncommon practice among married people."

"*Really*, Sybil!" Amelia put in, appalled.

Nell, too, was appalled. She had not known that her guardians were capable of such calculating heartlessness. "I could not live that way," she said quietly, turning away from them.

"You will have to, Miss," Sybil snapped. "It is necessary to us."

Nell merely shook her head.

"Is this the gratitude we should expect from a girl we took in and reared as our own?" her godmother demanded with a throbbing voice.

"I *am* grateful. Please believe that," Nell answered earnestly. "But you cannot wish me to sacrifice my life to permit you to *entertain* lavishly! Or to allow Charles to gamble away the fortune at his club! The price you ask is too high for that."

Charles indignantly stalked to the fireplace. Taking an authoritative stance, he faced his ward threateningly. "I've heard enough. We've spoiled you, Miss. We've indulged these whims long enough. Now I'm *ordering* you to obey me—you will agree to commision your god-mother to pay a call on Sir Nigel in the morning, when she will tell him that you've regretted your hasty words to him and that, if he will forgive you, you will never again behave in this way."

"No, I will not agree," Nell said flatly.

"I give you no choice in this matter. You will do as I say!"

"You cannot compel me, Charles. If Sybil *can* convince Nigel to give me another chance—which I very much doubt—I shall deny it *all* the moment he comes to see me."

Charles and Sybil exchanged looks of helpless frustration. Then Sybil, trembling, jumped to her feet and confronted her ward. "If you persist in opposing us, Helen Belden, we shall send you away! Far away from everyone and everything you've known. You shall live *alone*, with no one to talk to, with no shops, no libraries, no parties, no friends. We shall send you as far away as we possibly can. To... to... Charles, which one of the estates is the farthest from London?"

Charles looked at his wife admiringly. The woman was never at a loss for ideas. "Thorndene!" he answered promptly. "That ramshackle place we have in Cornwall."

"You can't send the girl to Cornwall—it's coming on *winter*! No one goes to Cornwall in winter," Amelia protested.

"Cornwall!" Sybil smiled in malicious delight. "It's perfect. It's as gloomy and lonely a place as one would wish. It's the end of the world, my girl, the end of the world! We'll just *see* how long you'll endure it there!"

Nell looked from one to the other undaunted. "Very well. If I must choose between living with Nigel or living alone at the end of the world, I choose the end of the world. Send me to Cornwall if you must."

"Very well," Sybil said curtly, "you've made your choice. I shall make arrangements tomorrow morning, if a night's reflection doesn't change your mind."

"I won't change my mind."

"I'd think on it, if I were you," Charles advised.

"Stubborn chit," Sybil muttered, crossing to her husband. "Don't trouble to argue with her, Charles. Let her go to Cornwall. She'll find herself so bored and lonely that, before a fortnight has elapsed, she'll *plead* with us to permit her to return."

Charles nodded agreement. Perhaps this extemporaneous plan would work. The girl could not be coerced, that much was clear. But banishment to a cold and lonely house, especially after the lively, crowded social whirl she'd been enjoying in London, might be the very thing to bring her round. His wife was clever, he'd say that for her. He offered her his arm. "Come, Sybil, let's go to bed."

Sybil accompanied him to the door, but before leaving she turned back to her recalcitrant ward. "Tell your abigail to begin packing," she said icily. "But don't imagine that I'll permit her to accompany you. You'll have to make do with the staff at Thorndene."

"Very well, ma'am," Nell answered with rigid formality.

"Aren't you coming up to bed, Aunt Amelia?" Charles asked.

"Not yet. I wish to discuss something with Nell first," the old lady said placidly. "We have some plans to make."

"Plans?" He looked at his aunt with suspicion. "What plans?"

Amelia busily fiddled with the teapot. "My plans to leave with her." She looked up at her nephew bravely. "You see, dear boy, *I'm* going to Thorndene, too."

"Wh-what?" Charles sputtered furiously. "To Thorndene? What do you mean? Are you trying to interfere with the disciplinary measures I see fit to administer to my ward?"

Sybil put a restraining hand on his arm. "Don't fly into a pucker, Charles. Let her go. We could not send Nell away unchaperoned. Amelia will serve very well."

Charles shrugged. "Oh, very well then. I don't suppose *her* presence will make a great deal of difference, one way or another."

"Amelia, dear, you needn't make such a sacrifice for me," Nell said quietly.

"Not all all," Amelia declared with unaccustomed spirit. "I make no sacrifice. There would be no one here I'd care to be with, once you were gone." And she threw her nephew and his wife a rebellious glance.

"Very well then, Aunt. Have it your own way," Charles said from the doorway. "I advise you both to take yourselves upstairs and arrange to have your things packed at once."

"We will," Amelia said, a new note of daring in her fluttery voice, "in due time. But first, Nell and I are going to...to..."

"To what?" Lady Sybil asked suspiciously.

Nell and Amelia looked at each other, their eyes smiling with affectionate understanding. "To have our tea, of course," Nell said contentedly.

Chapter Three

TRUE TO THEIR WORDS, Lady Sybil and Lord Charles sent Nell into exile. A week later, Nell was seated beside Lady Amelia in a rented coach crossing Bodmin Moor during a driving rainstorm. It had taken three days and two sleepless nights on the London-to-Exeter stage, another day to arrange for the rented hack, and another two days of bumpy riding to come this far. The coachman had assured her this morning that they were certain to reach Padstow before nightfall, but it was already darkening and (from what little Nell could see through the heavy rain) there was no end of the depressing Bodmin Moor in sight.

When Nell had first realized she was to be banished, she had been undismayed. To her lively, imaginative mind, the trip had promised adventure in a colorful and distant land. And she would not be alone; Lady Amelia's generous impulse to join her in her exile was extremely comforting. Amelia, who had a sensible mind and a gentle, generous spirit, would be, despite her seventy-some-odd years, a pleasant companion. But the length of the journey, the lack of sleep and the sound of the rain drumming with discouraging persistence on the roof of the coach all combined to depress her spirits. Amelia was drowsing beside her, thus offering no encouraging words. And the view from her window of Bodmin Moor, its bleak, solitary expanse stretching into infinity, sent a chill to her very bones. All this made Nell feel that perhaps Sybil had been right—she might not be able to withstand so much as a fortnight in this dismal place.

After a time, she noticed that the landscape had begun to change. The smell of the sea air pervaded the carriage, and through the coach window she could discern the dark shapes of the rocks and crags which lined the shore of the estuary of the River Camel. Her heart lifted, for the sea had always fascinated her, and the thought of living so close to it that the smell would always be in her nostrils and the sound of it in her ears made her pulse race in excitement. By the time they reached Padstow, her face was pressed to the glass and her eyes were shining.

But her renewed good spirits were not destined to last. The coachman, on making inquiries at a tiny inn, learned that Thorndene was still some distance away, along a difficult road. The driver muttered curses under his breath as he resumed his seat. Nell hadn't the heart to upbraid him. She knew he must be wet and chilled to the bone. Lady Amelia had awakened, and she, too, felt depressed. She wrapped her shawl tightly around her thin shoulders as the angry wind howled around the carriage. Nell could not find a cheerful word to say but merely stared out her window silently. The view showed only the silhouettes of misshapen trees outlined against a quickly darkening sky.

It was completely dark and still raining heavily when

they at last drew up before a large building whose grim aspect gave no encouragement for optimism. Not a light could be seen from the windows. No lantern had been placed near the doorway to welcome them. Nell, glancing at Amelia's face, could see that the old lady was worn out with fatigue. She squeezed Amelia's hand comfortingly. "Perhaps they no longer expected us today," she said encouragingly, "and they've gone to bed. Don't look so dismayed, Amelia dear. The coachman will rouse someone."

The coachman had gone carefully up the stone steps and he rapped smartly at the door. He stood there muttering and knocking for several minutes before a bolt was unlatched and the heavy door creaked open. "Who's there?" a boy's voice asked.

Nell could not make out the ensuing words, for the wind came up at that moment and drowned out the sounds. But the coachman soon turned and made his way back to the carriage. He opened the door and, touching his cap to Nell, said worriedly, "Beggin' your pardon, Miss, but you don't seem to be expected."

"What's that?" Nell asked in disbelief. "Stand aside, man. Let me settle this for myself!" She jumped out of the carriage and, disregarding the rain, ran up the steps. The lad, a boy of no more than thirteen years, was standing just inside the doorway, holding a lantern aloft and peering out the door which he held open just a crack. In the light, Nell could see that the boy was in his shirtsleeves, his straight, heavy blond hair falling in disarray over his forehead. "What is the meaning of this?" she demanded furiously. "Are you not expecting us? Didn't you receive a letter from Lord Charles Thorne?"

"No, ma'am, that we did not," the boy said, looking at her with suspicion.

Nell clenched her fists in bitter resentment. How like Charles and Sybil to order her from her home to this gloomy, impossible place and then to forget to make the proper arrangements. When she could control her voice, she said to the boy, "Well, letter or not, we are here! Open this door! And then go out to the coach to help Lady Amelia into the house. It's so dark out here, one can scarcely see the steps." She saw the boy hesitate, and her temper flared. "Do you *hear* me, boy?" she exploded. "*Hop to it!*"

The boy, responding to the ring of authority in her voice, jumped. He opened the door, stepped aside for her to enter and hurried out to the carriage. Amelia was soon ushered in, the coachman and the boy having assisted her up the steps. Then the coachman set about unloading the luggage. The boy stood uncertainly at the door, looking at the ladies helplessly, the light from his lantern throwing weird shadows on the floor. Nell and Amelia looked about them. They were standing in a great-sized hall, so large that its ceiling and far walls were too shadowed to be discerned. The nearer walls were of gray stone, covered here and there by tapestries in the medieval manner and looking as faded and dusty as if they'd hung there untouched through all the ensuing years. Nell half-expected the floor to be covered with rushes, as they must have been in the days of the Plantagenets, but she found that she was standing on a thin, oriental carpet which was frayed at the edges, worn in the center and so faded that all its once-bright colors had become a uniform gray.

"Well?" Nell asked the boy after a long moment of silence. "Where is the butler? What sort of staff have you here?"

"*Staff*, ma'am? There ain't no staff. There's only—"

But the boy was interrupted by the sound of a door opening somewhere behind them, and a beam of light shone forth. "Jemmy?" a woman's voice called. "Who have 'ee there?"

Amelia and Nell turned to find a woman approaching them, followed closely by a man carrying a candle. The woman's appearance was somewhat comforting to the weary travelers, for she looked as if she belonged in a civilized household: her hair was dressed in a tidy bun, her dark bombazine dress was neat and well-fitting, and the large apron that surrounded her ample form was crisp and spotless. She wore a pair of tiny spectacles which glinted in the candlelight. The man who followed her was not much taller than she. He had a bald head fringed with a row of gray hair, and held an unlit pipe between his teeth. They both were peering into the gloom with worried expressions.

"Two ladies, Mum," the boy was saying. "Say they was expected."

"Expected?" the woman said in alarm, coming forward swiftly. "No one be expected here!"

Nell had had enough. "Expected or not, we're here!" she said curtly. "And we'd like you to take our wet things and show us to someplace where we can be warm and dry."

"But . . . this be Thorndene, ma'am," the woman said, peering at Nell closely through her spectacles. "We ben't liberty to permit strangers to—"

"My good woman," Amelia said with unexpected acidity, "we are not strangers. I am Lady Amelia Thorne. And this is Miss Belden, Lord Charles Thorne's ward."

The woman's mouth dropped open. "Lady Amelia *Thorne*?" she asked, throwing a look of terror at the man behind her.

"Yes," said Nell in annoyance. "You, I assume, are the caretakers, is that right?"

"Yes'm," said the man, stepping forward and knuckling his brow. "Will Penloe's the name. This is Mrs. Penloe, and that'n is our boy, Jemmy."

The woman made a brief curtsy, but her expression was cold and unwelcoming. "'Tis sorry I be that we cain't make 'ee welcome. I mind as how you've come so far for nought, but I must tell 'ee that you cain't stay here."

"Can't *stay*?" Nell echoed. "Whatever do you mean?"

"We ben't prepared for visitors at this season. We've never had 'em in all the years we been here."

"Ridiculous!" Amelia said succinctly.

"It doesn't matter whether you've ever had out-of-season visitors or not," Nell declared, outraged. "This is *our* home, not yours. It's entirely up to *us* whether we stay or leave!"

The Penloes exchanged troubled looks for the second time. Then Mr. Penloe squared his shoulders and stepped forward. "Don't mean to sound toitish, ma'am," he said apologetically, "but Mrs. Penloe's right. You *cain't* stay here. There's nought been done to prepare for 'ee. The bedrooms ain't been made up, the larder's as good as empty—"

"And there's only Will, Jemmy and me to do for 'ee," Mrs. Penloe added hastily. "You cain't be wishful to stay. 'Twould not be all what you're accustomed to. There's no gentry for miles—not at this time o' year. No one to talk to or to call on. There'd be nought for 'ee to do from one day to the next."

"Nothing you are saying is at all to the purpose," Nell said impatiently. "We are here. We have nowhere else to go. Those are facts which cannot be changed. Therefore, we *all* may as well accept them. Now, here's what's to be done. You, Mr. Penloe, are to see to the coachman at once. His horses are to be stabled, and he's to be given a bed for the night. The poor fellow shall not be made to ride back to Padstow at this hour and in this weather."

The Penloes exchanged looks for the third time. *"At once!"* Nell said furiously.

There was a moment's hesitation. Then Penloe shrugged and beckoned to the coachman to follow him. "Very well, then, come along," he muttered, his teeth clamped hard on the stem of his pipe. "And you'd best come too, Jemmy. There's his bed to see to and the firewood, too. Leave Mum your lantern."

When the three had left the room, Nell turned to Mrs. Penloe. "Now, Mrs. Penloe, you may take us to the sitting room, if you please."

With her lips compressed into a tight line, Mrs. Penloe wordlessly led the way to a door across the hall. The room they entered was high-ceilinged, musty and forbidding, its furniture shrouded by Holland covers. Mrs. Penloe put the lantern on what seemed, under its cover, to be a table, pulled the cover from a sofa and gestured for the ladies to seat themselves. "If you'll hand me your things, I'll hang 'em to dry in the kitchen," she said grudgingly.

Nell removed her bonnet and pelisse and helped Amelia with hers. "Thank you, Mrs. Penloe," she said coldly, handing the things to her. "And when you've done that, please make our bedrooms ready."

"Wait, Nell," Amelia asked plaintively. "May we not have a tea tray before we retire?"

"Of course, dear," Nell said contritely. "You must be starved."

"No, no," Amelia assured her, "but a cup of tea would be so very soothing, don't you think?"

"I'd be happy to oblige 'ee wi' the tea tray, ma'am," Mrs. Penloe said, "but I beg 'ee to take your leave soon as your things be dry an' you be a bit refreshed." Her eyes met Nell's with a sudden, pleading look.

Nell's anger, which had flared up at Mrs. Penloe's words, died down again at the look of misery in the housekeeper's eyes. "I don't understand you, Mrs. Penloe," she said, searching the woman's face closely. "You seem a kind and sensible sort. Surely you cannot expect us to go back out into that storm—and at this hour of the night?"

Mrs. Penloe blinked at Nell with eyes that seemed to be about to fill with tears. She bit her lip and, clutching the damp clothing against her breast, shook her head. "But, you see . . . you *mustn't* stay! There be . . . reasons . . ."

"What reasons?"

Mrs. Penloe's eyes met Nell's imploringly for a moment and then fell. "I . . . I cain't say, Miss. Don't ask me. But you must not stay! You'll not be happy here."

"Our happiness is not your affair. I remind you, Mrs. Penloe, that this is *our* house, not yours. We are here, and we must all make the best of it, even you. After you've seen to our tea, I'd be obliged if you set yourself to preparing two bedchambers for us. And the first thing tomorrow morning, you are to send your husband into Padstow, or wherever it is you purchase foodstuffs, and stock up your larder with whatever is needed. Tell him to hire what household staff he may deem necessary to make this place livable for us. For we intend to remain for an indefinite period!"

Mrs. Penloe looked from Nell to Lady Amelia helplessly. "An indefinite p-period . . .?" she asked quaveringly.

"Mrs. Penloe, I don't wish to be unkind," Nell said patiently, "but you force me to say something unpleasant. I'm sure you have reasons to wish us to be gone—perhaps you and your husband are reluctant to buckle down to some real work after all these years of running Thorndene on your own—"

Mrs. Penloe gasped. "Mr. Penloe and me be honest, hardworking folk!" she declared tartly. "I don't take kindly to what you be sayin'!"

"And *I* don't take kindly to being told to remove myself from my family's house!" Nell answered with asperity. "I'm quite willing to take your word that it's not the work you're afraid of. But you can take *mine* that Lady Amelia and I intend to remain here. So you may as well go about your duties." And she turned her back on the unhappy housekeeper and strode to the curtained window. She pulled back the drapery, releasing a cloud of dust, and stared out at the rain, gnashing her teeth in irritation at the weather, the dust and the unpleasant welcome they'd received.

When she looked back, she found that Mrs. Penloe was still standing there, the wet garments clutched against her chest, looking at Nell with an expression of unhappy indecision. "Mrs. Penloe," Nell said, her voice quietly threatening, "I believe you have your orders."

Mrs. Penloe's eyes wavered and dropped. With a reluctant sigh, she turned and left the room.

Nell and Amelia spent the next few minutes in useless speculation about what had been Mrs. Penloe's purpose in attempting to drive them away, but the conversation soon flagged. Neither one had any plausible theory to offer, and both were too tired to encourage idle talk. They sat in silence, waiting impatiently for the comfort of a cup of hot tea, when there was a hesitant tap at the door. "Tea!" sighed Amelia. "At last!"

"Come in, Mrs. Penloe," Nell called.

But it was the coachman, not Mrs. Penloe, who entered. He took off his hat and approached them timidly. "I jes' came to tell you ladies that I'm off to Padstow now, if you was wishful to come with me," he said.

"Padstow? *Now?*" Nell asked. "But why? Surely the Penloes can find a place for you to bed down for the night."

"Oh, yes'm, they can. But I ain't wishful to stay, y'see."

Nell shook her head, puzzled. "But you can't wish to drive back to Padstow in this rain! You've been sitting on that box since six this morning, and it must be after ten by now!"

"Almost eleven, but I don't mind. Rather stay at the inn in Padstow, y'see. You'd best do the same. Be glad to take you there," the coachman said, edging toward the door.

"But . . . I don't understand . . ." Amelia said in bewilderment. "Didn't you tell me, not a half hour ago, that you were glad not to have to drive back tonight?"

"Aye, my lady, I did say that. But that was afore I heard . . ."

"Heard what?"

The coachman looked down at his hat, turning it around in his fingers uncomfortably. "What the Penloe boy was hintin' to me in the stable."

Nell sighed impatiently. "What tale did he tell you? That there are no clean bedrooms? It's ridiculous, you know. There's plenty of room in a great house like this. I truly believe that they just want to avoid the extra work we'll give them. Take my advice, coachman, and ignore them. Go to the kitchen and tell them I want you to be given something to eat and that your clothes are to be dried and pressed. Then get yourself to bed."

The coachman, disagreeing with Nell's assessment of the Penloes, shook his head disapprovingly and spoke up in their defense. "They already gave me a bite to eat, ma'am. Good Cornish pasty they brought me from their own supper, and a mug o' hot Shenagrum. And there's a warm, dry room they offered me over the stables. Good people they are, all three. But I'll not stay the night, not me."

Nell looked at him with a puzzled frown. "You're quite free to go, of course. But why would you wish to venture out on such a night?"

The man shuffled his feet uncomfortably but didn't answer.

"Seems to me you're acting like a fool," Amelia put in flatly.

The coachman's head came up in quick self-defense. "Foolish is as things turn out," he said truculently. "Mayhap some others be the fools for stayin' in this place. You can call me a fool, but I don't stay in a house what's got a ghost!"

"A *ghost*?" Nell gasped in amused surprise.

"What?" Amelia squealed, startled.

"That's right, my lady," the coachman said to Amelia, feeling a sense of satisfaction that he'd frightened her, "a ghost. The young lad didn't come right out with it, but I could tell he was tryin' to warn me. *Now* do you want to come back to Padstow wi' me?"

Nell laughed. "A ghost, eh? Is *that* what drives you out into the rain? Well, go ahead if you must, but we'll not go with you. It would take something much more real than a ghost to drive *us* out on a night like this."

The coachman shrugged and bowed himself out. But Amelia was staring at Nell with frightened eyes, not courageous enough to admit to the young, intrepid girl that she, for one, would quite easily be driven out into the rain if anything even *remotely* resembling a ghost should wander into her vicinity.

Chapter Four

MRS. PENLOE HURRIED down the stairs and into the kitchen, carefully shutting the kitchen door behind her. The damp outer-garments that the ladies had given her were still clutched against her chest, but she gave no thought to them. Her eyes were fixed on the man who sat at the large oak table in the center of the room. "Oh, Master Harry," she said in despair, "I be afeared we're in trouble!"

The man looked up at her and raised a quizzical eyebrow. "Oh?" he asked curiously. "Who was it at the door?"

"Two ladies!" Mrs. Penloe announced in a voice of doom. "Two ladies of the *family*!"

"Damnation!" the man muttered angrily. He was lean and tall and, even while sitting at the kitchen table in his shirtsleeves, had the look of a gentleman. His face was strikingly handsome, with dark, aristocratically arched brows and a strong, aquiline nose; his thick black hair was dramatically emphasized by a lock of white which grew from the center of his hairline and fell in disarray over his right eye; and his hands, while large and strong, were made surprisingly graceful by their long fingers. One hand was now supporting his chin and the other drumming impatiently on the table-top. "*Family,* you say?" he asked, looking up at Mrs. Penloe with a frown. "Who are they? Did you get their names?"

Before Mrs. Penloe could answer, the door opened and Will came in. Like his wife, he carefully closed the door behind him. He gave the man at the table a troubled look and, sucking at the stem of his still-unlit pipe, he asked, "Has she told 'ee?"

The man at the table nodded glumly.

"Well, you couldn't expect 'em to go out again on such a night," Will said, crossing the room to the box where the firewood was stored.

"What are we to do?" asked Mrs. Penloe, shaking out the pelisses she'd carried in and hanging them on the backs of two chairs. "Are we to let 'em stay?"

"No!" the man at the table said adamantly.

Will stopped stacking the small load of firewood he was gathering and stared at the man in surprise. "There ain't nothing else for it," he said. "Might as well face it. They're fixed here, for the night at least."

"Mr. Penloe!" his wife declared angrily. "Mind what you say to his lordship, if you please! There'll be no disrespect to him in this kitchen—or anywhere else in this house!"

Will Penloe stared at his wife in chagrin. Then, reddening, he glanced embarrassedly at the man at the table. He often forgot that this man, Captain Henry Thorne, was now the sixth Earl of Thornbury and the new Lord of Thorndene. Sitting here in the kitchen in his shirtsleeves, he was just like one of his family. In fact, at this time of his life, Captain Henry belonged more to the Penloe family than to the Thornes. Will Penloe very much doubted that the Thornes would even recognize him at this moment, if any of them should chance to wander in. It was not only in the recently acquired streak of white hair that Captain Henry had changed. He was much thinner than he'd been when he left for Spain, and his boyish look was gone. But the greatest change—the change that had brought him here to live in modest anonymity among the Penloes—was one that would not have been noticed except by the most discerning: the crutch that rested against the table was the only sign that the Captain's left leg had been replaced by one of wood.

Will Penloe had known Captain Thorne since he was a boy, and the intimacy of their present way of life made him feel very close to his lordship. Mrs. Penloe's reproof had cut him to the quick. After three months of intimate association with the young Earl, he often forgot to address him with proper formality. But he never crossed beyond the bounds of deepest respect, and he would rather have had his tongue cut out than to say anything offensive to the man he held in such high regard. "Disrespect?" he asked defensively. "Is it *you* who talks o' disrespect? 'Tain't me what calls him 'Master Harry' like he was still twelve years old."

"Cain't help it," Mrs. Penloe said shamefacedly. "I'm that used to't, I cain't seem to stop. You don't mind, do 'ee, Mas—your lordship?"

Lord Thorne looked up at the housekeeper, who was watching him with troubled affection. "I much prefer 'Master Harry' to 'your lordship,' I assure you," he said with an abstracted smile. "Now stop worrying about showing me disrespect (which neither of you has ever done, even when I was a boy), and let's set our minds to finding a way to rid ourselves of our unwanted guests."

"There ain't no way, my lord," Will muttered glumly.

"Not unless you face 'em and order 'em out." He sucked on his pipestem meditatively. "After all, Cap'n Henry, it *is* your house."

"No," Mrs. Penloe said sharply, "he cain't do that. 'Twould give the whole game away. We must think o' somethin' else."

The three fell silent. Mrs. Penloe studied the face of her adored "Master Harry" with heartfelt concern. She'd known Henry Thorne since he had first visited Cornwall, the summer after his father had died. The lonely, orphaned boy had touched her heart, and she had set about filling him with all the nourishing food and honest affection that he could absorb. She had taken an almost proprietary pride in his growth to praiseworthy manhood. She'd looked forward eagerly to his annual visits to Thorndene, had read, reread and treasured his occasional letters, and had looked at him in his first uniform with that mixture of pride and fear that a mother feels. Even the birth of her own son had not lessened the strong maternal affection she felt for him.

Her fears for his safety when he'd gone off to the Peninsula had turned out to be justified; the handsome, confident, happy Henry Thorne who'd gone to war was not the same man who'd come back. He'd returned with a face lined with pain, with eyes from which all the laughter had been washed away, with a streak of white hair cutting through the dark mass like a knife . . . and with his left leg cut off just below the knee.

Mrs. Penloe sighed deeply and set about preparing a tea tray for the new arrivals, though she did it with ill will. The ladies were obviously cold, fatigued and hungry, but she had no sympathy for them. They were causing trouble for her dear Harry, and therefore she had no room in her heart to care for *their* concerns. It was Harry for whom she cared—her dear, kind, good Captain Harry, who had come back from the war so altered in body and spirit.

It still pained her to look at him, even though the three months he'd spent here at Thorndene had brought some color back to his face and filled out the gaunt hollows of his cheeks. Although he was still the handsomest man she'd ever laid eyes on, the lines about his mouth, the weariness of his eyes, the awkwardness of his movements when he walked with the crutch under his arm, the tinge of bitterness in his attitude toward his future—all caused her heart to constrict. He wanted only one thing of life now: to live in solitary, undisturbed peace in this out-of-the-way place. She and Will had begged him, when they'd felt that he was restored to good health, to return to London and take his rightful place as his grandfather's successor, but he would hear none of it. As soon as he'd learned that the old Earl had died, his interest in the life of London had waned. London was the last place to which he wished to go. He wanted nothing to do with his family or friends. There was no one he cared to see. He wanted no attention, no pity. Let them think him dead, he declared. Let them give the titles to his Uncle Charles. He no longer cared about titles and estates. They were part of the past, like the leg he'd lost.

Convinced that a life of peaceful solitude was the only thing that would make Lord Thorne happy, Mr. and Mrs. Penloe and their son, Jemmy, joined forces to keep the knowledge of Henry Thorne's existence from the rest of the world. His name was never mentioned to outsiders. Their orders of food and necessaries, which they purchased in Padstow, were carefully planned to conceal the fact that anyone but the Penloes resided at Thorndene. Captain Henry ate the same food they did, and he took his meals with them in the kitchen or alone in the study he'd set up in the rear of the west wing. There he would not be discovered by any chance visitors. Much of the house was closed off and unused; no one could guess that a few of the rooms in the west wing had been made into a comfortably habitable apartment.

The only time Lord Thorne left the house was to ride his horse—a form of exercise he loved, but which he indulged in only in the very early mornings when the road was free of travelers. In the three months since his arrival his presence had remained undetected.

The unheralded arrival of the two ladies of the Thorne family was a severe blow to their sense of security. Mrs. Penloe, who by this time had developed so fierce a sense of protectiveness toward her "Master Harry" that she was not unlike a mother bear with a wounded cub, would gladly have locked the two intruders in the coal cellar or, better still, pushed them out of the house into the rain. But since such action would be only a temporary solution to the problem (for the ladies would be certain to return with the proper authorities, who would hold investigations and put their magisterial noses where they were not in the least wanted) she refrained from taking such drastic action. But what action she *could* take, she did not know.

Will Penloe took his pipe from between his teeth and spoke. "You may as well make up rooms for 'em, m'dear. They'll have to stay the night. Per'aps, Cap'n, you'll think o' somethin' by mornin'."

Lord Thorne nodded. Leaning on the table for support, he pushed himself up from his chair. "Will's right, I suppose. You may as well make them comfortable for the night," he told Mrs. Penloe with a sigh. He reached for his crutch and swung himself to the door. "I'll keep to my room until we find a way to send them packing. Put them in the east-wing bedrooms."

Mrs. Penloe hurried to open the door for him (a service which made him wince with irritation every time she performed it, for he was quite able to do it for himself), but the door opened before she reached it and Jemmy entered, his face lit with a self-satisfied grin. "Well, I scared the *coachman* off good and proper," he announced proudly. "The coach took off down the road so hasty-like, you'd 'ave thought the devil was after it."

"Did you indeed?" Lord Thorne asked admiringly. "How did you manage to accomplish *that*?"

"'Tweren't a bit hard, m'lord," the boy said proudly. "I just tol' him we had a presence."

"A *presence*?"

"Yes, sir. You know what I mean . . . a ghost."

Lord Thorne looked at Jemmy with interest. "Are you saying you told the coachman the house is *haunted*?"

"That's *just* what I tol' him. Turned a proper green, he did!" Jemmy bragged.

Will Penloe gave an amused snort. "You mean the fool heard 'ghost' and took to his heels?"

"Like a shot," Jemmy said proudly.

"That's most interesting," Lord Thorne mused. "The very *thought* that the house may be haunted sent him scurrying off in the rain . . ." He leaned comfortably on his crutch and smiled at the boy admiringly. "Jemmy, I think that was very clever of you: Very clever."

"Are you thinkin' what I'm thinkin', Cap'n?" Will asked eagerly.

Henry nodded. "I certainly am. Perhaps the same ghost will scare away our other intruders. "What do *you* think, my dear?" he asked Mrs. Penloe.

She shook her head doubtfully. "Those two be too stubborn-like and shrewd to take to their heels just because we tell 'em a ghost story."

Henry Thorne grinned. "But we'll give them *more* than a story, love. We'll give them a . . . a . . . what was it you said, Jemmy? A *presence*!"

Mrs. Penloe, picking up the tea tray to deliver to the visitors, paused and looked at him suspiciously. "I don't mind what you mean. Be 'ee plannin' some devilment, Master Harry?"

"Yes, I am, love," Lord Thorne said, his smile widening. "Real devilment. If they won't be frightened off by the *story* of a ghost, we'll give them a ghost in the flesh . . . if a ghost can be said to be 'in the flesh' at all."

Mrs. Penloe stared at him closely, peering through the tiny spectacles perched on her nose. She noticed that a spark of amusement had ignited in his eyes. For a moment she was reminded of a younger Master Harry, full of spirit and mischief. Could it be that he was *enjoying* this dilemma? If he could turn this disastrous occurence into a *lark*, there was real hope that the Harry of old was yet alive in him. She put down the tray. Her feeling of depression slid away, and although she did not smile, her eyes held an unmistakable gleam as she placed her hands on her hips and scowled at him in mock disapproval. "An' how do 'ee propose to bring in a *ghost*, I ask 'ee?"

"Never you mind, my dear. I have a plan. But I've decided that the ladies should not be given rooms in the east wing after all. Put them in the front bedrooms of the *west* wing, if you please."

Mrs. Penloe frowned in earnest. "The west wing? Are 'ee daft?"

"Not a bit. The large corner bedroom has a secret passage that will just suit my purpose."

"Aha!" Will Penloe nodded approvingly. "I begin to follow 'ee now."

Lord Thorne winked at him and started out the door. But Mrs. Penloe was not comfortable with the shift in plans. "But *I* don't follow 'ee at all!" she complained. "I don't like 'em bein' so close to 'ee. 'Tis a dangerous game you're playin'."

"Don't worry, love," Lord Thorne said, reaching over and chucking her affectionately under the chin, "there's nothing dangerous about it. I'll simply provide a few sights and sounds that the good ladies are not expecting, and by tomorrow morning they'll be *begging* Will to drive them into Padstow."

"But...which one do you want put in the corner room?" she asked, not very reassured.

"Either one. It won't make a particle of difference. When I send the lady you put in the corner bedroom flying out, screaming in fear, you can be sure that the other will follow." And with an almost hearty laugh, he left the room.

It was well past midnight by the time the bedrooms had been prepared for the newcomers and almost one before

Lady Amelia had found a warm nightgown in her voluminous trunk and had prepared herself for bed. She had fallen into a deep sleep when a strange clanking disturbed her. At first she thought she was dreaming and endeavored to ignore the sound, but the noise was quite real and very close. At last she realized that it was not a dream and opened her eyes. The clanking seemed to come from somewhere near the window—a casement which was set, dormer-like, into an alcove cut in the two-foot-thick wall. A heavy drapery curtained the window, and the arched opening of the alcove was dressed with a pair of sheer white curtains.

Her heart beat rapidly, for the sound was both unexpected and horrifying. It seemed to combine the rattle of chains and an unidentifiable clumping noise. But before she could shake off her paralysis of fear, something more horrifying occurred: a shimmering light seemed to materialize behind the curtain. At first it was faint, but it quickly brightened until...

Amelia gasped in terror. She could make it out distinctly. It was a candle... a candle floating in the air all by itself! It swayed back and forth behind the curtain, and with each sway it seemed to come closer. With eyes bulging in fright, a racing pulse and a scream which stuck in her throat, she threw back the covers, bounded out of bed with the speed of a much younger woman and flew to the door.

She slammed the door behind her and, in her bare feet, crossed the hall to Nell's room. Without bothering to knock, she burst in. "Nell, *Nell*!" she cried into the darkness. "Get up! Quickly!"

Nell woke with pulse-racing suddenness. "Amelia?" she asked tensely. "Is that you?"

"Yes, yes!" the old woman said breathlessly. "Where *are* you? I can't see anything in this darkness. Light a candle, quickly!"

Nell did as she was bid. With the first spark of the match, Amelia found her way to the bed. Tremblingly, she threw her arms around the bemused Nell. "Oh, Nell, I saw it! I *saw* it! The *ghost!*"

Nell stared at her in astonishment. "What are you talking about? Please, dearest, try to calm yourself. I can't understand a word of what you're saying."

"I tell you, it's true, Nell! There *is* a ghost—just as the coachman said!"

Nell, now fully awake, smiled at Amelia as if she were a child. "Goosecap!" she said affectionately. "You were only dreaming."

"No, no, Nell, I swear! I *thought* I was dreaming when I first heard it . . . You didn't hear anything, did you? A sort of clanking and thumping?"

"No, of course I didn't."

"No, I didn't think so. You couldn't have been sleeping so soundly if you had. It was a dreadful noise, I can tell you! Dreadful! It came from the window alcove. I know I didn't dream it because I heard it for several seconds after I had sat up!"

"Well, I suppose there *could* have been some noise," Nell said reasonably. "A bird trapped in the eaves, or the wind howling through some crack in the wall . . ."

"No, it wasn't like that. It wasn't like anything I've ever heard before."

"But Amelia," Nell comforted, taking the old woman's hands in hers, "there could be any number of explanations for strange sounds in the night. It's ridiculous to blame them on a ghost."

Amelia shook her head. "But I *saw* it . . . or at least its candle!"

"What? You *saw* something?" Nell asked in disbelief.

"Yes, *truly!* A burning candle, floating in the air!" She lowered her voice to a tense whisper. "Held aloft by an *unseen hand!*"

Nell could not help herself—she laughed. "Oh, Amelia, what nonsense! You sound like a character in a book by Mrs. Radcliffe."

Amelia sighed. "Very well, laugh at me. But I shan't

remain here another day. And I shan't permit you to stay, either. We are both going home. *Tomorrow!*"

"You're quite upset, dearest. Let's not talk about this now. Tomorrow the sun may shine. You'll feel quite differently then. In the meantime, let's try to get a little sleep. Here, take the candle with you, and keep it lit beside your bed. That should frighten any ghost away."

Amelia drew herself erect. "Are you suggesting," she demanded angrily, "that I *return* ... to ... that room?"

"Don't you wish to—?"

"*Wish* to! I'll never set foot in there again!"

"Very well, then, I'll go," Nell said firmly, climbing out of bed. "You sleep here."

"No!" Amelia screamed, grasping her arm. "You *can't* go in there!"

"I'll take the candle. Ghosts don't like the light," Nell improvised, trying to placate her.

"This one does. He carried his own candle, I tell you! Besides, I don't want to be alone. Please, Nell, stay here with me!"

Nell hesitated. But Amelia, sitting stiffly erect, the bedclothes clutched against her breast with one shaking hand while the other held on to Nell's arm with a grasp made firm by sheer terror, looked so pathetic that Nell weakened. "Very well, dear, we'll share the bed tonight," she said with a soothing smile. And gently loosening Amelia's hold on her arm, she climbed back into the bed again.

After a while, Amelia became calm enough to permit Nell to blow out the candle. But even in the darkness, neither was able to fall asleep, Amelia because she was watching and listening for the ghost to make another appearance, and Nell because she could feel the tension in Amelia's body as she lay rigidly beside her. "Can't you relax, Amelia?" Nell asked gently. "Do try to forget about the ghost. *I'm* here with you. The ghost won't dare to make an appearance while we're together."

Amelia sighed. "You don't believe me, do you?" she

accused. "I can tell. Do you think I've gone mad?"

"Of course not! But eyes and ears can play tricks on one, especially in the night, when one is weary to the bone, as you are."

"Hummmph!" the old woman grunted in annoyance. "You're trying to find excuses for me. But I don't want 'em. I know what I saw. I almost wish the ghost would reappear, so that you'd see him too!" With that, she drew the coverlet up to her neck and turned her back on Nell.

The two women lay silently beside each other and wished for sleep to come. But it was not until the light of dawn at last crept through the break in the draperies, and she realized that the ghost was not going to reappear, that Amelia finally drifted into sleep. And Nell, hearing the gentle snore from the lady beside her, at last permitted herself to do the same.

Chapter Five

THE RAIN HAD ceased during the night, and the morning brought a pale promise of sunshine. Mrs. Penloe waited tensely for some word from the new arrivals, but none came. Finally, well past nine o'clock, she went upstairs to peep into their bedrooms. Discovering the corner room deserted, she was not surprised to see the two ladies sharing the bed in the other room. What surprised her was the soundness of their sleep. Although the "ghost" had succeeded in frightening Lady Amelia from her bed, it had not managed to keep her, nor Miss Belden, from enjoying a deep and peaceful slumber.

Realizing that they were not likely to rouse themselves very soon, she prepared a breakfast tray for Lord Thorne and climbed the back stairs to his rooms. She found him awake, dressed and peering frowningly out the window.

"Good mornin', Master Harry," she greeted him. "Lookin' for somethin' out there?"

"I was hoping to see signs of activity in the stables. Aren't the ladies leaving?"

Mrs. Penloe shrugged. "Don't know for sure. They be sound asleep."

"They couldn't be! Why, I'm certain the poor thing was frightened out of her wits. Do you know who that old lady *is*? My Great-aunt Amelia! It gave me quite a turn, I can tell you, when I recognized her. I've no liking for what I did to her. If I'd known that it was my sweet old Aunt Amelia whom I was frightening half to death, I'd never have done it."

"Well, never mind, Master Harry. There weren't no real harm done that I can make out. She be sleepin' like a babe. Come to the table an' have breakfast. I've made 'ee some eggs and covered 'em with scrolls, just the way you like 'em."

Henry seated himself at the little table and picked up a fork. But his mind was not on eggs and bits of bacon, but on his unwelcome guests. "What am I to do now?" he asked, half to himself. "What if they *don't* leave today? They may go wandering through the house, or—"

"I'll keep an eye on 'em," Mrs. Penloe asured him. "An' you can try again tonight."

"But I don't want to frighten poor Amelia again. Who's the other one? Did you get her name?"

"Miss Belden, I was told. Lady Amelia calls her 'Nell'."

"Nell? Nell Belden? I don't believe I know who ... Wait, I seem to remember ... a scrawny little brat that Sybil took under her wing. Helen Belden, that's who she is. Perfect! Do you think, my dear, that you can persuade them to change bedrooms?"

"There'll be no need, I'll warrant. Lady Amelia was too frightened to return to her room last night—she bedded down wi' Miss Belden. If they *do* stay on another night, 'tain't Lady Amelia who'll be in the corner bedroom."

Henry Thorne smiled. "You may be right. Well then,

my dear, by this time tomorrow, our house will be free of unwanted visitors."

"'Tis a bit too cocksure you be, Master Harry," Mrs. Penloe cautioned. "Miss Belden's growed up since you last seen her, seems like. 'Tain't no scrawny brat you'll be dealin' with. Seems to me she's a good head on her, and a wide streak o' stubborn pride."

But Henry's expectations would not be dampened. "Have no fear, my dear. If the floating candle doesn't do it, I have one or two other tricks up my sleeve. They're bound to send her packing quickly enough." And he attacked his eggs with cheerful enthusiasm.

Amelia and Nell made no appearance until noon, when they came down the stairs and settled themselves in the sitting room which they'd occupied the night before. They had slept well into the morning and had dissipated the rest of it by arguing about remaining at Thorndene. Amelia was somewhat calmed by her few hours of sleep and by the fact that the daylight did indeed make the events of the night before seem like a dream. Nevertheless, she was all for making a quick return to London. Nell pointed out reasonably that such a course would result in her enforced marriage to Sir Nigel. Since no other course suggested itself, and since Nell offered to change bedrooms with Amelia (just as Mrs. Penloe had predicted), the elderly lady agreed to give Thorndene another chance.

Having instructed Mr. and Mrs. Penloe to meet with them in the sitting room, Nell set about making plans for the running of the household. It was decided that the dining room, the library, the morning room and the little sitting room in which they now sat should be cleaned and opened for their use, but that the rest of the house could be kept closed. Will Penloe was dispatched to Padstow with instructions to purchase sufficient provisions for their meals, to hire an abigail to assist the ladies with their clothing and comforts, and to aid Mrs. Penloe in tending to the expanded household. After he'd gone, the ladies asked Mrs. Penloe to prepare some sort of luncheon for them. Anything she had on hand would do, Nell told her, for they both were famished.

Mrs. Penloe, who had already opened and cleaned the dining room, set before them a modest luncheon of Cornish broth and something she called "Squab Pie." To the ladies, who had not eaten a proper meal since they'd left Exeter three days before, the luncheon was delicious. The ingredients of the broth were easily identified—carrots, cabbage, pork scraps and leeks. But the squab pie was something of a mystery, for although Amelia tasted apple, bacon and bits of mutton in it, and Nell was convinced that onions and cream were also included, neither could find a sign of squab, or indeed any poultry, in the concoction. Nevertheless, they ate every bit that was put before them and sighed with contentment when they had finished.

During the afternoon, while Amelia retired to her room to nap, Nell, noting that the sky had brightened considerably, requested that young Jemmy take her on a tour of the grounds. The lad seemed reluctant but was persuaded to agree. He led her through the Great Hall and out the front door. She found herself in a courtyard protected from the wind on three sides by the main house and its two wings, and on the fourth by a fortress-like building with a large archway in the center. It was through this archway that they had entered the night before. "This is quite like a medieval fortress," she exclaimed to Jemmy.

"Yes'm," the boy answered, "that just what it is. In old Cornish, it was called the Dinas of Thorne. That means the Thornes' Hill-fort."

"Why *Hill*-fort?" she asked.

"When we come round to the back, you'll see for yoursel'," the boy said with a smile.

They walked around the east wing of the house, through some well-planned but overgrown gardens, to the back. There the land sloped sharply down to the cliffs which edged the estuary. The grounds close to the house were beautifully terraced and dotted with fascinating, wind-blown trees like those she'd seen from the carriage the evening before. But what took her breath away was the sight of the wide Camel Estuary beyond the cliffs and of the Atlantic beyond, stretching in gray majesty to the far horizon. The height of the grounds on which she stood permitted her a panoramic view of land, sea and sky. "Now I understand about the Hill-fort," she told the boy with a smile of insight. "The Dinas of Thorne. *Thorndene!* The Thorne's fort on the hill."

She looked back at the manorhouse looming up behind her, its gray granite stone and mullioned windows shining in the light of the quickly setting sun. It was an imposing sight. "What are those buildings over there?" Nell asked, gesturing to her right.

Jemmy gave her a quick, nervous glance. "The ...stables..." he said hesitantly.

"Let's walk over to them, shall we?" she suggested.

"Well...I...'Tis a longish bit o' walk..."

"Nonsense," Nell said briskly, keeping her eyes fixed on his face.

He flicked her a worried look and then lowered his eyes to the ground. "'Tis close to dinner time. My mum may have need o' me in the kitchen."

"It *is* getting late," Nell agreed readily, "and I've kept you from your work too long. Go along to your duties, Jemmy. I'll walk over to the stables by myself."

Jemmy's face flushed with alarm. "Yoursel'?" he asked uncomfortably. "You don't want to do that! Why, 'tis...'tis..."

"What, Jemmy? What troubles you, boy?"

The boy kicked at a pebble underfoot. "'Tain't seemly, you walkin' about by yoursel'," he muttered.

She raised her eyebrows in cool rebuff. "There is nothing unseemly in my walking about on my own grounds. And it is much *more* unseemly for you to talk to me in that way," she said reprovingly.

"Yes'm, I'm sorry," the boy said sheepishly, but he didn't move.

"Well, go along, Jemmy. Your chores are waiting."

He sighed. "Best I go with 'ee," he said truculently. "Mum'd trounce me proper if I let 'ee go off alone."

"But why?" Nell asked curiously.

Jemmy, though a good, honest boy, was not at all lacking in imagination. The loneliness of his life in Cornwall encouraged his talents for pranks, storytelling and invention. So he was not long at a loss for words. "The *presence*, y'know," he said in a suddenly conspiratorial tone. "I didn't wish to frighten 'ee, but one cain't be certain when the...the presence will show himsel'."

"The presence? What do you mean?"

"The ghost, ma'am," he said, looking at her with wide-eyed innocence. "The Thorndene ghost, y'know. Sure, you must have heard o' the ghost?"

"More than I wish to," Nell answered drily. "You don't mean to tell me that a grown boy like you believes in ghosts?"

"Oh, yes'm, I do! An' so would 'ee, if you'd seen him as many times as I've done!"

"So you've seen him, have you? Well, well! You stir my interest, Jemmy. I quite look forward to meeting your ghost myself. But now, if you please, lead the way to the stables."

The reason for the boy's reluctance to show her the stables was not clear to Nell at first. The buildings were unexceptional, well-kept and orderly, the few horses housed inside were healthy-looking carriage horses, and, in a corner stall, Nell noted a graceful mare who seemed perfectly suited for her to ride when weather should permit. But the boy's unease did not abate. He stayed close at her side and seemed to be trying to hurry her out. A sudden, loud neighing cleared the mystery. Nell raised her head to trace the sound, but the boy tried to block her view. "What was that?" she asked, startled.

"Nought to trouble 'ee, ma'am," the boy said promptly. "We'd best start back."

Nell, ignoring his suggestion, thrust him out of her way

and strode to the stall behind him. "Good Lord! What a *magnificent* animal!" she exclaimed as her eyes fell on the great black beast whose existence the boy had evidently been trying to hide. It was the most splendid horse she'd ever seen, combining a feeling of tremendous power with a graceful beauty. "Whose horse *is* that?" she asked, awe-struck.

Jemmy's mind raced, but he could think of no explanation for the presence of such a horse. "Well, it . . . ah . . . it b'longs to the Thornes, o'course . . ." he said stumblingly.

Nell tore her eyes from the beautiful animal and fixed them on the discomfitted boy. "The Thornes, you say? How interesting. I'm surprised they keep him here, hidden away from the world, when he'd surely have been the talk of London had they taken him there."

The boy shrugged without attempting to answer.

"Who exercises him? Who rides him? Surely not *you*?" Nell asked.

The boy lifted his head proudly. "I ride him sometimes . . . when he—I mean, when I'm permitted."

"*He?* Who is it who permits you?"

Jemmy bit his lip. "My dad," he said, lowering his eyes to the ground again.

"Is it your *dad* who rides him?" she persisted, disbelieving.

He glanced up at her briefly. "Yes'm," he said shortly.

"I shouldn't think a man his age could manage an animal that size," Nell remarked.

The boy didn't answer. After waiting a moment she shrugged and turned back to the horse. "Well, he seems very well cared for, by the look of him. What's his name?"

"He's called Caceres."

"Caceres," Nell repeated lovingly. "That's Spanish, isn't it?"

"Yes'm. That's where he was bred," the boy said, stroking the horse's nozzle proudly.

Nell watched the horse for another moment. "He

certainly is a beauty," she said and turned to leave. With her hand on the stable door, she turned to look back at Jemmy, who was checking Caceres' stall door. "But I can't understand why you didn't want me to see him."

Jemmy opened his mouth to protest, but Nell stopped him with a motion of her hand. "Don't bother to deny it, boy. I'm not easily put off the mark by lies—or by ghost stories, either." And she turned on her heel and walked out.

Will Penloe returned before sunset, his wagon loaded with provisions and accompanied by the young woman he'd hired to be the abigail. The girl was called Gwinnys, a name taken from that of a Cornish saint, she promptly explained. Gwinnys had a broad, heart-shaped face, full lips turned up in a perpetual smile and hair that hung about her face in unkempt tendrils, as if she'd washed it in the sea and had let it dry without bothering to comb it. She looked about the house with eager interest, keeping up a flow of excited comments about her delight in being permitted to work in the "great house." Her thick West-country accent delighted the ladies, and by the time Amelia had helped her brush her hair and Nell had found a clean and proper dress for her to wear, they both agreed that they were pleased with her. The girl's persistent cheerfulness, her enthusiastic eagerness to perform any task assigned to her (and many that were not) made her pleasant to have about. She brightened up the gloomy house considerably.

Mrs. Penloe viewed Gwinnys' arrival with mixed feelings. While her presence would undoubtedly relieve Mrs. Penloe's load of work, it would, at the same time, make her life more complicated; she would have to take special care to keep Lord Thorne out of sight. His meals would have to be prepared and spirited up to him only at times when Gwinnys was not likely to pop into the kitchen. All the Penloes would have to put strict guard on their tongues when the girl was around. More and more, Mrs. Penloe wished her guests would go away.

Nevertheless, it was an excellent dinner she put before

the ladies that evening. The dining room, aired and dusted and gleaming, made Nell and Amelia glad they had worn proper dinner dress. They looked around in pleased surprise at the warm glow of the polished table, the epergne in the center filled with fruit and bright candles, and the cheerful fire in the hearth. The mutton, the smoked pilchards (a fish whose omnipresence any visitor to Cornwall soon learns to accept) and the Likky Pie were all deliciously prepared. Gwinnys helped Mrs. Penloe serve, her smile adding to the pleasant atmosphere. For the first time since their arrival, Lady Amelia showed signs of becoming her cheerful self. And after Nell suggested that Gwinnys be given Amelia's dressing room in which to sleep, she became almost reconciled to remaining. The suggestion was greeted with equal eagerness by Amelia and Gwinnys. Gwinnys had never had such a beautiful room before, she exclaimed, and Amelia, with Gwinnys so close by, could face the night with a feeling of security. At long last, Nell began to feel that their stay in Cornwall might turn out to be not so very bad after all.

When they retired for the night, Amelia made Nell promise to call out loudly if anything untoward should occur. "I'm a very light sleeper," she assured the girl. "The moment I hear you, I shall instantly rouse Gwinnys and we both shall come flying to your aid."

Remembering the shaken old woman who had burst in on her the night before, Amelia's brave words and vigorous tone made Nell laugh. She shook her head and assured her companion that she was not in the least worried about a ghost-visit. Then she went to her room and locked her door. Without the least hesitation, she crossed to the window and checked the latch. It was securely bolted. She drew the heavy drapes and closed the sheer curtains that covered the inner arch of the window enclosure. Then, true to her words, unperturbed by any nervousness or unease, she soon slipped into a deep, untroubled sleep.

When the ghost appeared, a little after midnight, he

found it necessary to crash his chains into the wall three or four times before the sleeping figure made any movement at all. Finally, however, the sound penetrated Nell's consciousness, and she sat up with a start. "Who's there?" she muttered sleepily.

There was no answer but the rattle of chains, a thump or two, and a dim light appeared behind the curtain. Then, just as Amelia had described, a candle floated into view, exactly as if it *were* being held by an unseen hand. "Come now, speak up," Nell demanded. "Who's there? What sort of hoax is this?"

Again there was no answer, but the candle began to swing to and fro alarmingly. Nell leaned forward. "Stop that this instant!" she ordered. "Do you want to set fire to the curtains?"

Nell was sure she heard a brief snort of laughter, but the sound became a moan before she had time to identify it with certainty. The moan was low and definitely masculine. "So, there *is* someone there! Is it you, Will Penloe?"

There was another moan, but this time with an unmistakably negative tone.

"Are you trying to make me believe that you really *are* a ghost?" Nell inquired of the candle.

This time the moan was affirmative.

"Are you going to do nothing but moan?" Nell asked querulously. "I don't see how we're going to converse at all sensibly this way. Can't you speak?"

There was another moan, but whether it was an affirmative or negative answer, Nell couldn't say. She tossed aside the bedclothes and swung her legs over the side of the bed decisively. "Can you see me, ghost?" she asked. "I give you fair warning that I'm getting out of bed. If you don't take yourself off this minute, I shall douse you with this pitcher of water." And she reached for the pitcher on the bedside table and held it up for the ghost to see.

There was threatening rattle of chains, but the candle remained swinging through the air in an arc-like motion.

"Very well, then," Nell said firmly. Grasping the pitcher in both hands, she crossed in her bare feet to the window enclosure. She reached out a hand to fling open the sheer curtains when a hideous wail stayed her. The sound made her courage flag, although it did not altogether fail. Without pulling back the curtains, she tossed the contents of the pitcher directly at the candle. To her astonishment, the flame remained lit. It was as if the candle were an illusion through which the water passed without effect. "Good God!" she gasped and backed away.

"Aha!" came a low, triumphant voice. "You *are* frightened after all!"

"I . . . I am *not*!" Nell declared. "It seems that you *can* speak, then."

"When I wish," the voice said.

"Well, then, I want you to know that I'm not in the least frightened. This is all some sort of trick."

"I can *see* that you're frightened," the ghost insisted.

"Oh? *Can* you see me?" Nell asked curiously, taking a step forward. "I didn't know whether or not ghosts can see—especially in candle form."

"Of course I can see you. Quite clearly," the ghost said in a matter-of-fact tone. "You are standing barefoot on this cold floor. Your right hand is clenched rather nervously at your side. And your nightcap's askew."

Nell's hand flew to her cap. It had slipped over her left ear. Tossing a challenging glance in the direction of the candle, she set the cap on her head firmly. "There, is that better? You know, you are quite a *rudesby* to spy on a girl in her nightclothes."

"Nonsense," came a prompt answer, the voice quite unghostly and with an unmistakable touch of amusement lurking in it. "Such things don't matter to *us*, you know."

"Well, they matter to *me*!" she said, pattering back to the nightstand and replacing the pitcher.

"Then why don't you hop back under the covers?" the ghost advised.

"No, I shan't. This nightgown covers me well enough."

The ghost chortled wickedly. "We apparitions have very good eyesight, you know. We can see through walls."

"What—? *Oh!*" Nell gasped, looking down at her thin linen gown in horror. Without another word, she dived for the bed and drew the coverlet up to her neck. The ghost seemed to be struggling to keep back a very human laugh. "You needn't laugh," she said, putting her chin up defiantly, "for I don't believe a *word* of what you're saying. Come now, be honest. Tell me who you are! I shan't call the magistrates if you're straight with me."

The voice became sepulchral. "I am the spirit of the late Harry D'Espry, smuggler and thief, born on the twelfth day of March, 1645, and died of sword wounds on the third of October, 1669."

"Died so young!" Nell said mockingly. "How sad! And have you been haunting this place ever since?"

There was an affirmative moan.

"Oh, dear," sighed Nell, "are you resorting to that dreadful moan again? What a pity!"

"You must go-o-o-o!" the voice said in a low, breathy wail.

"Why must I go?" she asked reasonably.

"This a place of danger!" he said in a frightening monotone. "You must go-o-o-o-o!"

"I'm not a bit frightened, Mr. D'Espry. And I intend to remain right here."

The candle began to swing crazily. "You must go-o-o-o!" the low voice insisted.

"Stop swinging that candle, you fool!" Nell said, alarmed.

But the light had disappeared. Nell peered into the sudden darkness. "Mr. D'Espry? Mr. D'Espry? Are you there?"

The answer came from a long way off. "You must go-o-o-o-o!" The voice wailed and faded away.

Nell jumped out of bed, lit her own candle and stared at the window alcove. She could see nothing behind the white curtains. Taking a deep breath, she moved carefully toward them. Bravely drawing them aside, she raised her candle and looked around. The heavy window drapes were drawn just as she had left them, but she opened them anyway. The window was firmly latched. There was no sign of anything at all out-of-the-way, except for the puddle of water on the floor. She carefully scrutinized the panels of the thick walls, but they offered no clue. With a shrug and sigh, she pattered back to her bed. This time she left her candle burning. She reviewed and reviewed the entire conversation with the "ghost," but sleep overtook her before she could make any sense of the incident.

While the rest of the household still slept, Mrs. Penloe carried his lordship's breakfast tray up the back stairs. She found him dressed in his riding breeches, waiting only for his breakfast before taking off on his morning ride. "Be 'ee set on ridin' today?" she asked in concern. "What if one o' the ladies should see 'ee?"

Lord Thorne felt no anxiety on that score. "No one will see me. London ladies are not known to rise before ten in the morning," he said cheerfully. "Besides, I'll stay close to the edge of the cliffs. Caceres and I are not likely to be noticed if we stay so far away from the house."

Mrs. Penloe took due note of his cheerful tone. She set down the tray and poured out a cup of steaming coffee for him. "Did your ghost do 'ee some good last night?" she asked hopefully.

He shook his head. "I'm afraid you were quite right about Miss Belden," he said, taking his place at the table. "She's an intrepid girl. I think it will take some doing to dislodge her. We'd better accustom ourselves to having them around for a while."

Mrs. Penloe stared at him in surprise. He seemed not only resigned to the invasion of his privacy—he was almost *cheerful* about it! Could it be that the challenge of frightening the visitors from the premises was a source of entertainment for him? Perhaps the presence of visitors— especially a young and pretty one—was a pleasant change from the boredom of the life he'd been living. For the first time, it occurred to Mrs. Penloe that the invasion of the Thorne ladies into their lives might not be a very bad thing after all. Her lips twitched in an almost invisible smile. "Very pretty little creature, Miss Belden be," she remarked casually, keeping her eyes fixed on his lordship's face.

"Mmmm," he assented noncommittally, absorbed in his breakfast.

Wisely, she said no more on the subject. She would watch and see. It promised to be a very interesting time.

Chapter Six

NELL WOKE ABRUPTLY that morning, as if some noise had sounded in her ears, but she did not know what it could have been. The room was absolutely still; no sound disturbed the early morning hush. A sudden recollection of the ghost-visit of the night before flashed into her mind. Was he back? She sat up and looked toward the window. There was no sound or sign of movement behind the white curtains—there was only a bit of pale sunlight which had crept in through a break in the drapes and painted itself on the curtains in a narrow stripe of light. Nell jumped out of bed, ran to the window and flung back the curtains. There was nothing at all out-of-the-way. The noise that had awakened her was probably something from a dream.

She opened the drapes to let the light in and stood gazing out at the grounds that stretched away from the manorhouse toward the distant cliffs. Through the morning haze she thought she saw a glint of the sea beyond. As she watched, she became aware of something moving along the cliffs. It was a horse, galloping at a good pace. From this distance if seemed to be dangerously close to the edge of the cliffs. Nell had no doubt that the large, sinewy animal was Caceres. She could not make out the rider clearly, but she was sure it was neither Will Penloe nor Jemmy. The rider appeared to be taller than either of them, and although she could not from this distance be certain, she thought he had dark hair. Before they disappeared from view, she received the distinct impression that the powerful horse was being guided by a rider of remarkable grace and strength.

Nell yearned to jump into her riding habit and make for the stables, but she didn't want to leave the house before seeing Amelia. She could not bring herself to waken Amelia, however, for the poor dear was evidently enjoying the first restful sleep she had had since leaving London. Nell found the wait unbearably long. Amelia did not make an appearance until the morning was well advanced. She found Nell pacing about the morning room impatiently. "Good morning, love," Amelia said cheerily, kissing Nell's cheek affectionately. "Have you been waiting long?"

"I've been up for hours! You must have slept well."

"Like a top. I'm quite refreshed, I'm pleased to admit. All I need to make me completely content is a cup of tea. But why did *you* not sleep well?" She stared at Nell in sudden alarm. "Heavens, I completely forgot! Did the ghost make an appearance? Oh, my dear, is *that* what drove you from your bed so early?"

"Oh, no," Nell assured her, "I slept quite well. It's only that I'm eager to try the little mare I saw in the stables yesterday."

"Are you sure?" Amelia asked, searching Nell's face closely. "You saw or heard nothing at all strange?"

Nell urged Amelia into a chair and poured a cup of tea

for her. "I believe you *want* me to have seen your ghost," she said, laughing. "You look almost crestfallen."

Amelia smiled wanly. "I suppose I do. But it's only because I wish that you'd believe me when I tell you that I *really* saw him."

Nell patted the old lady's hand sympathetically. "I know you did, my dear. You see, your ghost *did* pay me a visit last night."

"Nell! *Truly?*" Amelia put down her cup with a shaking hand and stared at Nell with an expression that combined alarm with a bit of self-satisfaction.

Nell laughed. "Truly. I saw and heard it all—the candle held by an unseen hand, the chains clanking, everything. I even *spoke* to him!"

Amelia gasped. "You *didn't*! You're trying to flummery me."

"Not at all," Nell said seriously. "He spoke to me. He said he is the ghost of a Mr. D'Espry, a smuggler who died in . . . when did he say? . . . 1669."

"Oh, Nell, how dreadful!" She stood up so precipitously that her chair fell over. "My dear, we must leave at once. We shan't spend another moment in this awful place!"

Nell rose, picked up Amelia's chair and gently urged her to sit down again. "Calm yourself, dearest, please. Nothing has occurred to cause us to feel the least perturbation."

"Nothing has occurred? Are you quite demented? Do you want to remain in a house that's *haunted*?"

"Yes, I do. Very much. I've not been so entertained since I was a child and my governess told me that Queen Katherine haunts a gallery at Hampton Court."

"Hampton Court? What nonsense!" Amelia declared, looking at Nell suspiciously.

"My governess did not think it nonsense. She claimed with great seriousness that poor Katherine comes shrieking through the haunted gallery with alarming regularity, wearing a white, flowing gown and a splendid jeweled hood and begging Henry for her life."

"Really, Nell, you cannot believe such a farrago of nonsense."

"Of course I don't. Any more than I believe in the ghost of Mr. D'Espry," Nell said pointedly.

Amelia blinked at her in perplexity. "But . . . you *saw* him . . . and *spoke* to him . . . ?"

"I saw *something* and spoke to *someone*, but I don't for a moment believe him to be a ghost."

"Then who—?"

"I don't know. But I have a theory," Nell said mysteriously.

Amelia leaned forward eagerly. "What is it, my dear? Tell me, please, or I shall imagine the most dreadful things."

"Well," Nell said, lowering her voice carefully, "I'm convinced that someone is living in this house who shouldn't be. And the Penloes are trying to pull the wool over our eyes."

Amelia's eyebrows came up in surprise. "Someone who *shouldn't* be? But who—?"

"I have no idea. But suppose that some relative of the Penloes—a younger brother of Will's or his wife's, perhaps—has been living here on the Thornes' largesse, eating food provided from the funds allotted for the upkeep of the house, sleeping in one of the bedrooms, using the Thorne stables as his own, and doing all these things without our family's permission. And suppose this has been going on for *years*. Then we happen along and upset the whole scheme. Wouldn't they want to frighten us off before we see for ourselves that they've been *embezzling*?"

"Embezzling!" Amelia was scandalized. "But . . . the Penloes don't seem to be the sort of people who would stoop to such dishonesty," she objected.

"Embezzlers never *seem* to be dishonest," Nell declared with the confidence of a complete lack of experience. "That's how they succeed in their odious plots."

"You may be right," Amelia murmured, stirring her tea absently. "But, my dear, I must admit than I don't feel any safer in this house with embezzlers that I do with ghosts! What shall we do now? Confront them with this information?"

"No, I don't think so. We haven't any *real* information, you see. Only a completely unsubstantiated theory of mine. I think we should keep this to ourselves. We'll watch carefully until we can *prove* what we say."

Amelia shook her head. "I cannot like this situation. Knowing that there's a strange man lurking about makes me extremely nervous. Why don't we return to London and tell Charles the whole story? Let *him* come here and straighten it all out."

"No, Amelia. I can't go back to London. There is no situation here in Thorndene that is more disturbing than the thought of returning to London and marrying the puffed-up Sir Nigel."

"But are you saying that we're to stay here? And say or do nothing? And that you'll sleep in that haunted room and let the ghost visit whenever he likes? You *couldn't*, Nell!"

"Why not? I don't believe we're in the least danger. And I truly find myself quite fascinated with this whole affair. I expected the sojourn to Cornwall to be dull beyond endurance, but this mystery is making our visit as exciting as a play at Covent Garden."

Amelia eyed the girl with horrified disapproval. "Your idea of excitement is much too wild, my dear. I'm afraid I cannot permit it. I look on myself *in loco parentis* as regards your welfare, and I must insist—!"

Nell jumped up and knelt beside Amelia's chair, placing a finger gently on the older woman's lips. "Don't insist, dearest, for it will only cause a break between us, and I should be unspeakably distressed to see that come to pass. If you could but agree to remain here with me, we shall have *such* an adventure!"

"An *adventure*!" Amelia exclaimed, removing Nell's

fingers from her mouth. "We shall be found *murdered in our beds*!"

"We shall have a *marvelous* adventure, and when we eventually *do* return to London, you'll have an endless supply of breathtaking stories to tell your friends over the teacups. And everyone will admire your youthful courage and remarkable intrepidity."

"Youthful courage, humph! Intrepidity indeed!" Amelia snorted. But a gleam of interest in her eyes indicated that she had succumbed to Nell's blandishments. "You'll probably have all the adventures yourself, and I shall know nothing of 'em. I shall be left to worry and imagine all sorts of dire events."

"Not at all. I shall tell you *everything* that happens. And, if you wish, you can share the haunted room with me," Nell said tantalizingly.

"Pooh," Amelia sneered, picking up her cup, "you know perfectly well that I won't spend another night in that room. If *you* insist on having adventures, go ahead and have them. *I* shall be quite content to hear about them at second hand. That is intrepid enough for me!"

Nell hugged her, laughing. "You are a *dear*! Thank you! And now, let's enjoy our breakfast. I think we're to have smoked pilchards again."

"I shall not be able to eat a morsel," Amelia grumbled. "Just pour another cup of tea for me."

"*Another* cup?" Nell teased as she poured the still-steaming brew into the proferred cup. "I begin to believe that you are quite addicted to this innocuous beverage."

"*Innocuous*! Did you say innocuous?" Amelia repeated in horror. "What blasphemy! I'll have you know that taking tea is one of God's true blessings. It is almost the only joy of life which is completely free of lust, gluttony or any taint of sin! I couldn't face a day without it! I warn you, love, that if you truly wish me to be intrepid—"

"I know, my dear," Nell interrupted, raising a

restraining hand and trying rather unsuccessfully to keep her smile from breaking forth into giggles, "I know. To keep you intrepid, I shall see that the teapot is always close at hand."

It was noon before Nell arrived at the stables. She had brought Will Penloe with her, telling him that she did not like to ride unattended on unfamiliar territory. He saddled the mare for her, while she looked around the stables. Caceres was in his stall, his coat freshly rubbed and gleaming. There was no way to determine if he had been ridden that morning.

Will took for himself an aging, mild-mannered hack and climbed into the saddle with a stolid clumsiness. Nell could not find in his movements any sign of the grace of the morning rider. They rode out together, but when Nell spurred her horse to a gallop, Will lagged behind. He seemed to be content to ride steadily at a slow trot. Nell watched him covertly throughout the hour she spent on her ride. By the time they'd returned to the stables, she was convinced that he could not have been the man she'd seen riding Caceres that morning.

The ghost made his next appearance that night, just at midnight, but to Nell, who had been waiting eagerly for him since ten, it seemed much later. She had been about to give up and permit herself to slip into sleep when the candlelight appeared behind the white curtain. "Good evening, Mr. D'Espry," she greeted the apparition cheerfully.

The answer was a low moan.

"Heavens, you sound ill," she declared briskly. "Tell me, do ghosts suffer from ill-health? Headaches, or fevers, or inflammations of the liver?"

"Inflammations of the liver?" the ghost asked with that tinge of amusement in his voice which she'd heard before. "What does a young woman like you know of such things?"

"*I'll* ask the questions, if you don't mind," Nell told him firmly. "Tell me about your health."

"I am but a shade, a shadow, a phantasm. Obviously, I cannot suffer from headaches or inflammations," the ghost explained patiently.

"Then, Mr. D'Espry," Nell responded promptly, "I'd be much obliged if you would refrain from that lugubrious moaning."

"I'm afraid I can't oblige," the ghost said sadly. "Moaning is quite natural to us—a kind of relief, like a sigh or a cough. I'm sorry if it frightens you."

"It doesn't *frighten* me at all. I just don't like it."

"I'll try not to do it too often," the ghost said apologetically. "Only when the pressure becomes too great."

"Thank you. That's very good of you."

The ghost moaned. "Sorry," he said when the moan had faded away.

"Don't apologize, Mr. D'Espry. I quite understand. You can't help it."

"You sound very cheerful tonight, Miss Belden. Am I to understand by this mood that you've decided to ignore my warning of last night?" the ghost asked in a deep, rumbling voice.

"Yes, I have. I can't see any danger in an illusory candle and a disembodied voice."

"You are being foolhardy, my girl," the voice said ominously.

"I am not foolhardy!" Nell said belligerently. "And don't call me 'my girl' in that avuncular way."

"I'll call you what I like," the ghost retorted, equally belligerent.

"I *knew* you were a rudesby!" Nell declared.

"A ghost's prerogative. Only the living must abide by the rules of polite society," the ghost responded, the amusement back in his voice.

"See here, Mr. D'Espry—would *you* like it if I called you 'my boy'?"

"It would be quite inappropriate, since I am about one

hundred and twenty-five years older than you. But you may call me Harry if you like."

"I do *not* like!" Nell said promptly. "In fact, I do not like your name or anything about you!"

"Dear me!" the ghost said in mock chagrin. "And after I've tried so hard to please you! What is it about me you dislike? It *cannot* be my appearance."

"That's just it, Mr. D'Espry. I dislike speaking to a disembodied voice. I would like to see what you look like."

The ghost moaned. "No, you wouldn't. I am a dreadful sight. I look exactly as I looked when the excise-man took my life."

"Oh?" asked Nell, her courage failing a bit. "And how was that?"

"Do you want to hear about my demise?" the ghost asked in surprise.

"I'm completely fascinated," Nell assured him.

"Very well then. It was in this very room, of course—" the ghost began.

"Of course," Nell said drily.

The ghost ignored the interruption. "I had hidden here behind the curtains. They were of a heavier material, then, and could not be seen through. Three excise-men burst into the room, swords drawn." The ghost moaned again. "Are you sure you can stomach the details?" he asked in exaggerated concern.

"Go on," Nell urged. "I'm all ears."

"Well, one of them must have seen the tips of my shoes sticking out below the hem of the curtains, for he laughed evilly and brandished his sword. Before I realized what he was about, he lunged at me through the curtain and ran me through."

"How *dreadful*. Just like Polonius behind the arras!"

"Exactly!" the ghost agreed.

"Do you mean to tell me that you have that sword sticking in you to this day?" Nell asked.

"No," the ghost said with a gurgle. "Only the hole."

Nell choked. "The ... *hole*?"

"Would you still like to see me?" the ghost taunted.

"Well, I..." Nell hesitated.

There was the sound of a snort. "Not quite so sure, my girl, are you?"

Nell put up her chin. "I don't believe you'd *dare* to show yourself! I hope you aren't deluding yourself into believing that I take a single word of your story at all seriously."

There was a threatening laugh, and the candle faded out. After a suspenseful moment of eerie silence, a ghostly figure came into view. It was dim and insubstantial and seemed to be floating about two feet above the floor. Nell felt a decided constriction in her chest. The figure was that of a tall man, his head shadowed, his trousers dark. The most clearly observable part of him was his white, belted smock, very much like a doublet, and over the belt was a gaping black hole surrounded by ugly bloodstains. Nell had all she could do to keep from gasping.

"How do you do, Miss Belden?" the figure said with a slight bow. "Are you satisfied now?"

"That is truly a *ghastly* hole, Mr. D'Espry," she managed.

"Harry," the ghost insisted.

"Harry," Nell begged, "do you think you could ...er...cover it up?"

The ghost laughed. "So you're frightened at last!"

"Not frightened at all," she declared stubbornly. "I know this is a trick of some kind, although I don't know how it's done."

"If you're so certain it's a trick," the ghost asked reasonably, "then why does the sight of my...wound trouble you?"

"It's so *bloody*," Nell said in a small voice. "Couldn't you wear a...a...waistcoat or something, to cover it up?"

"I must remind you that I'm only a shadow. One can't hang a waistcoat on a shadow, you know."

"Oh, I see," said Nell, trying to recover her composure.

"Would you rather that I disappear again? I'd be glad to return to my candle form," the ghost offered.

"No, thank you. I'll grow accustomed to your appearance."

The ghost shook his head admiringly. "You are a remarkable girl, you know. Most ladies run screaming from the room when they see me."

"Do they indeed?" Nell remarked, amusement having restored her equilibrium. "How very tiresome for you. Especially since you must have been a fine figure of a man when you were alive. I would imagine you were quite a favorite with the ladies."

The ghost laughed. "However did you guess? Well, my girl, I know it's immodest to admit it, but the ladies *did* adore me. I had scores of 'em dangling at my heels."

"Only scores of them? Not hundreds?"

"Oh, there *were* hundreds, if you count the married ones who offered to leave their husbands for me—"

"Let us count the married ones by all means."

The ghost put his hands on his hips, his elbows akimbo. She could almost see him looking at her askance. "I can see that you don't believe me," he said, a smile in his voice, "but many more ladies have made me welcome in their bedrooms when I was alive than have run away from me in the century and a half since my demise."

"I've no doubt of it," Nell said fastidiously, "but I don't find this an appropriate subject for discussion between a man and a young lady."

"Between a *ghost* and a young lady," he corrected, "*anything* may be discussed. As I pointed out to you earlier, there are no rules in this situation."

"If you insist on speaking in an unseemly manner, sir, I shall have to ask you to...er...evaporate, or vaporize...or do whatever it is ghosts do when they take their leave."

"Very well, we'll change the subject," he acquiesced. "I don't wish to be considered crude or vulgar, even though

I'm a ghost and therefore unaffected by such earthly epithets. However, in regard to taking my leave, may I remind you that I make my arrivals and departures only at *my* whims, not yours?"

"Hmmmph!" Nell snorted in annoyance. "Then there *are* rules for ghostly behavior. And they are very unfair, being designed for *your* convenience and not a bit for mine."

"Not *all* in my favor," the ghost pointed out ruefully. "There is one inflexible rule which is entirely in *your* favor. I may never touch you, you know, any more than a shadow may."

"What does *that* signify?" Nell asked thoughtlessly. "You can have no need or inclination to touch me, anyway."

"You can't know much about men—or ghosts—or how delightful you look sitting there in your nightdress, if you believe *that*," the ghost said with a disturbing sincerity.

Nell blushed and pulled the bedclothes up to her neck. For a long moment neither of them spoke. Nell, her eyes fixed on the bedclothes, was quite conscious of the ghost's eyes on her. "I wish you would not say such things to me," she said at last. "I am not accustomed to speaking so freely to gentlemen."

"But I am no gentleman, you know."

"You must have been, once."

"No, never. Only a poor smuggler."

"Rubbish! Your speech gives you away. But never mind that now. I've just realized something. You say that the rules make it impossible for you to touch me, is that right?"

"Yes."

"Then how can you claim I am in danger? You cannot be a danger to me if you can't touch me," she declared triumphantly.

"A ghost has ways, without using touch. Many ways.

That's why you must go...as soon as possible."

"What ways?" Nell asked.

"I shall now take my leave," he said, his voice deepening and taking on a ghostly monotone. "Just remember...you must go-o-o-o-o-o..."

The ghost slowly faded from view. "But *wait*, Mr. D'Espry!" she called after him. "You haven't explained—! Mr. D'Esp—? Harry! Come back!"

But he was gone. The room was in complete darkness. Nell didn't bother to look behind the curtains. She knew she would find nothing. But the "ghost" had given her much to think about. Who was he? And of what was he trying to warn her? Was he, as she suspected, a trespasser who wanted her out of the house? Was he truly a danger to her? And how had he created those frightening illusions of floating candles and ghostly presences?

She slid down under the comforter and snuggled into the pillows. Her pulse was racing, but she could not tell if the pounding in her blood was caused by fear or excitement. There was only one thing she knew with certainty: she had not the slightest intention of leaving this house, no matter what danger loomed before her. She was having much too beguiling a time.

Chapter Seven

GWINNYS TAPPED LIGHTLY on Miss Belden's door and, without waiting for an acknowledgement, went in. After more than two weeks of service to the ladies of Thorndene, she knew what to expect. Miss Belden would be awake and stationed at the window, as usual, watching for the mysterious early morning horseman. It was her morning ritual. Miss Belden had revealed to Gwinnys, in the strictest confidence, her suspicions that the rider was a trespasser, hiding under this very roof.

Gwinnys, energetic, curious and not at all lacking in courage, had frequently suggested to her young mistress (of whom she had grown very fond, and to whom she felt a strong loyalty) that they search the house. But the young Miss had not seemed to take a real interest in the suggestion. Although it was quite clear that Miss Nell was eager to discover what she could about the trespasser, she seemed, on the other hand, to wish to avoid any action which would disturb their precariously balanced co-existence. She could have hidden herself in the stables and confronted the man on any morning during the past fortnight, but she had not wanted to do so. And Gwinnys had told her more than once that she had seen Mrs. Penloe go up a staircase behind the kitchen, carrying a loaded tray, but Miss Nell had not gone to explore the stairway and had forbidden Gwinnys to do so. The young abigail could not have put her feelings into words, but she understood instinctively that Miss Belden wanted to hold on to the magic and romance of the unsolved riddle. A mystery, once it is solved, is nothing more than a group of facts which must be dealt with. Gwinnys suspected that her beautiful, lively mistress was enjoying the mystery too much to wish to solve it.

Miss Nell was indeed standing at the window. Gwinnys came up behind her. "There's naught to see out there, Miss Nell," she remarked, "with the mist so thick."

Nell sighed. "Yes, you're right. Besides, the rain is too heavy for anyone to ride in. I may as well give up for today."

Gwinnys busied herself readying Nell's clothes while Nell made her ablutions in the icy water from the pitcher on her nightstand. "Tell me, Gwinnys," she asked, toweling her face briskly, "have you had an opportunity to ask Mrs. Penloe about her family?"

"Ais, I did an' all," Gwinnys nodded, "but 'twas a waste o' time. She says she has a sister lives at Carthamartha, and Will as a deal o' relations—brothers and sisters and what-all—but none as is a proper fit to our man."

"If 'our man' is *not* a relation to the Penloes," Nell mused, stepping out of her nightgown with a shiver, "I cannot conceive of who he can be."

"I've asked 'ee afore," Gwinnys pointed out, "to come wi' me up the back stairs, or to let me go alone. Here, let me help 'ee into that petticoat—you're all of a shrim."

"Well, who wouldn't shiver on so cold a morning?" Nell said, hurrying into her clothes. She turned her back on the girl so that Gwinnys could button the back of her burgundy-colored muslin dress. It was a good choice for this chilly day, with its long sleeves and high-necked, gathered bodice, for it gave warmth without being as heavy or scratchy as wool. While Gwinnys devoted her attention to the tiny buttons at the back, Nell's thoughts reverted back to her abigail's suggestion. "As for those back stairs, Gwinnys," she said firmly, "I insist that you stop nagging at me about them. I do not wish for a confrontation with our trespasser—at least, not yet. When I've made up my mind about how to handle the situation, I shall let you know."

Gwinnys shrugged. "I mind what you say, Miss Nell. No need to be sniffy."

"I'm not being 'sniffy' at all. I just want to be sure that you don't take it into your head to explore those back stairs without my permission."

"Don't trouble yourself about *that*," Gwinnys assured her. "I'm too timmersome to do it alone."

"Timmersome!" Nell exclaimed with a smile. "Is that your Cornish way of saying 'timid'? You, my girl, have not a timmersome bone in your body!"

Gwinnys ignored the teasing, completed the buttoning and stepped back to admire her handiwork. "There you be, all buttoned." She circled her mistress admiringly. "An' I'd *lay* you be a pretty sight! You look *tremmin!*"

"Tremmin?" Nell asked. "Another of your Cornish barbarisms? What does it mean?"

"It means, Miss, that you're a sight for sore eyes, as any man who saw 'ee would agree."

"Well, thank you, Gwinnys," Nell said with a little, mocking bow. She stepped into her sturdy half-boots and went to the door. "But as Jemmy Penloe is the only unmarried male who is likely to see me, it hardly seems worth all your effort."

* * *

It was a long, dreary day, the westerly wind whipping up to gale force by nightfall. Amelia and Nell sat near the fire after dinner, passing the time playing backgammon and trying to ignore the howl of the wind in the chimney. Mrs. Penloe, assisted by Gwinnys, brought the tea tray at ten as usual. It had become a habit to take their tea and retire, but tonight Amelia asked Nell to play another game. Nell complied, telling Gwinnys not to wait up for them.

When she at last entered her bedroom, it was almost midnight. She was struggling with the undoing of her buttons when the ghost appeared. She had not expected him quite so soon and gave a little cry of surprise.

"Oh, sorry," the ghost said politely. "I seem to have startled you."

"Well, isn't that what ghosts are supposed to do?" Nell asked saucily.

"Yes, that's true. But it's been many days since I've been able to arouse any sort of proper reaction from you. You've grown quite complacent in my presence."

"Yes, I have, haven't I? I suppose that means you are not succeeding very well in your ghostly role."

"I am a positive failure," the ghost agreed ruefully. "If word of this leaks out among the society of ghosts, shades and phantoms, I shall not be able to hold up my head."

"I most sincerely feel for you," Nell said with patent insincerity. She picked up her hairbrush, took down her hair, which had been pulled back in a tidy knot at the back of her head, and began to brush vigorously.

"This is the first time I've seen you dressed," the ghost remarked. "I must say you look..." he hesitated for a word.

"Tremmin?" Nell offered.

"Yes, indeed. Tremmin! The very word."

Nell turned and peered at the faint light behind the curtain, where the shadowy, now-familiar figure of Harry D'Espry stood watching her. "Oh? Do you know that word?" she asked curiously. "It's a Cornish coinage, I think."

"Of course I know it. I *was* a true Cornishman, you know."

"Were you? That's another one of your claims which I'm inclined to doubt."

"Why do you doubt me?"

"Your speech. It has always puzzled me. It seems excessively cultivated, for a smuggler."

"That is quite easily explained. The language was spoken with more polish a century ago, for one thing. For another, I've haunted a number of the gentry all these years, and their ways rub off on one. Ais, 'tis a lot I've learned, to be sure, but I reckon I ben't such a jinny-ninny that I cain't bring the owld words to m' tongue."

Nell giggled. "You did that very well. I could *almost* believe that you were a Cornishman if you spoke that way consistently."

Harry sighed. "What a suspicious female you are, to be sure. Is there *nothing* I say that you believe?"

"Nothing," Nell said bluntly.

"But you *must* believe that you are tremmin, my dear. Your dress is a lovely color—it suits you. It's like wine. It makes your cheeks glow."

The hand wielding the hairbrush wavered. Harry's compliment had thrown Nell into confusion. Although the shadow behind the curtain seemed very like a ghost, Nell had no doubt the illusion was created by a real man, a person with the abilities, qualities and feelings of any living man. There was an attraction between them—a spark that flamed up from time to time so brightly that it broke into her consciousness. Ordinarily, she would let herself forget his reality and simply accept, and enjoy, the ghost-visits. But when the spark ignited between them, she became uncomfortably aware that this was her *bedroom*, that he visited her here *nightly*, and that she was permitting a grossly improper relationship to develop. If she had any character, if she were not a wild, irresponsible, shockingly fast female, she would force a confrontation with this imposter, make him admit his crimes (whatever they were) and turn him over to the magistrates.

But she could not do it—not yet. His nightly visits were her only source of pleasure in this cold, dreary place. She counted the hours each day until she could retire and wait for him. When he was with her, something bubbled inside—something which was a heady combination of excitement, nervousness and laughter. Every once in a while, he would remind her that he represented a danger that loomed over her, but she never felt threatened. They were comfortable together, as if they'd been friends for years. Nell began to realize that her life had been a lonely one—she had no sisters or brothers, and her guardians had not encouraged her to make intimate friendships. For the first time in her life, she had found someone she could talk to in intimate, honest exchanges. She did not want to give up this experience.

"What is it, girl?" Harry asked suddenly. "Have I said something to upset you?"

She shook her head and resumed brushing. "No, not at all. It's only that you make me uncomfortable when you . . . flirt with me."

"Flirt with you? Is *that* what I'm doing? Nay, lass, that can't be so. I'm only a ghost, after all. There can't be any such nonsense between you and me."

"Can't there?" Nell asked, raising a challenging eyebrow. "Are you sure of that?"

"Are you disbelieving me again? Of course I'm sure."

She eyed him speculatively for a moment. Then a gleam of mischief flickered in her expression. She put her hands behind her and began to struggle with her buttons. "Sometimes it's too bad that you're a ghost," she sighed.

"Why?" Harry asked suspiciously.

"Well, if you were real, you could help me with these."

"With what?" the ghost asked. "What *are* you doing?"

She turned her back to him, to show him. "I'm undoing these blasted buttons, you see? There are dozens of them. If you were real, you could—"

"But why are you undoing them *now*?" the ghost asked in some chagrin.

"Why not now?" Nell asked, turning an innocent face in his direction.

"Because... because..." Harry muttered uncomfortably.

"Well?" she insisted, continuing to undo the buttons.

"I say!" he exclaimed, outraged. "You don't mean to undress while I'm *here*, do you?"

"Of course I do. You're only a ghost, after all. You can't touch me or flirt with me, or—"

"Never mind all that. It is not *proper* to—"

"Don't be silly," she insisted. "You told me yourself that you can see through walls. Therefore you've probably been seeing through my *clothes* all this time. Surely there's no need *now* for me to behave like a simpering miss—!"

"Good Lord, woman!" the ghost exclaimed, sputtering. "You surely don't believe that I've been... *oggling* you through your clothes all this time! Like... like a blasted Peeping Tom!"

"What else am I to think?" she asked with exaggerated reasonableness. "I've become quite accustomed to the thought of it by now. So there's no need to fall into a taking over my undressing, is there? Not after all this time." Most of the buttons had, by this time, been unhooked, and Nell daringly pulled the gown from her left shoulder.

"Nell," Harry growled, "you go too far. *Stop that*!"

Nell merely tossed her head and bared her shoulder even more.

"Very *well*. Miss," Harry said furiously, "I bid you *goodnight*!" And he faded away.

Nell laughed. "Oh, very well, Harry, I'll stop." She pulled the dress back up to her neck and quickly rebuttoned the back. "You can come back now."

But there was no answer, and no light glowed from behind the curtain.

"Harry? Harry! Come back! I promise to behave." But the ghost had gone for the night.

The gale continued through the night, and the wind still raged the next morning when Mrs. Penloe brought Lord Thorne's breakfast to his room. She found him lounging on the window-seat, an open book forgotten on his lap, staring out the window at the rain lashing against the pane. But instead of the gloomy expression which she thought the inclement weather would bring to his face, she noted that a faint smile curled his lips and his eyes were bright and amused. "Don't see what there is about the rain to make 'ee smile so," she remarked as she set his table.

"It isn't the rain, love," he said, rousing himself from his reverie. "Only a bit of a memory."

"Oh?" Mrs. Penloe asked, looking at him with interest. "Somethin' you mind from your chiel'ood?"

"No. More recent than that," he explained as he hobbled over to the table.

Mrs. Penloe set the coffee pot at his elbow and uncovered the eggs. "I'm surprised at 'ee bein' so cheerful, what wi' the weather so nasty-like, and the ladies still hangin' about."

He buttered a hot biscuit generously and smiled up at her. "I don't mind the ladies. They don't seem to pry or get in my way. As for the weather, well, what can one expect in Cornwall at this time of year? Sit down, Mrs. Penloe, and have a bite with me. You've brought enough food to feed six."

"You *don't* mind the ladies?" Mrs. Penloe asked in surprise, sitting down at the table opposite him.

"No, not at all. Why should I?"

"Well, you're stuck in this room so much, for one thing. I was sure you'd get housey."

"No, I don't mind. I have my books. And you, Will and Jemmy pop in often enough to cheer me. So long as our visitors don't come poking about where they're not wanted, I don't mind having them here."

Mrs. Penloe propped her chin on her hand and fixed her eyes on his face. "But what if they *should* come pokin' about?"

"I don't see why they should, if they haven't so far," he said carelessly, lifting a forkful of egg. But suddenly his hand stayed. "Why?" he asked, his complacent expression gone. "Do you think they will?"

She shrugged. "'Tis the only thing that keeps me afeared. Do 'ee still pay the girl ghost-visits?"

He looked at her guiltily and nodded.

"Don't seem to frighten her, do they?"

"No," he admitted.

She reached for a biscuit and said with elaborate casualness, "Then I don't see why you bother."

He shifted in his seat uncomfortably. "I enjoy the game. Do you think I should stop?"

"'Tis not for me to say."

He looked at her, his eyebrows raised. "Tush, woman, I've never known you to hold your tongue when you've something on your mind."

"You reckon I've somethin' on my mind?"

"Yes, I do. You've been sitting there tearing that biscuit to shreds without eating a crumb. So speak up, love. Tell me what's troubling you."

"'Tis you an' the young woman what's troublin' me. Seems to me you're *both* enjoyin' these ghost-visits. That's why she's not pokin' about—she has no wish to upset the applecart."

"Yes, I suppose that's true. Go on."

She lifted her head and looked at him levelly. "It seems to be you've a real likin' for one another. Then why not face her in the open? Cain't you be abroad wi' her?"

Harry stared at her for a long moment. Then he put down his fork, rose and limped to the window. "No," he said at last, "I can't be 'abroad' with anyone. Nothing has changed. Nothing *can* change."

"I been watchin' the young lady for more'n a fortnight," Mrs. Penloe said gently, coming up behind him and putting a hand on his arm. "She ben't a giglot. A good, strong girl she be. 'Twould not matter to her that you've only one leg."

Harry turned and looked down at the little house-keeper, a mockery of a smile on his face. "Are you trying to be a matchmaker, my dear?" he asked with forced humor. "There's no use, you know. I'm determined to remain a bachelor." He turned back to the window. "And don't trouble yourself about my ghost-visits," he added softly. "I'll do what I can to end the game we've been playing. She'll find herself bored to distraction soon enough and will take herself off to London."

Mrs. Penloe's heart sank. Not only had she failed to change his mind about facing the outside world, but she'd spoiled his happy mood. "Oh, Master Harry," she asked miserably, "be 'ee nipped wi' me?"

Harry, with a great effort of will, pulled himself out of the doldrums and turned to her with a smile. "Of course not, love," he said, lifting her chin and bending to kiss her cheek. "Nothing you'd ever say could vex me. Come, give us a smile and put this business out of your mind."

She tried to comply, but the heaviness of her heart could not be pushed away. The hopeful feeling she had nurtured during the past fortnight was gone, and a depression such as she'd not felt since the ladies had arrived settled on her spirit like a black cloud.

The ghost did not make an appearance for the next two nights. By the third night, Nell was in such a state of nervous anxiety that she trembled at every sound. Even Amelia noticed her agitation and made a comment at the dinner table. Nell excused herself shortly after nine o'clock and ran upstairs. What could have happened? she asked herself over and over. Was Harry angry with her because of the rather tasteless teasing she had indulged in when she'd pretended to undress? Gwinnys tapped on the door, but Nell dismissed her for the night. She undressed quickly, put on a very proper, starched white nightdress and her prettiest lace-trimmed cap, and climbed into bed. It was only a little past ten. She plumped the pillows and sat back against them primly, waiting with a beating heart for the light to appear.

Midnight came and went. When the hall clock struck one, and the ghost had still not made an appearance, Nell turned her face into the pillows and wept. But suddenly she heard the thumping footsteps that always heralded his appearance, and she sat up abruptly, the tears still wet on her cheeks. "Oh, *there* you are!" she exclaimed in tremulous relief. "Wherever have you *b-been*?"

"Good Lord!" the ghost blurted out incredulously, "have you been crying?"

"Of c-course I've been c-crying. I . . . I've been worried about you."

"Worried? About *me*? Don't be daft, girl. No one worries about a ghost."

"I do. I was afraid something dreadful had happened to you."

Harry laughed. "But, my dear, *nothing* can happen to a phantom. We merely go on and on through the centuries, untouched, unharmed, unchanged—"

"Then why didn't you come?" she demanded petulantly. "Did you wish to punish me?"

Harry was startled. "Punish you? Why would I wish to punish you?"

"You know very well why!" She looked down at the bedclothes embarrassedly. "Although I didn't dream you could be such a . . . a prig."

"Prig?" asked Harry completely puzzled. "I don't know what you're talking about."

"You are equivocating, sir. Surely you are fully aware

of the incident to which I refer. And only a prig could have believed that I would *really* undress in front of a man—ghost or no ghost."

"Oh, *that*!" Harry said with a laugh. "You surely don't believe I stayed away for such a ridiculous reason as that. Good God, girl, you looked so charming that night, it was all I could do to force myself to leave!"

"Oh," said Nell in a small voice, blushing hotly.

"I suppose I *did* sound like a prig," Harry admitted ruefully. "I was merely trying to prove to you that, sometimes, I can behave like a gentleman."

"Perhaps you can," Nell admitted, "but I'm not at all certain it was gentlemanly to stay away for two nights when you knew I was expecting you. Why *did* you—?"

"I was busy. I had some thinking to do."

"Thinking? About what?"

"Well, to be quite honest, about *you*, my dear."

She looked up at him with interest. "Why were you thinking about me?"

"I was trying to find a new scheme to use to frighten you off."

Nell's face fell. "To...frighten me? I don't under-stand—"

"I have my reputation to think of," he explained. "My ghostly reputation. The word is spreading among my...er...ghostly confreres that I have not succeeded in dislodging you, even after all this time. I think, therefore, that the time has come for me to buckle down seriously to work."

"But...but I thought you'd given up trying to frighten me off. I've told you from the first that I don't intend to be driven from this house. I thought you'd accepted that fact."

"No, my dear, I've not accepted it. Not as a fact or even as a possibility."

"You *must* have!" she insisted. "You haven't even *tried* to frighten me since your second visit. I was convinced . . . I felt sure that . . ." She faltered.

"What?" he asked cautiously.

"Well, you see, we've been getting on so well, laughing and joking together . . . that I thought we'd come to . . . an understanding . . ."

"Only a temporary truce, I'm afraid," Harry said gently.

The words sent a chill through her. Something was happening that threatened to change everything, and she was not yet ready for a change. "Do you . . . w-wish to be rid of me?" she asked, vulnerable as a child.

There was a momentary silence. Then the ghost said quietly, "It is my job to be rid of you. That is what ghosts are meant to do, is it not?"

She stared at him, biting her underlip to keep it from quivering. She had been rejected! And not by a ghost—by an ordinary man! A worse than ordinary man! He was a vulgar, dishonest, thieving trespasser! And yet the pain she now felt was stronger than anything she'd felt before. Three broken betrothals and any number of flirtations with gentlemen of quality had not prepared her for feelings like this.

But Nell had pride and spirit. She'd rather have died than let him see how he'd hurt her. She lifted her head and sat up, erect and cold. "You can stop spouting rubbish about ghosts, Mr. D'Espry. Do you take me for a fool? I told you a fortnight ago, and I tell you now—I am here, and here I shall remain!"

Harry sighed. "I suspected you'd say that."

"Well, then—?" she challenged.

"Then it seems the truce is over, and the battle lines are drawn. Sorry, girl."

"No need to be sorry for me, sir! I can take care of myself very well—especially against a mere ghost."

The ghost rubbed his chin regretfully. "Well, then, I suppose there's nothing more to say. Goodnight, my dear."

Nell didn't care to watch him fade away. She blew out her candle, flounced down into the bed and turned her back on him.

"Won't you even bid me goodnight?" the ghost asked, hopefully. "Just once more, while the truce is still in effect?"

"You can go to the d-devil!" she threw at him over her shoulder.

"Not only was that *unkind*," the ghost said reprovingly, "but quite unladylike."

"Unladylike!" she cried, sitting up and staring at his fading form. "I can't afford to be ladylike. This is *war*!"

Chapter Eight

NELL'S FIRST ACT to mark the opening of hostilities was to indulge in a bout of hearty tears. After her good, long cry she lay awake until the dawn, trying to guess what new strategies her ghost might devise to drive her away, and to concoct defenses against them. For it was plain that Harry had the advantageous position of offense. He could attack at will; *she* would have to engage in a defensive war.

But her thoughts were muddled, her logical thinking processes confused by the emotions which interfered with her usual rationality. An irrelevant question kept inserting itself into her mind: *why had Harry suddenly changed?*

By morning, no satisfactory answer had presented itself. Noticing that the rain had stopped at last, she dressed quickly and slipped out of the house. She walked briskly down the back slope and along the edge of the cliffs. The sky was gray, and the wind whipped at her hair and skirts in a most satisfactorily violent way. The sea below her roared in angry ferocity against the rocks in a manner completely appropriate to her mood. She found a rocky ledge, somewhat sheltered from the wind, and sat down, her eyes fixed on the waves thundering against the rocks far below. They crashed with such vehemence that she could feel the bite of spray on her face. The turbulent beauty of the scene fascinated her, and, surprisingly, that very turbulence had a soothing effect on her spirits. With her eyes fixed on the churning sea below, her mind calmly reviewed her strange situation. Why had Harry, the so-called ghost, so disturbed her? What had given him the power to hurt her so? She had no idea who he was. She had never even *seen* him clearly. They had, of course, spoken together often, and the conversations had been amusing and entertaining, but not of such depth and seriousness as to account for what she now suffered at his withdrawal. She was behaving as if . . . the thought caused her to gasp! . . . as if she'd been rejected by a *lover*!

Had she become *attached* to her ghost? The question, now that she had actually faced it, was profoundly disturbing. She really knew nothing about him—not even what he looked like. It was only his voice she knew. But the voice had spoken words, and the words had revealed thoughts and feelings. If she were to be completely honest, there was a great deal about Harry that she knew. He was clever, yet kind. He was amusing, yet gentle. He had warmth and strength. She was as sure of these things as if she'd known him all her life.

But oh, there was a great deal she didn't know. Who was he? Why was he hiding at Thorndene? Had he a family? *Good Lord,* had he a *wife*? Why, the man could be anything—a thief, a smuggler, a . . . a *murderer*, for all she knew! Yet he had handled his visits to her bedroom with great tact and delicacy—he'd never done anything to cause her the least discomfort or embarrassment. In short (and despite what she'd said to him in her teasing fashion), he was a gentleman.

All these thoughts, however, were quite beside the point, she reminded herself. He had declared himself her enemy. He wished to drive her from Thorndene. He, who was a trespasser and an imposter, had declared that *she*, who had the right and authority to be here, must go! She could not, if she had a grain of sense, permit him to take such advantage of her. She should set about discovering his identity, his whereabouts in the house, and the reason for his ghostly deception. Or, if she were *truly* sensible, she should turn the entire matter over to the authorities at Padstow.

It didn't take much thought to dispense with *that* idea. Such action would surely be too precipitate. She didn't want the man imprisoned—at least not yet. She wanted to be fair. She had no certain knowledge that he was a criminal. She could always go to the magistrates as a last resort. In the meantime, she could plan a counter-strategy...

Nell was a girl with many inner resources. She had a lively and imaginative mind, and a number of schemes suggested themselves to her. She analyzed them one by one, discarding some as implausible, smiling at others that were too ridiculous for serious consideration, and thinking of ways to implement the good ones. Absorbed in these plans, she didn't hear the sound of hoofs until the horse was quite close. The sound made her jump up in panic. The dark powerful horse was galloping along the cliffs and coming toward her at an alarming speed. It was Caceres.

Before she could see the rider clearly, he saw her. He reined in the horse so suddenly that the beast reared and neighed terrifyingly. For a moment, Nell was certain that both she and the rider would be trampled beneath the hoofs of the enormous, rearing animal. But before the scream which had begun to form in her throat could be released, the rider had brought the horse under control, turned him round and was riding back the way he'd come. Nell stared in sudden recognition at the back of the tall, dark-haired rider rapidly disappearing from her sight. She leaned back against a rock to recapture her breath. Then she laughed. "You don't fool me, Harry!" she shouted into the wind. "I'd know you anywhere!"

Her first plan was to place two large candelabrum behind the white curtain, hoping that the bright light would reveal both the man and the mechanism by which he made his ghost-figure fade in and out. But Harry did not appear while the light remained, and she eventually gave up the plan.

Her next scheme was to spread a coating of a greasy substance on the floor in the window embrasure. In that way, Harry would leave visible footprints on the floor, and she could confront him with the evidence of his physical existence. The problem was that she didn't have a greasy substance to use. After giving the matter much thought, she went to Amelia. Claiming to be looking hagged (which was not difficult, since Amelia had been remarking on that very fact several times during the last few days), she asked to borrow a lotion for her complexion. "But of course, dear," Amelia said, eager to share her knowledge of cosmetics with Nell. "I have several. Which would you like? I have Denmark lotion, of course. And an ointment Mr. Keypstick made for me—an elixir of apples and asses' milk. Then there is a lotion of my own concoction, made of white flowers, cucumber water, lemon juice and minced pigeon meat—"

Nell shuddered. "Minced *pigeon* meat?"

"Oh, yes, dear. They say that pigeon flesh is as beneficial to the skin as crushed strawberries, you know—"

"Never mind," Nell interrupted. "Give me the thickest lotion of the lot, if you will."

Amelia blinked at her in surprise. "The thickest? What a strange request."

The Denmark lotion proved to be the best, and Nell spread a coat of it carefully on the floor before the window. Then, to ease her conscience at having deceived her dear Amelia, she spread some on her face as well. Promptly at midnight, the sound of Harry's approach reached her ears. She sat up with an eager smile, but Harry did not materialize. Instead, she was subjected to a series of groans, squeaks, grunts and cries which were obviously designed to frighten an innocent victim out of her wits. Nell put her hands to her ears and laughed. When at length the noise subsided, she demanded loudly, "Did you really think, you fool, that I would be frightened by that child's trick?"

Harry's voice was rueful. "No, I suppose not," he admitted.

"Where are you?" she asked. "Why aren't you showing yourself?"

"No need for that. Since the noise didn't do the trick, I may as well go."

"No, don't go just yet," Nell urged, trying to ensure the success of her footprint trap. "Stay and talk for a moment."

"Why?" he asked suspiciously. "Are you up to something?"

"Of course not. I'm sitting right here in bed, exactly as I always do."

"I know that," he said crossly. "I can see you. What *is* that on your face, by the way?"

"On my face?" she asked puzzled. "What—?" She put her fingers to her cheeks and felt the lotion. "Oh, that. It's only a lotion for my complexion," she said in some embarrassment.

Harry let out a snort. "What nonsense," he said disparagingly. "You women are such gullible fools."

"What do *you* know of the matter, sir? I have it on good authority that this lotion gives excellent protection against age-spots and wrinkles."

"Age spots and wrinkles, eh?" Harry asked, his grin apparent in his voice. "Well, then, I sincerely apologize.

Obviously, the lotion is a necessity for such a wrinkled old hag as yourself."

"Oh, take a damper!" Nell muttered in annoyance. "Not only are you behaving with irritating male superiority, but you're being cowardly as well."

"Cowardly, ma'am? In what way?"

"Why are you afraid to show yourself?"

"Afraid? Not at all. Only suspicious. I know you're up to something. But rather than succumb to my suspicions, I'll prove my courage. There!" And the ghostly figure slowly appeared.

Nell was sure she'd heard a match being struck. But she did not bother to mention it. She merely smiled to herself. Surely she had his footprints now! "Thank you, Harry," she said sweetly. "Now you may go."

"Oh, I may, may I? Now that you've had your way with me? Very well, ma'am, I'll go. I take no pleasure in looking at your lotion-covered face with that irritating smile of *female* superiority. Goodnight, my dear."

No sooner had he faded from view than she jumped out of bed, snatched her candle and ran to the window. Pulling aside the curtain, she examined the floor minutely. Not a mark disturbed the lotion-covered surface of the floor!

Nell was nonplussed. She spent the following day in brooding silence. She paid scant attention to Gwinnys's chatter or Lady Amelia's attempts to tease her "out of the sullens." By the end of the day, she had determined to take the most drastic step of her entire anti-ghost strategy: a head-on confrontation! The next time he appeared, she would choose a moment when he was absorbed in conversation, dash out of bed and fling open the curtains before he'd had a chance to escape.

That night, sitting in bed as usual and awaiting the hour of twelve, she found that she was trembling. She knew her plan was weak and fraught with danger. In the first place, she had no idea what trick *he* had devised for tonight. She could not count on his appearing at all, or, if he *did* come, that he'd show himself in the usual way. In the second place, she was not at all sure that he couldn't make himself disappear even in the few seconds it would take for her to race across the floor to the curtain. Perhaps, if she took a stance somewhat closer...

Harry's thumping footsteps sounded just as the hall clock struck twelve. She was standing three steps from the curtain when the first faint flicker of light appeared. "Good evening," came his voice. "I see that you're not in your bed."

"And *you* are not showing yourself," she accused.

"No. Nor do I intend to, while you stand so close."

"Oh? Why not?"

He didn't deign to answer. "If you want me to stay, get back into bed," he said coldly.

"If I do, will you show yourself?" she asked, hampered but not foiled.

There was a silence while he considered. She could almost read his mind. He knew she was up to something. "Oh, very well," he agreed, succumbing either to the temptation of her companionship, to the challenge of her threatened trap, or to some purpose of his own.

She pattered back to bed, settled herself against the pillows and smiled innocently at him. "There, is that better?"

"Much better," he said shortly, and slowly came into view.

She looked at him curiously. "You seem much the same as usual," she said in some surprise. "Haven't you devised any new horror with which to attack me tonight?"

"No. I've decided to try to reason with you."

"Don't waste your time. I can imagine no reason that a ghost could present that would logically convince me to surrender my bed and board—my *home*, in fact—to a mere spectre."

"Nevertheless, I *do* have good and valid reasons—"

She shook her head. "I wish I understood you," she said plaintively. "Why is it so important to be rid of me?

Am I in your way? Do I disturb your life? What is it you want to do that I prevent you from doing?"

"I was thinking of *you*, not of me," the ghost said, with convincing sincerity. "You cannot be happy here. You've been here for several weeks, during which time the weather has been abominable, there hasn't been a visitor from the outside world, you haven't a hope of a party or ball... This must be an impossibly dull place for you. Surely by this time you must be homesick for the liveliness and gaiety of London."

"My happiness is none of your affair," she said rigidly.

"Perhaps not. But it occurs to me that you may be forcing yourself to remain here in some stubborn desire to prove yourself stronger than I. It's nothing but foolishness, you know, to cut off your nose to spite your face."

"You exaggerate your importance to me, Mr. D'Espry," she said cuttingly.

There was a wistful sigh. "That's a facer," Harry admitted with a touch of regret. "Nonetheless, you must realize that it cannot be healthy for a lovely young girl to bury herself away from all possibility of social encounters. You should be in London, in the midst of a whirl of activity, surrounded by beaux and—"

"How dare you, sir!" Nell hissed furiously. "The matter of my beaux is none of your affair! Who are you to speak to me so? I've never known a ruder, more encroaching, interfering, insulting thatchgallows, man *or* ghost, than you!"

"Thatchgallows?" Harry exclaimed, trying unsuccessfully to hold back his laughter. "What an epithet for a smug—"

But Nell had bounded out of bed as soon as the last word had left her tongue. She flew across the floor in four leaping steps and threw the curtains aside. Her speed kept her moving forward and, before she could see what her action had revealed, her head came into crashing contact with what seemed to be a solid glass wall. She felt a flash of searing pain, pieces of glass went flying through the air, and she felt herself falling. A dark pit seemed to loom around her, slowly trying to swallow her up. *"Nell!"* she heard a voice cry in agony.

The pain in her head was excruciating, she was surrounded by blackness, and she knew her consciousness was slipping quickly away. But she felt her shoulders gripped by a strong arm, and a shoulder was slipped under her head to support her. All the while, the voice cried urgently in her ear: "Nell, *Nell!* Oh, *God*, what have I done? Please, girl, open your eyes! Speak to me, Nell! *Please!*"

She could not refuse him. She clung to consciousness with all her will, and, with tremendous effort, opened her eyes. A man's face was bending over hers. His dark eyes were staring in anguish into hers, and his mouth was compressed into a tense line. But the handsome face, with its black, white-streaked hair, its lean, lined cheeks and high forehead was just exactly what she'd imagined it would be. She slowly and painfully lifted her hand and touched his cheek. The skin was warm, rough, unshaven... and very, very real. *"Harry...!"* she whispered weakly, with the tremor of a smile on her lips. Then she turned her face into his shoulder and let the blackness envelop her.

Chapter Nine

SHE HAD A dim awareness of faces bending over her from time to time. Mostly she saw Gwinnys, her eyes tearful and full of affection. Then there was Mrs. Penloe, warm and protective, lifting her from her pillow to force soup into her mouth. There was Amelia, looking fluttery and nervous, and a gray-bearded man who frowned at her and senselessly kept passing his hand in front of her eyes. And Harry, staring at her with that look of agony. But most of the time she lay in a comfortable blackness, unaware of anything except a persistent pain in her head.

Then, after what seemed a very long time, she opened her eyes and found herself looking at the familiar ceiling of her bedroom. She evidently was safely in her bed. The flickering shadows that danced across the ceiling came from the fire, she knew. Was she alone? She tried to sit up, but a pain in her forehead stabbed her. She groaned, raised her hand to head and felt, to her surprise, a heavy bandage.

"Miss Nell, be 'ee awake?" Gwinnys appeared, smiling down at her.

"Gwinnys..." Nell tried to say in greeting, but her voice was only a croak.

Gwinnys patted her shoulder. "Evenin', Miss Nell. 'Tis good to see 'ee come round."

"But... what happened...?"

"Seems a mirror crashed down from the wall and hit 'ee on the head," Gwinnys explained. "Leastways, so Mrs. Penloe says. How do 'ee feel, Miss Nell? Still hurtin'?"

"Not unless I move," Nell replied, turning her head gingerly. "A *mirror*, you say? What mirror?"

Gwinnys shrugged. "The one that hung on the wall over there."

Nell lifted her head and stared at the spot Gwinnys indicated. "Nonsense," she declared with her old spirit. "I was struck over *there*—at the window!"

Gwinnys regarded her mistress speculatively. "That cain't be. Nothin' there to break on one. 'Twas a mirror struck you, Miss Nell. I swept up the pieces mysel'. Only..."

"Only?"

"There's somethin' havey-cavey 'bout this, I seem. When I heard the commotion that night—"

"*That* night? You make it sound so long ago..."

"Three days since, Miss Nell," Gwinnys explained, smiling at Nell's look of surprise.

"I see. Well, go on."

"Like I said, I heard a noise, an' I come runnin' to your door. But someone's locked it. 'Get Mrs. Penloe, quickly,' a man says through the door."

"Who was it, do you know?"

"Mrs. Penloe says it was her Will, but..."

"But you don't think it was?"

"No, Miss. The voice, well, I'd *lay* it didn't belong to

Will Penloe. Then Mrs. Penloe goes in, payin' no mind to what I'm shriekin' at her, and locks the door. They they send Will for a doctor, all the time keepin' the door locked and lettin' me weep an' wail outside. By the time the doctor leaves, Lady Amelia's up and demandin' to be let in. Well, they open the door and there's no one there but Mrs. Penloe and Will, an' 'ee layin' there white as a sheet, a big bandage on your head. And there, along that wall, is the bits of broken mirror, which Mrs. Penloe tells me to sweep up. But the queer thing was..."

"Yes?"

Gwinnys narrowed her eyes and lowered her voice histrionically. "I was sittin' wi' 'ee last night—we all take turns, you see—and seen somethin' gleamin' on the floor near the window. 'Twas a bit o' mirror. Now, I reckon broken glass can fly about a bit, but 'tain't likely it can fly clear 'cross the room, can it?"

"Did you ask Mrs. Penloe to explain?"

The girl shook her head. "No, not yet. I was wishful to talk to 'ee first. Do you suspicion she's up to somethin'?"

"I don't know, Gwinnys," Nell said abstractedly, trying to piece together a coherent sequence of events from the bits she remembered and the story Gwinnys had told her.

"I suspicion somethin' else, Miss Nell," Gwinny added. "The man what locked me out...I reckon he's your mysterious horseman."

"And...you've not seen or heard this man since?" Nell asked carefully.

"No, not a sign."

Nell tried again to sit up but a spasm of pain made her groan. Gwinnys clucked guiltily. "Listen to me, runnin' on an' on, an' 'ee in pain. I'll fetch Mrs. Penloe. She's had a pot o' broth simmerin' all day, waitin' for 'ee to open your eyes."

"Yes, thank you, Gwinnys. I'm feeling surprisingly hungry. A bowl of broth is just what I'd like."

Nell, alone for a moment, pulled herself to a sitting position. When Mrs. Penloe bustled in a few moments later, carrying the steaming broth, her eyes behind the little spectacles shone with pleasure at seeing Nell. "Well, Miss, I call it *tremmin*, seein' 'ee sittin' up so!" she exclaimed delightedly.

Gwinnys, who had followed her in, nodded in enthusiastic agreement. "Tremmin is the word!" she chortled. "I was afeared that sittin' up would be a twister for 'ee yet awhile."

"A twister?" Nell asked.

"'Tis Cornish for somethin' hard to do," Mrs. Penloe explained, tying a bib round Nell's throat and perching on the bed at her side.

"Now, you drink all o' that broth, Miss Nell," Gwinnys urged, leaning over Nell on her other side. "Doctor says 'ee have need o' nourishment."

Mrs. Penloe looked up at the abigail in annoyance. "Hold your clack, girl," she chided. "You'll be givin' Miss Belden a headache worse'n she has already."

Nell looked up at the abigail kindly. "Please, Gwinnys, leave us for a bit. I'd like to talk to Mrs. Penloe alone."

The abigail's eyebrows shot up. "Oh?" she asked curiously, looking from one to the other. "I mean, o' course, Miss Nell. I'll run down the corridor and tell Lady Amelia that 'ee be awake."

"Yes, do that," Nell agreed. "And tell her that I'd love to see her . . . er . . . *after* I've . . . finished my broth."

Mrs. Penloe gave Nell a sidelong glance and busied herself with the broth. After Gwinnys had shut the door behind her, Mrs. Penloe lifted the spoon and tried to feed her patient, but Nell could see that her hand trembled slightly and that she was biting her lower lip nervously. Nell gently pushed the spoon away. "Not yet, Mrs. Penloe. There's something I wish to ask you first."

"*Ask* me, Miss Belden?" Mrs. Penloe quivered.

"Where is he?" Nell demanded without hesitation.

"*He*? Who?" Mrs. Penloe said, her eyes on the soup.

"You know who! Harry!"

"Drink your soup, Miss, afore it cools," Mrs. Penloe begged, lifting the spoon to her mouth again.

Nell thrust the spoon aside again. "You're *not* going to pretend he doesn't exist, are you? I've *seen* him, you know."

Mrs. Penloe looked at Nell levelly. "I've nought to say, Miss. 'Tis sorry I be."

"Nothing to say!" Nell cried in exasperation. "Then perhaps you'd better *find* something! If you won't talk to me, you'll have to talk to the magistrates. You've been hiding a trespasser here, feeding him from the Thorne larder and supplying him with horses from the Thorne stables! And now, you keep silent after he very nearly *kills* me—!"

Mrs. Penloe, who had remained remarkably calm through most of the accusations, drew herself up angrily at the last one. "Miss Belden," she exclaimed furiously, "you cain't b'lieve that! 'Twas an accident—a terrible accident! No one's more upset than he—"

Nell watched the woman closely. "*Is* he upset? I don't believe it. He hasn't even been here to see me since the accident, Gwinnys says."

"Precious little *she* knows about it!" Mrs. Penloe declared. "He's been here every night, after th' others 've gone to bed. The way he sits there, holdin' on to your hand an' starin' at your face—'tis enough to break my heart!"

"So," Nell said firmly, trying not to be moved by Mrs. Penloe's description of the events, "there *is* someone, isn't there? Who *is* he, Mrs. Penloe?"

Mrs. Penloe stared down at the bowl in her lap. "Cain't say, Miss."

"Can't—or won't?"

Mrs. Penloe looked up at Nell sadly. "I cain't. I . . . promised."

"You know, Mrs. Penloe," Nell asserted, "I'll find out the truth whether you tell me or no."

"I wish 'ee would!" the little housekeeper said

earnestly. "I truly wish 'ee would. Now, please, Miss, let me feed 'ee this broth. 'Twill help us *both* to feelin' better."

Harry did not make an appearance, either in ghostly or fleshly form, after Nell regained consciousness, but Nell did not inquire about him further. As soon as she was well enough to stand, almost a week after her accident, she made a thorough investigation of the window embrasure. She knew that the door to a passageway must be concealed somewhere within the alcove. The possibilities were limited; there were only two narrow walls, one on each side of the window. They were both paneled, and even close examination revealed no hinges or latches of any kind. However, the wall farthest from her bed sounded hollow when she tapped it. That was obviously the door, but she could find no way of opening it. Probably it had been designed to be opened only from within the passage itself.

Nell had not forgotten the stairway that Gwinnys had urged her to explore. The stairway now seemed to Nell the most accessible route to Harry's whereabouts. That night, when she was sure everyone was asleep, she put on a dressing gown and slippers, lit a candle and stealthily crept down the stairs to the kitchen.

There, in the back of the house, she found the staircase Gwinnys had described and, pausing at the foot, held the candle high. It was a steep stairway with a door at the top. She started to make the climb, but on the second step she hesitated. Harry would no doubt be asleep. Would it not be awkward to wake him? Perhaps she would not like the answers he would give to the many questions which troubled her. Besides, she was not properly dressed. Her courage failed her, and she turned away. As she did so, she glanced back over her shoulder at the door. In the darkness she noticed a faint light shining from beneath the door. Someone up there was awake.

With renewed determination, though quaking in every limb, she softly mounted the stairs. After the briefest hesitation at the top, she blew out her candle, pushed open the door and peered inside. She found herself on the threshold of a large, paneled room, furnished much like a library. There was a wide fireplace in which a fire was dying. One wall was covered with crowded bookshelves. In the center of the room was a long table, books and papers strewn about on it in careless profusion. At the far end of the table, an oil lamp burned dimly, lighting the head of the man she had come to see. He had fallen asleep, his head on the table resting on one arm, the other arm stretched out before him, the fingers clutching an empty wine glass. An open book and several large maps lay spread before him and a half-empty decanter was within reach.

Nell coughed gently. Harry stirred. "Is't you, Mrs. Penloe?" he muttered sleepily. "Yes, yes, I know. 'S late. I'll take myself t' bed." He raised his head, smiled sleepily and nodded at the shape he could barely discern in the gloom.

"It's not Mrs. Penloe," Nell said quietly.

The man at the table stiffened. "Then, who—?"

Nell smiled to herself and gave a low moan. "I am Helen D'Espry," she said in a low, wailing monotone. "Born 1647, died 1668, having been murdered in my bed by a smuggler."

"Nell?" He gasped. *"Nell!"* He jumped up in awkward haste. "What—? Why did you come? Damnation, I'm so befuddled by sleep...I don't know whether or not I'm dreaming—!" And he lifted a shaking hand to his forehead and brushed aside the tousled hair that had fallen over his eyes.

"I think you are befuddled with more than sleep," Nell said in amusement. "Don't you think you should ask me to sit down?"

"Yes, of course...No, wait! Good Lord, why can't I *think*! No, you can't sit down and visit as if this were a tea party. It's the middle of the night!"

"The hour never seemed to bother you before, when it

was *you* who paid the visits," she pointed out calmly.

He frowned at her. "Never mind. That was different."

"Why?" She came forward to the table, moving into the circle of light from the lamp.

He stared at her with a bemused intensity, noting the soft ruby color of her dressing gown, the glow of her face in the lamplight, the loose profusion of her curls which only imperfectly concealed the bandage she still wore on her forehead. "Your head . . . ?" he asked. "Is it better?"

"Yes, much better. I'm almost good as new. Why did you not come to see me, to find out for yourself?"

"I came to see you," he said shortly. His eyes, which had been searching her face, fell. "Nell, you *do* realize that I never intended to hurt you. I'll never forgive myself for—"

"It's not necessary to tell me that," she assured him. "There are, however, many other things I think you should make clear to me. May I *please* sit down?"

He sighed. "Yes. I suppose this meeting is inevitable." With obvious reluctance, he came round the end of the table to assist her into a chair. It required half a dozen steps to reach her. Holding on to the table with his right hand, he limped to her side. As he approached, she was able to see him clearly for the first time. Although bleary-eyed and unshaven, he was in her eyes breathtakingly handsome, his appearance dramatized by the streak of white in his hair. He was even taller than she'd expected, with beautiful, broad shoulders and an erect, soldier-like bearing. But the limp drew her eyes down to his legs. Her cheeks whitened as she saw for the first time the wooden stump that was his left leg.

He met her startled glance with an imperturbable expression and held out the chair wordlessly. For a frozen moment they stared at each other, the sudden closeness emphasizing the reality of a relationship that, until that moment, had been only a game. She wanted desperately to say something . . . something amusing and casual . . . to bring things back to the way they'd been before . . . before she'd touched his cheek, seen his face, learned that he'd suffered the tragic loss of a limb. But no words came to her, and her throat constricted painfully. Unable to say anything, she took the seat he held for her, folded her hands on the table, lowered her eyes and waited.

He limped back to his chair. Shoving aside the books and papers carelessly, he faced her with a mocking smile on his lips. "Well, my girl, you've found me out at last. What is it you want to know?"

She flicked a quick glance at him, feeling suddenly shy. "Everything—what you are doing here, why you want to be rid of us, how you managed your ghost impressions, how I was hurt—everything. But first, of course, I want to know who you are."

"Do you want a *name*? What difference can *that* make? Won't the name Harry D'Espry do?"

"No, it won't. D'Espry, indeed! Did you think I wouldn't guess that you chose *esprit*, the French word for *spirit*?"

"That was clever of you," he said drily. "Such a clever young lady must have fabricated some theory concerning my identity. Who do you think I am?"

"I truly don't know. I *did* think, at first, that you were a relative of the Penloes..."

"But you don't think so any more? Why not?"

"It's obvious, isn't it? You're a man of education and breeding—anyone can see that. So I haven't a clue as to who you are and why you are hiding away here."

"What makes you believe I'm hiding away?"

"Well—" she began, then paused and glanced at him guiltily.

"Don't pull your punches, girl," he urged. "I won't take offense, I promise."

"Very well, then," she said bravely, going on to reveal the problem that most worried her. "Clearly, you did not want us to know of your existence. In fact, you went to great lengths to drive us away. What else can it be but that you are hiding from...from..."

"From . . .?" he prodded.

She took a deep breath. "From the authorities."

His mocking smile became more pronounced. "From the authorities, eh? You're convinced that I'm the perpetrator of some dastardly crime, is that it? What sort of crime had you in mind? Poaching? Smuggling?"

Nell was inexplicably overwhelmed with shame. She shook her head and lowered her eyes to her hands.

"Not smuggling?" he asked sardonically. "Did you think I was a highwayman? No? *What*, then?"

"Oh, nothing so paltry as a highwayman," she admitted, trying to shrug off her guilt-feeling with a jest. "Nothing less than murder would do for you."

He stared at her for a shocked moment and then a laugh burst out of him. "You thought me a *murderer*? Oh, poor Nell. What a dreadful time I've given you!"

His reaction made it clear that he was not a criminal. She sighed in relief. "Then . . . if you're not hiding from the authorities, why *are* you hiding here?"

"But I'm not hiding at all," he said simply. "I *live* here."

"You *trespass* here, you mean," she said bluntly. "This is *my* house."

"No, you're quite out there, my girl. It is not your house, it is *mine*."

Her eyes narrowed suspiciously. "Yours? Don't be ridiculous—it belongs to the Thornes."

"Does it?" he asked quizzically.

"Of course it does! Well, that is, it belongs to the Earl, but . . ."

"Exactly. The *Earl*. Well, it was he who gave it to me."

"Did he *really*?" Nell asked amazed. "How can that be? He's in the army in Spain—or at least he was . . ."

"I'm well aware of that, my dear. I was in the army with him."

Her eyes widened. "But of *course*! You're a *soldier*! That's where . . ." she faltered.

"Yes, that's where I lost my leg."

She nodded solemnly. "I'm sorry," she said quietly. But after a moment of thought, her brow wrinkled in suspicion. "But, Harry, I don't understand. If this house *is* yours, why were you hiding?"

"I've told you I *wasn't* hiding," he said impatiently.

"Not hiding?" she challenged. "Do you mean to deny that you didn't want anyone to know of your existence?"

"I merely like my privacy," he said defensively. "Is there anything wrong with that?"

"*Privacy?* Is *that* what you call it?" she asked incredulously. "You've hidden yourself away in a secret part of the house, you've made the Penloes lie for you, you've tried to frighten me out of my wits and almost killed me . . . and all for *privacy?*"

His eyes met hers defiantly, then wavered and dropped. "Well, you see," he muttered, "it all got a bit out of hand . . ."

"So it seems," she said curtly. She propped her chin on her hand and regarded him closely. "Why do you *need* all this privacy? What is it you do here? These maps and charts and books . . . are you doing something secret?"

He looked up again, amusement in his eyes. "You, my dear Nell, are an incorrigible romantic. You could not make me into a murderer, so now you are trying to make me a *spy*, is that it?"

She had to laugh. "Am I wrong again? Are you *not* a spy?"

Smiling at her indulgently, he reached across the table and took her hand. "Please believe me, Nell. There's no great, dark secret here. I like my peace . . . my privacy. Perhaps I'm excessive, but not wicked. All I do here is pass my days studying military history. That's what the maps and books are all about. Some day, when I've learned enough, I may write a book myself. Do you believe me now?"

She stared at the hand clasping hers. She wanted to believe him. But somehow, his story didn't make sense. One didn't need to hide from the world just to study or write a book. "I believe that what you've told me is *part* of the truth," she said thoughtfully.

He withdrew his hand abruptly and his smile faded.

"It's as much of the truth as you're going to get from me tonight," he said brusquely. "If you will hand me that crutch leaning on the wall behind you, I shall escort you back to your room."

But Nell didn't budge. "I think you *are* hiding," she said gravely, "and I think I know why."

"And *I* think I've heard enough of your theories for one night. Come, I'm taking you back to your room." And he pulled himself up from his chair.

She stood up and faced him. "It's your leg, isn't it? You're *ashamed* to be seen with a wooden leg!"

"Have you quite finished?" he asked her coldly. "If so, I suggest that we conclude this interview for tonight."

"I've hit on it, haven't I?" she insisted, driven on by an unaccustomed sense of righteousness. "Your reactions prove I've hit right on the mark. But Harry, how foolish of you! No one who knows you will think less of you for that! How can they? It is *ennobling* to have sacrificed a leg for your country!"

He glared at her with icy disdain. "I don't believe my behavior or my personal life need be a concern of yours, ma'am. It seems to me that your remarks show a great deal of presumption."

She gasped and flushed shamefacedly. "Yes, you're quite right. I . . . I'm sorry."

"Then shall we go?"

She looked up at him and lifted her chin in the defiant way he'd seen so often before. "There is no need for you to escort me, sir," she said with the same icy formality he had used. "I can find my own way. If you will be so kind as to light my candle, I shall take my leave."

He bowed stiffly, pulled a match from a pocket of his breeches and lit her candle. "Goodnight, then, ma'am. Please accept my good wishes for the continued improvement of your health," he said, putting the candle in her hand.

They stared at each other coldly for a moment. Then Nell went quickly to the door. There she paused and looked back at him. "There's something else I've had the presumption to discover about you," she said in cold triumph. "I've guessed your true identity at last. Goodnight, *Captain Thorne!*"

Chapter Ten

A TROUBLED AND confused Nell approached the breakfast table the next morning, her mind a mass of indecision. If Captain Thorne—or, rather, the Earl—did not want her here at Thorndene, it was *she* who was the trespasser. Should she pack immediately and take her leave? Should she bide her time and wait until Harry ordered her to return to London? In the meantime, should she tell Amelia of Harry's true identity? Hours of sleeplessness had not brought answers to these and several other troublesome questions.

Unaware that the solution to these problems waited right outside the morning-room door, she accepted a cup of tea from Amelia with a wan smile. At that moment, Mrs. Penloe bustled in. The housekeeper's face was transformed. Her eyes shone behind the little spectacles, her cheeks glowed, and her buxom breast heaved in joyous gasps. "Lady Amelia, Miss Belden..." she said breathlessly, "I have a request from his lordship! He asked permission to...*to join 'ee at breakfast!*"

Nell gaped. *"Join us?"*

Lady Amelia merely raised her brows questioningly. "What are you talking about, Mrs. Penloe," she asked, mystified.

"Never mind, love. I'll explain in a moment," Nell said quickly. "Tell him we'd be delighted, Mrs. Penloe."

Mrs. Penlow beamed at Nell adoringly. "Oh, Miss, *thanks to 'ee*" she breathed.

"Don't be silly, Mrs. Penloe. There's no need to thank me. This *is* his home, after all."

Now it was Amelia who gaped. "*Whose* home? What are you *talking* about?"

But Mrs. Penloe had eyes only for Nell. "You don't *know*...you cain't *conceit*..." she muttered, tears welling up in her eyes. "'Tis the first time since the war...! Oh, Miss Nell, I don't know what you've done...or how 'ee managed it, but 'tis truly *arear*!" And dabbing her eyes with her apron, she ran from the room.

"Arear?" Nell asked no one in particular.

Amelia shrugged. "It's the Cornish way of saying 'wonderful.' I've heard Gwinnys use it from time to time. It's truly *arear* how Mrs. Penloe lapses into Cornish when she becomes emotional. But tell me, Nell, what *is* all this?"

Nell reached across the table and grasped Amelia's hand. "I've news for you, dear, that may come as quite a shock. The man who's been living right here in the house—the ghost, you know—"

"Nell! Have you *discovered* him? We must call the magistrates at—"

"Wait, love, you must hear the whole, and we haven't much time. The man has more right to be here than we have. Amelia, it's your *nephew*, Captain Thorne!"

Amelia could only gape while the import of Nell's words sank in. *"Henry?"* she breathed incredulously. "My dearest Henry, *alive?*" Clasping her hands to her breasts, she rose from her chair and tottered to the door. "Alive! Oh, the dear boy! Where *is* he? I must see—!"

"Wait, Amelia," Nell cautioned. "Please, there's something else you must know."

"Yes, of course, dear. But later. You must tell me everything, of course, but first I want to *see* him with my own—"

The door opened and Harry stood on the threshold. He was clean shaven, combed and dressed in modest elegance in a russet wool coat, tan breeches and gleaming riding boots. The only sign of his impairment was the crutch under his right arm. "*Henry!*" Amelia screeched joyously.

Harry held out his left arm and Amelia fell into his embrace. Only after she finally let him go did she notice the crutch. "Henry, you're *wounded!*" she cried in her fluttery voice.

Harry led her to the table, all the while giving a calculatedly casual account of his "wound," and although Amelia shed some bitter tears when she realized the full extent of his injury, his determined cheerfulness made her cut short her grief. Telling herself that she was grateful he was alive, she forced herself into control, and a semblance of a normal breakfast ensued. Harry permitted his doting aunt to load his plate with heaping servings of coddled eggs, herby pie, smoked pilchards and thick slices of country ham. As if these were not enough, Amelia called for Mrs. Penloe to bring out some hot biscuits from the kitchen. These were served by a goggle-eyed Gwinnys, who was so overwhelmed by the sight of a real Earl (a fact she'd learned from the overwrought Mrs. Penloe) that she was, for once, struck dumb.

When at last Mrs. Penloe had dragged the stupified Gwinnys from the room, and Amelia had calmed herself with her ubiquitous cup of tea, Harry was able to turn his attention to Nell. She had sat back quietly, observing the proceedings with a great deal of amusement, noting with a surprisingly possessive feeling of pride Harry's tact and grace in handling the excessive blandishments of three adoring females. "You have been unwontedly quiet this morning, Miss Belden," he said to her blandly.

"I do not crow when I have won a point," she retorted.

"Won a point? Which one is that, ma'am? You've won so many victories over me that I cannot guess which one you mean."

Nell cast a glance at Amelia who was attending their conversation with much interest. "You shall have Amelia believing that we've been engaging in some sort of war. I only meant to say that I'm delighted you've decided to heed my advice not to hide from us any more."

"Nell is quite right, Henry dear," Amelia said, putting down her cup to emphasize her words. "I cannot *imagine* why you didn't make yourself known to us when we arrived."

"Because, my dear aunt, I didn't—I don't!—want the family to know of my existence. I want nothing to do with their problems, their finances, their lawyers, their bailiffs, their schemes, their antics—in short, their lives. Forgive me, Aunt. I hope you will take no offense, and I trust that when you return to London you will not give me away."

"But that's impossible!" Amelia declared earnestly. "You *must* tell them you're alive. You are now the head of the family. They *need* you."

"Rubbish!" his lordship responded flatly. "Let them make Charles the head of the family. It's an honor I've no wish for."

"Your wishes have nothing to do with it," Amelia said sensibly, picking up her teacup again. "It's a matter of duty. Besides, Charles would squander away the entire estate within a year, if he were put in charge."

Harry shrugged. "I'm afraid that the condition of the estate no longer interests me, Aunt Amelia."

Amelia drained her cup and rose. "You are entitled to a time of withdrawal from the world, Henry, especially under the circumstances. I don't blame you. But you'll not feel this way for long. In any case, I have no wish to argue with you—I'm too delighted at having you restored to me. But all this has been quite agitating to an old woman. If you will both excuse me, I shall lie down for a bit."

Left alone with Nell, Harry turned to her with a smile. "I'm glad we have this chance to be alone. I must apologize to you for my churlish behavior of last night."

"There's no need. Your appearance this morning has more than made up for it, my lord."

"Tush, girl, you'll not take such paltry revenge on me by calling me 'my lord'," he said, horrified.

"Surely you don't expect me to call you 'Harry'—as if you were still the ghost of an impudent, unmannerly smuggler?"

"Why not? All my friends call me Harry. Did you really think poor D'Espry was impudent and unmannerly? I rather liked the fellow."

Nell smiled at him warmly. "I did, too. In fact, I shall probably miss him, even though he gave me quite a headache. How did that happen, by the way? You haven't explained it to me."

"It was all quite simple. The ghost you saw was really a mirror-image. There's a passageway from my sitting room to the window-alcove in your bedroom—"

"I guessed that," Nell said with self-satisfaction, "but I couldn't manage to find the door."

"It only functions from the passageway side. Short of pulling off the wall, there is no way you could have opened it."

"So you came down the passage and opened the door. And then?" Nell asked curiously, leaning toward him with eager attention.

"It was all done with mirrors. I could stand near the open doorway, right inside the passageway, which was black as pitch. Whatever I chose to light with my candle would be reflected in a mirror which I'd attached to the inner side of the door. That reflection in turn would be caught by a *second* mirror which, on my nightly arrival, I would hang from a hook in the alcove ceiling—"

"A hook? I never noticed it!"

"I counted on that. It was *that* mirror-image you saw, and it was that mirror which you ran into when you so impetuously dashed through the curtains that night." His expression darkened at the recollection. "I haven't ceased to berate myself about concocting that ridiculous scheme. I might have killed you!"

"Yes, you might have. But since I am quite alive, you needn't make a to-do over the incident," Nell said, dismissing her injury with a toss of her head. "I'm more interested in the manner in which you created the illusion. Do you mean to say that it was only a mirror-image of you that I conversed with all that time?"

"Exactly. That's how I appeared to be floating above the floor. The mirror hung about two feet above the floor."

Nell's brow wrinkled in her effort to understand. "I'm afraid I can't quite envision how it worked," she complained.

"Would you like me to show you how it was done? If you're not afraid of coming down the passageway, I'll let you see the whole process for yourself."

Nell eagerly agreed, and the pair promptly left the table. Harry escorted Nell to his sitting room, lit a lantern and opened a narrow door in the window alcove which Nell noted was quite like the one in her room. He was about to lead her into the passageway when he remembered that one of his mirrors had been broken. Excusing himself, he quickly went to his bedroom and removed a mirror from the wall. "This is a bit smaller than it should be," he explained on his return, "but it will serve well enough for a demonstration."

He led her down a long, dark, windowless corridor. When they reached the end of it, he showed her his paraphernalia which was hung neatly on hooks in the wall: the six-foot-high mirror-frame (from which the broken mirror-glass had been removed) hanging by a ring screwed into the top of the frame; a white, smock-like

shirt on which he'd crudely painted a huge, gaping
wound; and a candle which he'd fastened to the end of a
long black pole. "This was the floating candle," he
explained as he held the lantern high to show her the
second mirror which he'd hooked to the door.

He removed the ring from the empty mirror frame and
screwed it to the top of the frame of his bedroom mirror.
Then he unlatched the door and Nell found herself
looking into her bedroom. With the ease that comes with
frequent practice, Harry swung the mirror into the alcove
by means of the pole and hung it on the hook which, just
as he'd described, had been fixed in the ceiling in the
center of the alcove. Then he lit the candle and swung it
around until it was reflected in the door-mirror. He
adjusted the angle of the door until the second mirror
picked up the reflection. "There's the ghost-candle," he
said. "If you perch on your bed you'll see it quite plainly."

"And you haven't stepped into the room!" Nell
marveled. "No wonder you didn't leave footprints!"

To Harry's vast amusement, Nell told him about the
grease-trap she'd set for him on the alcove floor. Then he
donned the gruesome shirt, and Nell sat on the bed
watching the ghost appear. It was done by placing the
lantern on the floor, covering it with a cloth until Harry
was costumed, and then, when he was ready, slowly
pulling the cloth away with his crutch. As the light slowly
brightened on him, it made him appear in the mirror as if
he were "materializing." "It's the thin fabric of the
curtains that gives the final touch," he told her. "Only the
objects which are clearly lit are visible through the
curtains. You saw the candle but not the pole."

Nell applauded the apparition admiringly. "Just like a
magician," she said gleefully. "May I try it?"

"Please do," he urged. "I've never had a chance to
admire the effect. I'll sit on the bed and let you haunt *me*."

In order that Harry might enjoy the full effect, they
drew the draperies to darken the room and closed the
white curtains. Harry perched on the bed, and Nell

disappeared into the darkness of the passageway. In a few moments, to Harry's delight, a faint, wavering figure appeared behind the curtains, seeming to float insubstantially above the floor. Her face was shadowed, but he could make out the female form. On her head she had tied an enormous bandage with a bloody smudge on one side. "You are in great danger," she said in a wailing monotone. "You must go-o-o-o-o!"

Harry fell back against the pillows, overcome with laughter. "It's marvelous!" he crowed. "I had no idea my illusion worked so well."

"*Your* illusion!" the ghost said, offended. "This time it is *my* illusion, if you please."

"I beg pardon, ma'am. But what is that dreadful thing on your head?"

"It's a head-wound, sir. I look exactly as I did when the smuggler took my life."

"Poor girl! How did the brute do it?"

"It was done with a mirror which he let fall upon me," she said maliciously.

"What an unkind ghost you are," Harry remarked wryly.

"Ghosts *must* be unkind," she reminded him. "It's our job. Oh, by the way, sir, I'm pleased to note that I cannot see through walls—or anything else."

Harry snorted. "Aha! I *did* frighten you with that suggestion!" he chortled triumphantly.

"Well," Nell admitted, "although I didn't believe you, the suggestion of the mere *possibility* of such a . . . a talent rendered me quite uncomfortable."

The badinage continued until the two of them were weak with laughter. At last, however, the ghost of Helen D'Espry vanished, and Harry led the way back to his room. When they had stepped from the passageway into Harry's sitting room, he took down a key which hung on a long chain from a hook in the alcove, and with great ceremony locked the door to the passageway. Smiling, he turned to her and made a courtly bow. "There, my dear,"

he said, handing her the key. "Now you need never fear
that unwanted visitors will find their way to your
bedroom in future."

The key was of silver, with an unusually long shaft and
an ornate head, and it hung on a lovely silver chain.
"Thank you, sir," she said with an answering curtsy. "I
can only marvel at the odd fact that I never before
concerned myself about my vulnerability to...
er... *invasion* because of that passageway."

"That's because your instincts told you that I would
abide by the rules."

"Rules? What rules?"

"I was playing the game of being a ghost, and therefore
could only behave in a ghostly way. But now the game is
over. Now it is recognized and acknowledged that I am a
man, therefore..." He shrugged and left the rest unsaid.

"Therefore, the key," she finished for him with a small
smile. "I am truly grateful, my lord, and I'll wear the key if
you wish. It is very unusual and will make a pretty
ornament. But the gesture was really unnecessary. You
see, even though the ghost-game is over, *other* rules now
apply."

"Other rules?" he asked, cocking an eyebrow at her
quizzically.

"You are a gentleman, as I always knew you were. And
that implies rules even more strict than those set for
ghosts."

He grinned at her wickedly. "Perhaps so, but wear it
nevertheless. So long as it hangs around your neck, you
can be sure that neither ghost nor 'gentleman' shall come
down that passageway again."

Nell nodded meekly, but while he took the key from
her hand and hung it about her neck, she decided to
broach the subject still uppermost in her mind. "This
gesture of yours," she began, fingering the key shyly,
"makes it seem as if you expect me to remain in this house.
But I realized last night, to my shame, that I—not
you—am the trespasser here. Aunt Amelia and I... we

would not wish to take advantage of your hospitality. I know you find us in your way. When do you wish us to leave?"

"Now that you know of my existence, you are not at all in my way," he said reassuringly. "As I've said to you often, in my guise as the ghost, I cannot understand why you should desire to hide yourself away here, so far from the excitements and amusements of London, but if you wish to remain, please accept my hospitality for as long as you like."

"Thank you, my lord," she said with another curtsy. "I shall be most grateful. As to your question about why I desire to 'hide myself away here,' I seem to remember putting the same question to you. You didn't choose to answer me in any satisfactory way. I hope you'll not be offended if my response to you is equally unsatisfactory."

He smiled wryly. "*Touché*, ma'am. I shall not raise the question again."

Nell turned to the door. Just as she was about to leave, her eye was caught by a miniature hanging on the wall. "Oh, how lovely!" she couldn't help exclaiming. "Who *is* she?"

Harry came up behind her. "It's a portrait of a lady I once knew," he answered briefly.

"But I think I *know* her!" Nell leaned closer and examined the tiny features. "Isn't that Edwina Manning?"

"Yes, that is Miss Manning," Harry said shortly, turning away.

Nell wheeled around. "But how did you—? I mean, how is it that—?"

Harry went to the window and stood looking out at the gray mist beyond. "Miss Manning and I were once betrothed," he said in a tone that clearly indicated his dislike of discussing the matter further.

"Betrothed?" Nell asked in astonishment. "You and Edwina? I had not heard—"

"It was arranged some time ago." His voice was cool, warning her clearly that she was trespassing on private preserves again.

But Nell could not help herself—she had to pursue the matter further. Her high spirits were rapidly evaporating with this new discovery, leaving her feeling numb and empty. It was as if there was suddenly a void where her stomach had been—a void she seemed impelled to fill with words. "But what happened?" she asked with what she knew must sound like vulgar curiosity. "Surely if she had cried off, I would have heard. When I broke with Lord Keith the tale was one of the favorite *on dits* in every drawing room in London."

Harry turned to face her. "Miss Manning did not 'cry off,' ma'am," he said coldly. "May I suggest that this is also a subject we would be wise to avoid?"

Nell ignored the warning in his voice. "But if she did *not* cry off, you must still be betrothed," she said, her heart sinking. The full realization that Harry belonged to someone else—to one of the loveliest girls in England— had reached her spinning brain and its effect on her spirit was devastating. She did not know why the news had affected her so strongly, but standing here facing Harry's icy stare was not the time to find the answer. All she could think of now was Edwina Manning, waiting in London for a man who was hiding from her in Cornwall. Suddenly she looked up at Harry in horror. "Does she not know you've come back from the war?"

Harry was glaring at her, but soon his eye wavered under her direct gaze. "The matter of my return can no longer be of interest to her," he said, turning back to stare out the window. "After all, it has been a long, long time. She *must* have become attached to someone else long since." He lowered his head. "Perhaps she's already wed," he added quietly.

"She's *not* wed. Nor is she betrothed, as far as I know. Of course, she is much sought after, but she is known to have excellent principles. Oh, Harry, she *must* be waiting for word of *you*! How can you remain hiding here—?"

Harry turned again, his lips compressed, his cheeks pale. "You go too far again, ma'am," he said in the icy tone she'd heard before. "I must insist that you refrain from meddling in my private concerns."

Nell reddened, her spirit quailing before the coldness of his manner. "You are quite right, my lord. I beg your pardon. I shall not—to use your own words—raise the question again."

She fled without another word. When she reached her own room, she flung herself across the bed, troubled by a sharp and spreading pain which she was reluctant to identify. It was a pain quite new to her, and one which she would readily have exchanged for the physical one which recently had troubled her head. The severe headaches she'd suffered during the past week were nothing compared to *this*, which she knew was not physical. This anguish was of the *feelings*, and as she fingered the key which hung about her neck, she began to suspect the cause. If her suspicions were correct, she had not the slightest idea of how to effect a cure.

Chapter Eleven

THE SCENE IN Harry's room did not augur well for the future of the new relationship between Nell and her moody host. But to her surprise, he appeared at dinner that evening in a cheerful mood and spent the hours before bedtime with the two ladies in perfect amiability. The next day, which was unexpectedly bright and sunny, brought Nell an invitation to ride with him. Then, on the day following, during a rainy afternoon, he invited her to assist him in his researches into the military strategies of Marlborough. Before a week had passed, they found themselves enjoying a stimulating and pleasantly friendly intimacy.

Nell kept a strict guard on her tongue. As Mrs. Penloe had learned before her, Harry was immovable in his determination to cut himself off from his previous life, and Nell wisely decided to abide by his wishes. Once it became clear that neither would try to influence the other's life, they were able to discuss even their pasts without embarrassment. During the following weeks, they spent part of each day in each other's company. They talked incessantly. Nell told Harry about her feelings when she'd learned about her parents' death in a terrible accident in their coach, and about the difficulties of life with Lady Sybil. She revealed, to Harry's hearty amusement, the shocking facts of her three broken betrothals and the resulting ruin of her reputation among the ladies of Quality. On his part, Harry kept Nell fascinated with tales of his exploits on the Peninsula, the battles, the customs of the Spanish people he'd met, and the strange sights he'd seen. And one day, to his own surprise, he revealed to her the story of how he'd been wounded, how he'd hobbled for miles, delirious, parched and agonized, until he'd been found by a Spanish peasant who'd taken him in and whose wife had nursed him back to health. It was the first time he'd told the tale.

It had happened on a morning which was gray and threatening. Ignoring the ominous clouds, they had decided to ride. With Harry on Caceres and Nell on the mare, they had ridden out along the cliffs and finally stopped in the sheltered area that Nell had found so many days before. Sitting on the rocks and staring at the churning sea, Harry had found it soothing to tell the wide-eyed girl of his experiences—experiences that he'd relived so often in nightmares. As he spoke, his eyes fixed on the water below, he almost forgot she was there. Details of those terrible days, things he'd thought he'd forgotten, came back to him. He remembered the heat, his parched lips, the excruciating pain in his leg as the wound slowly festered. He'd found a tree branch to use as a crutch, but it was so rough that his hand and underarm were cut and blistered. After a while, his delirium took over. He imagined he was on a fox hunt, that he'd been unhorsed, and when he'd come upon the Spanish farmer he'd shouted, "Which way, man? Which way have they gone?"

There had been no doctor, and, in a moment of lucidity, he'd realized that his wound had become gangrenous. Under his direction, the Spanish farmer had been the surgeon. He had no doubt that the surgery had saved his life.

A low moan from Nell brought him back to the present. Aghast that he'd revealed so much, he stared in horror as she dropped to her knees beside him, her eyes brimming with tears, and laid her head gently on his left knee. "Oh, Harry," she sobbed, "thank God you had the courage."

"Confound it," he muttered, trying to lift her head, "what a crack-brained fool I am! I should never have let my tongue run on so. It's no tale for a young female to stomach. Forgive me, Nell."

But she merely stared up at him, her eyes wide and full of something he refused to acknowledge to himself. Neither of them seemed able to move. At that moment, the storm which had been threatening all morning broke around them, the rain and wind whipping at their heads and backs. He put his hands on her shoulders to urge her to her feet, but their eyes remained locked, and she did not budge. There seemed to him to be nothing else to do but cup her face in his hands and bend his head to hers. It was natural to kiss her, as instinctive and artless as the violent waves below and the rain beating down on them.

After a long moment, a trickle of rain found its way behind his coat collar and ran down his back, bringing him back to sanity. He let her go abruptly. "We're *both* crack-brained," he said with an embarrassed laugh. "Get up, girl, quickly! Let's get back before you're drenched through!"

She let him throw her on her horse without a word. He jumped on Caceres with an agility she always found amazing, and they galloped for home. By the time they dismounted in the stable, his manner had so completely reverted to pleasantly cordial friendship that she almost believed she'd dreamed the incident. Wet and shivering, she followed him back to the house, trying to ignore the feelings of confusion and anguish which his unaccountable behavior had roused in her.

During the morning, Amelia and Mrs. Penloe had also been having an intimate conversation. The weeks since Lord Thorne had revealed his presence had brought the two women into a close friendship. Initially, it had been their mutual affection for and interest in the young Earl that had brought them together, but time had revealed other compatabilities. Mrs. Penloe, well aware that her Cornish cooking had severe limitations, was delighted to learn that Lady Amelia was a collector of unusual recipes, and Amelia was only too happy to share her knowledge. The sharing of recipes soon led to a sharing of knowledge of medicinal and cosmetic concoctions, both women feeling a growing respect for the other's aptitudes. And when Amelia discovered that Mrs. Penloe felt it necessary every few hours (just as Amelia did) to restore her spirits with a cup of hot tea, the budding relationship flowered into friendship.

It became their habit to cease their activities at mid-morning and take their tea together. Amelia insisted that Mrs. Penloe ignore her position as housekeeper, take off her apron and sit down at the tea table in the morning room as if she were one of the family. The tea was served by Gwinnys who was too ignorant of the ways of the gentry to be at all surprised by the procedure. After Gwinnys was dismissed, the two women enjoyed a comfortable "coz" on one or more of their various mutual interests. This morning, however, the topic had been Harry.

Mrs. Penloe had felt positively euphoric over Master Harry's emergence from seclusion, but when day after day had passed without a real change in his attitude toward his inheritance, his responsibilities and his London life, she began to feel discouraged again. "I see nought to make me b'lieve he'll ever take up his old life again," she confided to Lady Amelia.

"Tush, woman," Amelia objected, refilling both their cups, "you're worrying needlessly. I have no doubt that he'll come round in a month or two."

Mrs. Penloe shook her head. "The boy can be stubborn as any nogglehead when he sets his mind to somethin'."

"Rubbish! When Nell and I go back to London, I have no doubt at all that Henry will go with us."

Mrs. Penloe peered over her spectacles at the lady opposite. "Be'ee plannin' to leave soon?"

Amelia shrugged. "We've had no word from Lady Sybil and Lord Charles since we arrived. I tell you, Mrs. Penloe, a more ramshackle, thoughtless, irresponsible pair than they do not exist! But they can't leave poor Nell to wither away here indefinitely. Not that I think she's withering away at all, but as far as Charles and Sybil know she is. In any case, they are bound to relent and send for her sooner or later."

"An' you reckon Master Harry'll go wi' 'ee when you're called back?"

"It's my guess that something will happen *before* Charles and Sybil relent. Nell will persuade Henry to take us back as soon as she's had her fill of Cornwall. With Henry with us, Charles and Sybil's permission is completely unnecessary. Henry is the head of the family, after all."

"Seems he's the head of the family only if he wants to be. An' he don't want to be."

"Don't underestimate Nell's influence with him, Mrs. Penloe," Amelia said with a knowing smile. "She's a strong-willed, persistent chit with taking ways. She'll manage him, see if she won't."

"She hasn't managed him yet," Mrs. Penloe said dubiously.

"Give the girl a little time," Amelia insisted. "A little more time is all she'll need. We're not in the suds yet, Mrs. Penloe. Just leave it to Nell."

But Nell herself had no confidence that she had any influence with Harry. The times when she felt close to him occurred only when they discussed their pasts. The subject of the future was closed. If ever she broached it, his manner would become icy and she would retreat in haste.

When they returned from their rain-drenched ride, she quickly parted from him, claiming the necessity of changing her wet clothes. But she needed time to think, to try to understand the meaning of his conduct and the state of her own emotions. But Gwinnys hovered solicitously over her, prattling distractingly about the problems caused by her naggy relationship with Mrs. Penloe and her irritation with Jemmy, who was always under foot and who taunted her with the unmerciful glee of a little brother. By the time Nell was able to dismiss the abigail, she realized that it was time for luncheon and Amelia would be waiting.

Harry did not join the ladies for luncheon, but he found Nell soon afterward and bore her off to his study to show her a new map he'd discovered of the land surfaces of Blenheim, and she found herself alone with him without having had a chance to sort out properly the confusion of her feelings. Harry had obviously decided to treat the events of the morning as if they had not happened. Nell, however, had no wish to follow his lead. She had been kissed by several men in her rather wild past, but no kiss had so disturbed her equilibrium. She had no intention of ignoring so momentous an occurence. She fixed her eyes on him determinedly. "Are you going to spend the entire afternoon prosing on about Blenheim?" she asked bluntly.

He was standing opposite her at his work table, pointing out places of significance on the map he'd spread out between them. He looked up from the map in some dismay. "I didn't know I was 'prosing on.' I'm sorry to be such a bore," he said, mildly affronted. "I thought you were interested."

"Of course I'm interested, ordinarily. But not today."

"Oh?" he asked curiously. "Why not today?"

She frowned at him irritably. "Today was a bit unusual, was it not?" she asked candidly. "It's not every day that I'm kissed like that."

He glanced quickly at her, flushed and dropped his eyes. "Oh. I . . . I'm truly sorry about that. I hope you'll forgive me. Can't think what came over me, but I assure you I'll not let it happen again."

"Why not?"

This time he looked up at her incredulously. "What do you mean?" he asked, arrested.

"You heard me, my lord. *Why* won't you let it happen again?"

His stare became suspicious. "Come now, Nell, don't run sly with me. What mischief are you brewing?"

"No mischief at all. I've asked a simple question. *Why*, sir, is kissing me such a blunder that you must apologize for it? I can name several gentlemen who would give much for such a chance."

"You needn't bother to name them—I have no doubt their number is legion," he said drily. "Now let us have done with this conversation. I find it most improper."

"Do you indeed? Well, I'm not accounted a very proper young lady, so I don't intend to 'have done.'" She put her hands on the table and leaned across toward him. "The matter is important to me, Harry," she said earnestly. "Why can't you answer me?"

Her sudden seriousness discomfitted him. "You know the answer," he muttered, turning his back on her and sitting on the edge of the table. "Why do you taunt me with it?"

"But I don't, Harry, truly!" She sighed helplessly. "Is it . . . has it anything to do with Miss Manning?"

He lowered his head. "It has to do with *me*, don't you see?" he said miserably. "I have nothing to offer to you *or* Edwina."

"Nothing to offer?" Nell asked incredulously. "What do you mean? Good heavens, Harry, are you speaking of your *leg*?"

"I am only part of a man. You deserve more, my dear. Much more. And when you go back to London, you'll realize I'm right."

She clenched her teeth, strode around the table and confronted him. "You are a fool, Lord Thorne," she said flatly. "A complete fool! You've exaggerated the significance of your impediment out of all proportion. And when *you* go back to London, you'll realize that *I'm* right."

He met her eye with a sigh of patient but dogged stubbornness. "I shan't go back to London, girl. It will avail you nothing to keep insisting upon it. Do you think the *ton* would enjoy the sight of a cripple marring the festivities of their balls and squeezes—?"

"A *cripple*?" She winced at the word.

"Yes, a cripple. You've grown accustomed, here in our isolation, to my crutch and my clumsiness—"

"Clumsiness? I've never seen a *sign* of clumsiness. I constantly marvel at your adept management of your movements!"

"Perhaps, here in my own home, where my activities are limited to what I can easily manage. But can you truly see me at Almack's? Or making my way through the crowds at Drury Lane? Or hobbling along the red carpet they roll out in front of Carlton House when a ball is in progress?"

"Yes, I can see you in *all* those places! Why not?"

"I'll tell you why not," he said bitterly. "Because the *ton* of London are frivolous pleasure-seekers. They do not want their amusements sullied by reminders of war and mutilation. Just as the blemishes on their faces are covered over with cosmetic waxes and the distortions of their figures are masked by girdles and braces, the sick, the ugly, the deformed are at best pitied and tolerated, but are more often hidden away or covered over or ignored. I want no place in such a world."

Nell was pale and shaken by his words. "You cannot believe what you are saying! How can you think so little of the people of your own class—your own *family*, even. It would not be *at all* the way you think. People would honor you, admire you, seek you out! You would be welcome anywhere!"

Harry smiled mockingly. "What a romantic, childish bit of nonsense that was, my dear. You really should try to grow up a bit."

"You may ridicule me if you like, my lord," Nell said furiously, beginning to tremble at the knees, "but I think it is *you* who should grow up. You are like a spoiled little boy, sulking because his perfection has been impaired. I think you're nothing but a *coward*!"

Harry laughed. "A *coward*, ma'am? You think to rouse me into changing my mind by infuriating me? It won't work, you know. I've too many battles behind me—"

"Bravery in battle is child's play compared with the bravery of facing one's peers when one feels at a disadvantage," she said quietly. "To go to London, now, feeling as you do—*that* would be true courage."

"Perhaps," he said and turned away from her with a deep sigh, "but I have no wish to test my courage in that arena. Have done, girl. This conversation is too painful for both of us."

"Yes, I've done," she said, clenching her trembling hands behind her. She went slowly to the door. "But I cannot stay here and watch you hide from the world like this." She turned to face him once more. "I shall return to London as soon as it can be arranged."

"As you wish," he said with a nod, his lips compressed tensely. "It will no doubt be best for us both."

"B-best?" she asked, dismayed, blinking her eyes to keep back the tears. "It's the very *worst* that could happen

to us, as you'll f-find out to your sorrow before very
l-long. But I . . . I d-don't know what else to d-do." She
ran out, closing the door quickly behind her so that he
would not see the tears which she could no longer keep
from spilling over.

The next two days were the most painful Nell had yet
lived through. Her abrupt decision to depart caused an
almost hysterical flurry throughout the household.
Gwinnys burst into tears at the news and would no sooner
calm down when some reminder—seeing an open trunk in
a bedroom, or overhearing a discussion of travel
plans—would bring on a fresh outbreak of waterworks.
Amelia took the news calmly enough but felt it was too
precipitate, and she tried to urge Nell to postpone action
for a while. Her suggestions were listened to politely—
and ignored. Mrs. Penloe was beside herself with
disappointment. Her beloved Master Harry had retreated
to his apartment, and she was convinced that he was now
in worse condition than before.

Harry kept to his rooms, insisting on the strictest
privacy. Knowing that Mrs. Penloe couldn't face him
without haranguing him to accompany his aunt to
London, he requested firmly that she refrain from
bringing him his meals until she could accept his decision
with complaisance. In the meantime, the only persons
permitted to enter his rooms were Will and Jemmy,
neither of whom saw anything amiss in his lordship's
desire to remain at Thorndene, and neither of whom
would have dreamed of taking the liberty of discussing the
matter with him.

Even his Aunt Amelia was denied permission to visit
him. As a result, she spent the greater part of the few days
left in trying to find a way to confront him. Finally she
decided to write a letter to him. The day before they were
to depart, she composed a lengthy letter which she slipped
under his door. The letter, full of tear-spots and
cross-hatched deletions, pleaded with him to Reconsider

his Responsibilities, predicted that his continued Withdrawal would bring Dire Results for the Family, and
begged him to do Something to prevent his Shockingly
Cruel Aunt and Uncle, Lady Sybil and Lord Charles,
from Forcing her Beloved Nell into an Unwanted
Betrothal.

As a result of her emotional epistle, Lord Thorne
emerged from his apartment on the morning of their
departure. He found the members of the household
gathered in the great hall. Before announcing his
presence, he stood in the shadows watching them. Mrs.
Penloe, red-eyed and overwrought, was embracing Lady
Amelia fondly but despairingly. Jemmy, who had made
Miss Nell a bouquet of evergreens, clutched the greens
behind his back until he could work up the courage to
present them to her. Will was assisting the coachman of a
hired hack to carry out the trunks. The only cheerful
countenance belonged to Gwinnys, who had managed to
convince her mistress that she was indispensible and, to
her unbounded delight, had been granted permission to
accompany the ladies to London. The prospect not only
of remaining in her mistress's employ but of seeing the
Great City, was so thrilling that even her beloved Miss
Nell's obvious unhappiness could not dampen her
excitement.

Nell, enveloped in a numbing misery, stood near the
open doorway, staring at nothing. Harry watched her
from the shadows. She was dressed for travel in a hooded
blue fur-trimmed cloak, her hands hidden in an enormous
muff. The blue of the cloak and the dark fur circling her
face suited her. It seemed to him he'd never seen her look
so lovely. But he knew that it did him no good to stand
there staring at her like a goggle-eyed schoolboy, and he
roused himself abruptly. With an embarrassed cough, he
came forward. The eager cries with which his appearance
was greeted by his aunt and Mrs. Penloe made him brace
himself with fist-clenching fortitude. "I've written a letter
to Mr. Prickett," he said to Nell, holding it out to her. "It

authorizes him to pay Charles' and Sybil's debts and to increase their allowances. It also provides for an independence for yourself."

Nell, her expression stony, shook her head and refused to take the letter. Harry shrugged and turned to Lady Amelia. "Here, my dear, *you* take it," he said, smiling a little at her eager acceptance, "but I hope you'll warn the Thornes that this does *not* mean I will countenance any communication from them, or any visits either. If they *must* reach me in an emergency—and *please*, Amelia, make it clear that only the most dire of circumstances should make this necessary—they should do so through Mr. Prickett. Oh, and most important of all, Amelia—no one else is to be told of this. No one at all!"

He accepted his aunt's grateful embrace, wished them both a safe journey and stepped back. Will ushered Gwinnys out to the coach and helped her aboard, while the coachman performed the same service for Amelia. Jemmy, realizing that time had run out, thrust the bouquet into Nell's arms and ran out the door, his ears red. Mrs. Penloe hugged the girl and turned away, weeping. Then Nell lifted her eyes to Harry's. They stared at each other wordlessly, and she turned and walked swiftly out the door. Harry didn't move until he'd heard the coach begin to crunch down the drive. Then he turned on his heel, hobbled quickly down the hall and up the stairs to his rooms, shutting the door behind him with a loud, reverberating slam.

Chapter Twelve

LADY SYBIL STOOD before the wall mirror in the small saloon trying on one of half a dozen new bonnets. The floor around her was littered with open handboxes, mounds of tissue-thin paper and hats of every description. Lady Amelia, who was sitting at a small table near the window with a tea tray before her and a cup of the hot brew in her hand, shook her head in disapproval. The small chip hat that lay near Sybil's left foot must have cost more than Lady Amelia would spend on an entire costume, and with its ridiculous covering of long feathers, it would no doubt fly away at the first wind.

Sybil, her head covered with a dress bonnet which looked like a tight bell decorated with colored stones, turned to face Amelia. "Well, what do you think of this one? Shall I keep it to wear with my new plum-colored ball gown or shall I send it back?"

Sybil was impaled on the horns of a very difficult
dilemma. She had been ordered by her husband to return
four of the bonnets without delay, and she found herself
quite unable to decide. Why was Charles making her life
so difficult?

The answer was obvious. Nell and Amelia had
returned from Cornwall with the news that Henry Thorne
was quite alive, and Charles had had to learn to accept the
fact that he would never have control of a large sum of
money. Although Henry had authorized the payment of
their debts (which he might never have done if he had
been aware of the extent of their indebtedness) and had
thereby given them *carte blanche* to begin to compile new
ones, Charles was nevertheless quite irritable. Sybil, on
the other hand, had immediately gone on a shopping
spree, the six bonnets being only a small portion of her
purchases.

Unfortunately for Sybil, the six bandboxes had been
delivered at just the moment when Charles had been
departing for Brooks's. The resentment that he nurtured
in his breast against the fates—for making him a second
son, for giving him the damnedest luck at the gaming tables,
and for endowing him with a wife whose proclivity for
spending was nothing short of prodigious—seemed to
break forth at the sight of the bandboxes. Ignoring the
butler, the other servants, the liveried delivery men and
anyone else who might have been within earshot, he had
roared for her appearance and had delivered a scold in so
stentorian a tone and with such abusive language that, for
the first time in her life, she'd been left in a quake. Now
there was nothing for it but to do as she'd promised and
return four of the six bonnets without ado. "Well,
Amelia," Sybil asked impatiently, "what do you think?"

Amelia looked at the conglomeration of beribboned,
bejeweled, flowered, feathered headpieces and shrugged.
"You can return all of 'em, if you truly want my opinion,"
she said bluntly.

Sybil glared at her. "I don't know what's come over you

and Nell since you've returned. I barely know either of
you. You, Amelia, have become as rude and outspoken as
an old harridan. I've never known you to speak at all
brazenly, and now you're bold as brass. And as for
Nell..." Sybil paused and wrinkled her brow thoughtfully.

"What about Nell?" Amelia asked interestedly. Nell's
behavior troubled her, too.

"I don't know," Sybil faltered, "but she's different,
somehow. Haven't you noticed it? She doesn't laugh and
joke as she used to. She hardly speaks a word to me—"

"What can you expect, after the way you've treated the
poor child?"

"No, that's not it," Sybil said in perplexity. "She
doesn't seem to bear a grudge about being sent to
Cornwall. It's something else. I can't put my finger on it,
but it's as if she were watching us all the time, measuring
us with...with..."

"With new eyes?" the old lady put in shrewdly.

Sybil stared at her aunt with dawning respect. "Yes,
that's exactly it! With new eyes." Sybil tossed aside the
dress bonnet carelessly and sat down with Amelia at the
table. "What *happened* to you in Cornwall?" she asked,
leaning forward eagerly and studying Amelia curiously.

Amelia calmly sipped her tea while Sybil waited
impatiently for a reply. After a pause, Amelia looked up
from her cup and smiled enigmatically. She was enjoying
to the full a new sense of importance in the family. Since it
was she who had carried Lord Thorne's letter to the
family, and since Nell did not say one word about the
Earl, all questions concerning him were put to Amelia. If
Amelia was indeed in the Earl's good graces (and that
was certainly the impression that Charles and Sybil had
received), they could not afford to offend her. Amelia, so
long neglected, insulted and shunted aside by her niece
and nephew, played her new role to the hilt. "Nothing
happened in Cornwall," she said to Sybil, carefully
permitting just a hint of mystery to creep into her voice.

She looked at her niece with a touch too much of innocence in her eyes. "Nothing occurred that was at all out of the way," she repeated, protesting just a bit too much.

Sybil jumped up in irritation. "Very well, *don't* tell me!" she muttered, going back to her looking glass. She pulled from its box a flowered bonnet with an enormous poke, pulled it on furiously and stared into the mirror. But all she could see was the reflection of her aunt behind her, calmly lifting her teacup, her lips curved in a very slight (really, it was barely discernable) but, in Sybil's eyes, a most self-satisfied, vexatious smile.

Nell had truly changed. Sybil and Amelia were not the only ones to notice. Even Beckwith, the butler, remarked on it. The young Miss, with whom he'd had such a comfortable relationship in the past, was quite withdrawn. She still greeted his pleasantries and quips with a smile, but it was wan and abstracted. Something had occurred to affect the girl. That much was obvious. Under normal circumstances, he would have attributed her melancholy preoccupation to love, but there was no young man hanging about, and she could hardly have met an eligible young man in Cornwall, for he'd learned from her new abigail, the lively Gwinnys, that they'd never had a caller in all the time she'd been in service at Thorndene.

That Nell might be mourning for the poor, crippled Earl she'd left behind in Cornwall occurred to nobody but Amelia. Amelia had seen the two of them together often enough to suspect that Nell had been profoundly moved by the Earl's plight. If Nell had not assured her that her feelings for Harry were not those of a lover but a sister, Amelia would have been quite troubled by Nell's wistfulness. But she completely accepted Nell's tale that Harry was in love with the girl to whom he'd been betrothed so many years ago, Edwina Manning, and that Nell had only a sisterly concern for his welfare.

Nell, however, had had plenty of time to realize the

truth. She'd been charmed by Harry since his first
appearance as ghost. And when he'd kissed her on the
Cornish cliff, with the waves pounding below them and
the rain pelting them in icy unconcern, she knew that the
moment had had a significance for her which was beyond
that of any kiss she'd known before—or, she guessed, any
she might know in the future. Throughout the long trip
back to London, her anger at what she called Harry's
cowardice kept her from seeing what that kiss had
actually signified. But after many restless, unhappy
nights, she admitted to herself that she loved him. She
recognized the feeling as irrevocable, overpowering and
hopeless.

Nell wanted only to return to Cornwall, to throw
herself into his arms and to convince him that, to her, he
was more of a man with one leg than all the others in the
world with two. In other circumstances, she would have
told him so long since. She knew she could convince him,
because it was true. The two of them would be together in
blissful companionship instead of living in this miserable
separateness. But circumstances had conspired against
her. They had made him fall in love with Edwina
Manning. And because he had implacably decreed his
own isolation, they were *all* doomed to unhappiness.

London was rather thin of society in the wintry
months, and January of 1810 did not offer many
diversions. Nell attended one dinner at Sybil's insistence,
and she found herself listening to the conversation as
Harry might, had he been there. She was appalled at the
triviality of the talk at the table. For most of the evening,
the talk centered about Frederick, the Duke of York, and
his mistress, Mrs. Clark, who was rumored to be up to her
pretty neck in the illegal sale of military commissions.
When the talk temporarily veered to the war itself, the
only comments made were to disparage Lord
Wellington's lack of activity on the Peninsula. Nell could
easily imagine what would be Harry's chagrin at these
remarks—he had often spoken to her of his high regard

for the man he still referred to as Sir Arthur Wellesley. He'd explained to her often that Sir Arthur—or rather, Wellington—was wisely training his troops, building up a first-class medical corps and waiting for the proper moment to make his move.

Later, conversation turned to the French blockade, which had eased in recent months but which threatened soon to affect their lives again. The loud complaints made by the elegantly gowned ladies and the well-fed gentlemen about extortionate prices for laces and liquors, left Nell wondering uncomfortably if Harry might have been right after all in rejecting London society.

Nell's one other venture into the social whirl also failed to drive Harry from her thoughts. Lady Holcombe held a dress ball in honor of her husband's birthday, and almost every member of the Quality (and several who were not) who had remained in town during the winter months had been invited. Nell, who had been coaxed by her godmother to buy a new gown for the occasion, had determined to put Harry out of her mind and to conduct herself with the vivacious gaiety which had distinguished her behavior in the past. She would laugh and dance and flirt until she was able to convince herself that she was happy again.

The ball was a dreadful squeeze. When the Thorne party arrived, the stairway leading up to the Holcombe's drawing rooms and ballroom was crammed with people pushing their way up to the receiving line. How would Harry have managed in such a crush? Nell found herself wondering. She moved slowly up the stairs, finding every moment distasteful. When she at last was seated beside her aunt, trying to recover her breath from the effort of the stairway, she looked up to find that Sir Nigel Lewis was approaching with a triumphant smile lighting his face. He would not accept her awkward refusal to stand up with him, and rather than engage in senseless argumentation, she endured an interminable and embarrassing dance with him. The elaborate figures of the dance did not permit much conversation between them, but from his arrogant smirk and a few of his remarks, she deduced that Sybil had hinted to him that her return from Cornwall might indicate a willingness on her part to resume their betrothal. Before she could phrase a denial of something hinted at rather than stated, Nigel laughed confidently. "Of course you needn't say anything at all yet," he said smugly, "for a resumpt on of our relationship must be well considered by *all* parties."

Nell reddened in fury. "There is nothing at all to be considered—" she sputtered, but a movement of the dance separated them, and when they came together again, Nigel spoke of other things. Nell decided to let the matter drop. She had no intention of resuming any sort of relationship with Sir Nigel, but if he chose to delude himself, she didn't care.

It was only a little later, while she was dancing with a shy young man who seemed much younger than she but who was obviously smitten with her, that she recognized Edwina Manning on the dance floor. Since Nell's partner (content to gaze at her wordlessly) did not require her undivided attention, she was able to study Miss Manning covertly but thoroughly. The lady was taller than most of the other women on the floor, and the poise of her bearing and the regal carriage of her head gave her the elegance of a princess. Her smoky hair was drawn back from an oval face into a smooth knot at the back of her head, but one thick curl had been permitted to hang loosely and enticingly over her shoulder. Her eyes were a startling blue and seemed to give the impression of great feeling and sensitivity. She wore an azure satin ball gown which was cut low over her graceful, milk-white shoulders. Nell was not at all surprised to note the great number of admiring glances cast at her by the men who passed her by. She was undoubtedly the most beautiful woman in the room.

When the throng of guests were making their way to the supper tables, Nell sought out her godmother. "Tell me, Sybil," she whispered, "have you heard anything about Edwina Manning? Is she betrothed, or about to be?"

Sybil studied Nell curiously. "Why do you want to know?"

"No particular reason," Nell said, trying to appear offhand. "Only idle curiosity. She is so beautiful that it is hard to credit her prolonged resistance to matrimony. One would imagine that some dashing gentleman would have carried her off long since."

"Well, you needn't make her sound decrepit. She's been out for a few seasons, but she can't be much above twenty-two or three. It's said that she feels herself bound to Henry, although it is almost two years since she's seen him. The Mannings were always excessively proper. The poor girl will probably not be permitted to accept any offer until Henry has been declared legally dead. I wonder what she'd say if she discovered that her betrothed was hiding away from her in Cornwall."

Nell wondered the very same thing. How long could one expect a lovely young lady to languish in unmarried loneliness waiting for a lover who failed to appear? Nell watched Miss Manning for the rest of the evening. Edwina favored every gentleman who approached her with a warm, detached politeness. She was the very model of a woman whose hand had been given to an absent suitor. Nell felt a grudging admiration for her. Whatever else Edwina Manning might be, she was certainly steadfast.

She did not think it possible, but Nell's spirits were even further depressed by the evening of the ball. She realized at last why Harry was still attached to Miss Manning. The lady was indeed beautiful, in face and in manner. There was an air of polished perfection about her. No wonder Harry was reluctant to face her with what he regarded as a terrible and permanent flaw.

*   *   *

A cold and rainy January became a freezing, snowy February. Nell retired more and more into herself. She rejected all Sybil's urgings to pay calls, to venture out to the shops and bazaars, or to engage in any of the other pastimes in which her godmother indulged. She sometimes joined her on excursions to the lending library, but more often she spent her days in her room or with Amelia, quietly sipping tea but speaking very little.

One afternoon, when Nell was reading quietly on the window-seat in her bedroom, looking up periodically to stare out at the thickly falling snow, Gwinnys came in hurriedly, carrying a Venetian-red velvet dress over her arm. "Mind you'd best dress up a bit tonight, Miss Nell," she advised, laying the dress carefully across the bed.

"The red velvet?" Nell asked in surprise. "Whatever for?"

"The whole fam'ly's dinin' *in* this night," Gwinnys explained. "Wi' the snow so heavy an' all, Lady Sybil ain't goin' off to the Petershams' and even Lord Charles stays in. Lady Amelia says to tell 'ee that everyone's havin' dinner right here at home."

Nell and Amelia had grown accustomed to dining alone at the long table of the Thorne House dining room, for Charles spent every evening at one or another of his clubs, and Lady Sybil managed to wangle an invitation to one social affair or another almost every evening, even in the off-season. The two ladies who were left behind did not mind the peace and comfort of their simple dinners, for they were quite content with each other's company. But Nell understood the message Amelia had sent. The fact that Charles and Sybil would be dining with them did make the evening seem a bit festive. Although she overrode Gwinnys's choice of evening attire, she agreed to the mauve silk, and Gwinnys was satisfied.

The dining room did indeed have a festive air. A great fire blazed in the hearth and three branches of candles lit the table. Lord Charles, however, was not in a festive mood. He could not bear to miss even one night of cards. He sat at his place at the head of the table sulking and drinking too much wine. Sybil, too, was sulky and petulant. She had not bothered to dress but sat glumly at her place wrapped in a dressing gown, her hair carelessly tousled and unkempt. She complained that the sauce the cook had prepared for the fish was too bland, the ragout too peppery, and the roast too rare. And to make matters worse, Beckwith was serving them in his shirtsleeves. Nothing he did infuriated her more than his carelessness in matters of his attire. But knowing that a scolding would not have any effect on him except to heighten his glee at causing her displeasure, she gritted her teeth and said nothing.

By the time they had been served the second course, Nell found herself wishing the meal were over. Any attempt of Amelia's or her own to open up avenues of conversation was met with a grunt or a monosyllable from either Sybil or Charles. Sybil's complaints spoiled the others' enjoyment of what was really an excellent dinner. The wind howled mournfully outside the windows, and the fire and the candles seemed to burn less brightly. The family dinner was proving to be a deplorably dismal experience.

Into this dreary atmosphere, a timid maidservant entered, tiptoed to the coatless Beckwith and whispered something into his ear. The butler raised his eyebrows in surprise and hurried out of the room. "What is it, girl?" Lord Charles asked the little maid.

"'Tis a caller, m'lord," the girl said with a curtsy.

"A caller? In this weather?" Sybil exclaimed in surprise, her hand flying to her disordered hair.

"At this hour? Ridiculous! I wonder who—?" Charles scratched his head in puzzled annoyance.

He was not kept wondering for long. A few moments later, Beckwith reentered, flinging open both the large doors dramatically. His eyes were shining excitedly, and his mouth was stretched into a gleeful grin. Sybil was started to see that he'd gotten into his coat and looked quite unexceptional. Taking a deep breath, the butler held his head high and announced in a voice of unaccustomed formality, "Ladies, Lord Charles, I have the honor to announce the arrival of his lordship, *the Earl of Thornbury!*"

Chapter Thirteen

FOR A FROZEN moment no one moved. Lord Charles' wineglass fell from his fingers and broke on the floor, but no one paid the least attention. They were all preoccupied with their own reactions to the shocking news. Lady Sybil was excruciatingly aware of her inappropriate costume and slovenly appearance, and she alternately paled and reddened as her fingers fumbled nervously with her hair. Charles, whose mental processes were always rather sluggish (except when he'd drunk too much wine, and they were positively slow), merely gaped stupidly at the door while his brain attempted to ascertain the significance of Beckwith's announcement. There was a glad cry from Amelia, her eyes eager for the first glimpse of her dear nephew in his premier appearance as the new Earl. As for Nell, she could not account for her emotions. No sooner had Beckwith made his announcement when she'd felt the blood drain from her face and congeal somewhere in her chest. But whether this strange constriction inside her signified joy, surprise or terror, she could not tell.

Every eye was fixed on the doorway, but when the gentleman made his appearance on the threshold, he seemed a complete stranger. Even to Nell, who had seen him most recently and most closely, he was scarcely recognizable. The man in the doorway was an elegantly dressed, imposing Corinthian. His modish, many-caped greatcoat was so splendidly stylish that even the snowflakes melting on the shoulders in no way detracted from its magnificence. His hair was flatteringly cut in the popular "Brutus," and he carried a tall, curly-brimmed beaver in one gloved hand. He leaned casually on the cane held in the other hand and surveyed them all with amused, imperturbable aplomb. "Good evening," he greeted them affably. "I regret that the snow delayed my arrival long enough to cause this interruption of your dinner."

These words seemed to shake his audience from their stupefaction. There was a sudden babble of welcoming words, and Charles jumped up from his chair. "Not at all, not at all," he said heartily, hurrying to his nephew's side and clapping him on the shoulder fervently. "Devilish glad to see you, boy! Devilish glad!"

Sybil, laughing with rather hysterical excitement, rushed to Henry's other side. Combining her declarations of joy at his appearance with apologies for her own, she covered his cheek with kisses. Beckwith hovered about behind his lordship, trying to wrest the greatcoat from his back and the hat from his hand. And Amelia sprang up from her chair with unusual agility and threw her arms around him in an enveloping hug. Completely surrounded by people as he was, Lord Thorne managed to meet Nell's eyes. Over Amelia's shoulder, he grinned at her—a rather sheepish grin which told her as clearly as if he'd spoken that he had at last accepted her challenge.

It seemed to Nell that she had not drawn a breath since

Beckwith had made his startling announcement, and she now permitted herself a long sigh. She could feel the lump inside her melt away. What she'd felt before did not matter—she was now filled with a joyful pride in him. He had come! He had reconsidered and decided to face the world. And he had done it with courage and style.

She remembered the bitterness of his description of London society. What a struggle he must have had to overcome those feelings! Her throat tightened with suppressed tears, and she stared down at her hands, still clenched tightly in her lap, and tried to compose herself. But a tear escaped from the corner of one eye and slid down her cheek. She brushed it away hurriedly and glanced around guiltily, hoping that none of the servants had seen the small emotional display. But the only one looking at her was Harry.

He separated himself from the others and crossed to her chair. For a moment he stood smiling down at her. "Save those tears, girl," he said in an under-voice. "I may need them later."

Charles came up to the table and insisted on Henry's taking his place at the head. Although Charles had felt resentment in his breast against the system which had given the titles and wealth to a younger man, he had no personal animosity toward Henry himself. (If he had been endowed with any talent for self-analysis, he would have realized long since that he was secretly relieved not to have been saddled with the many serious responsibilities which accompanied the inheritance.) He was truly delighted to see his nephew looking so well. He expansively ordered every platter to be removed and replaced with freshly prepared hot food, and the dinner was resumed.

The change of atmosphere in the room was remarkable. Everyone but Nell tried to speak at once. Henry was bombarded with questions. Why had he come? How long would he stay? What were his plans? How was his health? What was the state of his body and mind? He did his best to answer them all, and his replies were so politely, casually or humorously phrased that only one person was aware that they were somewhat evasive. When the last course had been eaten and the wine decanters had been placed on the table, no one dreamed of suggesting that the ladies withdraw, so amicable and entertaining had the conversation become. There was much laughter and chatter, and the decanters were repeatedly refilled. It was not until the mantel clock struck midnight that the assemblage realized how many hours had passed.

Nell had not said much but had spent the evening drinking in every one of Harry's words. Now, she pushed back her chair and asked to be excused, pleading weariness. Her real reason for breaking away from the cheerful gathering was a sudden need to be alone, to think, to determine how to comport herself in this new situation. To her surprise, Harry rose and offered to escort her to the stairway.

It was the first chance they'd found to speak in private. As he hobbled down the corridor at her side, she noticed that he leaned heavily on his cane and that the knuckles of the fingers he'd bent round the handle were showing white. "Don't you use your crutch any more?" she asked, trying not to show undue concern.

"What a provoking wretch you are!" he declared in mock reproach. "I've spent *weeks* perfecting this technique. It's much more difficult to maneuver with the cane than with the crutch, you know. But nothing escapes your notice, it seems. It took you only a moment to see how short my new technique falls from perfection."

"Don't be absurd. You handle yourself beautifully," she assured him. "But I fail to understand why the change was necessary. If the crutch is more comfortable, I don't see why you bother with the cane at all."

"Don't you?" He regarded her candidly. "As I told you before, you are a romantic. You mustn't assume that, because I've come out of my retreat, I've changed my view of London society. I still cannot accept your romantic view of it. Therefore, I've switched from the crutch to *this* inadequate thing because a cane is a less pitiable object than a crutch."

Nell almost winced. "Oh, Harry..." she murmured, shaking her head in discouragement, "I wish you were not so ... so censorious."

"What a tyrant you are, my dear," he said, his grin reappearing with captivating charm. "You demand complete capitulation. It is not enough for you that I have *acted* according to your wishes. You now demand that I *think* as you wish."

"I did *not* demand," Nell said with an answering grin. "I only *wished*." But her smile vanished, and she asked him frankly, "If you haven't changed your mind about how people will behave, why did you come?"

"Because of you."

Her eyes flew to his face. "M-Me?"

"To prove to you that I'm not as cowardly as you seem to think," he said, smiling at her discomfiture.

"I *never* believed you to be cowardly," she denied saucily, "so if that *was* your reason, you might as well have saved yourself the trouble." She ran up the stairs, but before turning at the landing she looked down at him. "But I *am* glad ... very glad ... you decided to come," she added, smiling mistily down at him, and with a wave, she disappeared round the turn, her voice floating down to him as she called over her shoulder merrily, "Goodnight, my lord."

Henry's first excursion into society did not occur for two days, the snow keeping all of them prisoners indoors. But no sooner had the storm abated and the roadways cleared than Charles declared his intention to spend the evening at White's. He urged Henry to accompany him. Henry had as yet no great confidence in his ability to handle himself in society, but he realized that an evening sitting at a card table would not be beyond his capabilities, and he agreed to go.

His entrance into the club rooms caused no great stir at first, for his face was not familiar to most of the men present. Charles introduced him to a few of his cronies who welcomed him warmly and made a place for him at their table. But when, a short while later, Sir Owen Alcorn left the table to greet a friend across the room, his arm was grasped by the elderly, very deaf Lord Billingham, who demanded to know the name of the gentleman with the military bearing. "Oh, you must mean young Thorne," Sir Owen said loudly enough for Lord Billingham to hear. "He's just back from the Peninsula."

"Young Thorne?" shouted Lord Billingham, in the manner of the very deaf. "I thought 'e was dead."

"Confound it, Billingham," Sir Owen said disgustedly, "you can *see* he's alive, can't you?"

"Eh? Alive, you say? Good news, that," Billingham said loudly. "Glad the fellow came through it all right and tight. Good sort of fellow, if I remember 'im rightly."

"He didn't come through it all right and tight, old man," Sir Owen corrected him. "Left a leg in Spain, you know."

"No! A leg, y' say? Damned shame!"

Since this exchange was heard throughout the room, it was not long before Henry was surrounded. Old friends pressed round to welcome him back with eager, enthusiastic affection. Strangers demanded introductions and shook his hand warmly. Shy youths looked up at him with unmistakable admiration, and distinguished gentlemen sought him out to ask his views on the progress of the war. And two members of Parliament who were present engaged him in debate over Wellington's inaction and Napoleon's intentions. It was heartening to be lionized and to realize that he'd been missed and was truly welcomed back. But to be causing a stir and to find himself the center of attention was also somewhat disconcerting, and as soon as he could politely do so, he took his leave.

As he was about to descend the front stairs, he came

face to face with a young dandy who sported a pair of mustaches of elegant proportions. The fellow was about to brush by when he stopped and gaped at Lord Thorne in astonishment. The surprise immediately changed to delight. "Harry!" he shouted gleefully. "*Harry*, you crusty old *clunch*!"

"Roddy?" Harry asked in equally delighted surprise. "Is that *you* behind those enormous mustaches?" The two men laughed and pounded each other's shoulders with an enthusiasm bordering on hysteria. "Roddy, you jack-a-dandy popinjay!" Harry exclaimed when the excitement of their greeting had spent itself. "What are you doing in London looking like a damned coxcomb?" He fingered the lapel of his friend's coat of shiny green Ducapes with amusement. "I never dreamed that the Honorable Roderick Driffield, late of Sir Arthur's personal staff, had such a talent for alamodality."

"Never mind my alamodality, you make-bait. I've been trying to find you for *months*! Where've you been hiding, man?

"You'd heard I had it?" Harry asked, his smile fading.

Roddy nodded. "Ran into Algy Blount in Scarborough last fall. He was on leave. Told me they'd had to leave some of the wounded behind at Talavera, though everyone on staff who could be spared searched for you wildly before pulling out." He frowned and shook his head. "Talavera was a bloody disaster. Don't know why they keep calling it a victory."

"Only because the French fared worse," Harry said wryly.

"What happened to you?" Roddy demanded.

Harry tapped his leg against the banister, and Roddy nodded silently. Forgetting his intention to spend the night gaming, Roddy asked Harry his direction and turned to walk along with him. Sir Roderick Driffield had been with Sir Arthur's staff during the early days of the Peninsular War, but when his father had died, he'd had to sell out to help his mother. The two men had not laid eyes on each other since. As they walked along, companionably filling in the gaps that time and distance had made in their relationship, Harry realized how much he'd missed the close comradeship that soldiers find in each other. Of all the men he'd conversed with that evening, it was only now, with Roddy, that he felt completely without constraint.

Their conversation continued the following day, when Roddy appeared at Thorne House before eleven and the two ex-soldiers closeted themselves in the library. There they remained for the rest of the day. The only signs of their existence were the repeated requests for madeira they sent out and the sound of their voices and their raucous laughter. Finally, at twilight, they emerged hungry and happy. For both of them, it had been a most satisfying day.

Roddy was easily persuaded to remain to take dinner with the family. Since Lady Sybil was engaged to dine elsewhere, and Lord Charles had already left for the club, a small party of four took their places at the long table. Harry had made the introductions earlier, but now Roddy looked accusingly at Nell. "I've been introduced to you before, Miss Belden," he reminded her. "In fact, you stood up with me for a country dance. It was at the Denholm's ball last year."

"How flattering that you should remember after all this time," Nell said by way of apology.

"Not at all. You are not a partner one easily forgets," Roddy said fulsomely.

Harry chortled. "Evidently you *are*, old boy," he teased.

"Oh, Harry, how unkind," Nell remonstrated. "The only reason I don't remember—"

"—Is that all those fellows with mustachios look so damnably alike?" Harry supplied mischievously.

Nell looked at him in disgust. "No, of course not! I was going to say—"

"—That you've danced with so many, you can't be expected to remember every Tom, Dick and Roddy who comes along?" Harry said incorrigibly.

"I am quite capable of finishing my own sentences, my lord," Nell said quellingly. "What I started to say, Sir Roderick, is that the only reason I don't remember you is that I was betrothed at the time, and it would not have been seemly for me to have taken *particular* notice of *any* young man."

"Oh, what a shocking bouncer!" Harry hooted. "Everyone knows you are an incorrigible flirt, betrothed or no."

Nell turned to Roddy for support. "Really, Sir Roderick, are you going to permit him to malign me in that way?"

Roddy looked away in feigned embarrassment, his eyes glinting with amusement. "What can I do, ma'am? In the first place, he is my host. In the second place, you *did* flirt with me a bit on that occasion."

Nell drew herself up in offended dignity. "I can see that the military has allied itself against me," she declared. "Come, Amelia, we shall have to join forces to achieve a strategic balance. Can *you* not find something to say in my defense?"

Amelia looked up from the slice of roast goose she was contentedly devouring and smiled at them benignly. "I can only note," she said mildly, "that you all seem to be in remarkably high spirits. It is quite entertaining listening to you."

The two men burst into laughter and Nell gave up in disgust and turned her attention to her dinner. Her attempt to cut and eat her food while maintaining an expression of lofty indifference caused the men to laugh even more. By this time, even Amelia began to giggle. Nell finally surrendered to her urge for laughter, and they all made a very merry meal. Harry was much inclined to think it was the very best day he'd had since Talavera, until Roddy, taking his leave, remarked that Miss Belden was a regular out-and-outer. For some reason, this simple little comment bothered Harry. Why it should have bothered him, he had no idea, but he couldn't help being aware that it took a bit of the brightness out of the day.

Chapter Fourteen

THE NEWS SPREAD quickly that Captain Thorne, now the sixth Earl of Thornbury, had returned from the wars. Henry realized that word would soon reach Edwina, if it had not already done so. The necessity for him to pay a call on the Mannings became more and more pressing. He was aware of a certain reluctance to do so, but attributed it to the discomfort of having to tell the girl he'd dreamed of for so long that he was not the same man she'd agreed to wed. But he knew he could procrastinate no longer.

Nell, who had taken note of all Harry's comings and goings with great interest, was fully aware that he had not yet arranged a reunion with his betrothed. However, when she saw him one morning in the breakfast room, dressed with more than his usual care and looking complete to a shade, she knew what his destination must be. He wore a perfectly fitting morning coat of gray superfine, a striped yellow waistcoat, pale yellow breeches fitted smoothly on shapely thighs, and a pair of gleaming Hessians. He carried a high-crowned beaver in one hand and his inevitable cane in the other. Although it took more courage than she thought she could muster, she managed to tell him that he looked at home to a peg.

"Do I?" he asked with a grateful smile. "Thank you. I made an herculean effort, I assure you. I want to cut a dash today."

"Well, in my view you have succeeded admirably. A veritable Pink of the Ton. Even your tie. What do you call that intricate fold?"

"Charles' fool of a valet instructed me in the method of achieving these convolutions. He tells me it is called the *trone d'amour*," Harry said with a sheepish grin. "If Roddy should see it, I'd be roasted unmercifully. However, if you find it acceptable, I shall be satisfied."

She reassured him with such sincerity that he was emboldened to adjust his hat to a rakish angle. He touched it with his cane in a gesture of adieu and left. Nell watched him limp down the street and out of sight, her emotions in a turmoil. She tried with all her heart to wish him well in his romantic venture, but a diabolical selfishness which she could not control kept her hoping that something would occur to prevent the resumption of Harry's betrothal to the beautiful Miss Manning.

The meeting between the two lovers was not quite as dramatic as either Harry or Nell had anticipated. Sir Edward and Lady Clara, Edwina's parents, greeted him with great affection. They were joined by their daughter in their tasteful, Egyptian-style drawing room, and the four engaged in warm reminiscences for fully an hour. So delighted were the Mannings to see the long-absent Lord Thorne that they agreed to permit Edwina to speak to his lordship in private for as long as they liked—even as much as half an hour.

When her parents had closed the drawing-room door behind them, Edwina looked up at Henry meltingly. "Oh, my dear," she said tenderly, "how good it is to have you back."

Henry merely smiled and took a seat beside her on the sofa. "It is good of you to say so," he said after a pause, "but we both know that it has been a very long time since . . . since our last meeting. And much has changed."

"Changed?" Edwina asked carefully.

Harry faced her with a level look. "You may already have heard that I've been wounded," he began.

She lowered her head and nodded. "Your leg," she said tremulously, pulling a handkerchief from the cuff of her sleeve. "I was most dreadfully pained to hear it." She dabbed at her eyes which were moist with tears. "How you must have suffered!"

"There's no need to cry, my dear," Harry said, taking her hand consolingly. "That is all behind me now. I manage quite well without it."

"Yes, I see that," she said, smiling through the tears that still glistened on her lashes. "You are remarkably brave and strong. You have my heartfelt admiration."

Uncomfortably, he let her hand go and stood up over her. "Edwina, let us be frank. It's been almost two years since our betrothal was announced. Much has happened, no doubt to you as well as to me. You must not feel bound by the promises we made so long ago. If you have formed another attachment, or—"

"*Henry,*" she exclaimed, horrified, "how can you *think*—?"

"I don't mean to say these things in any sense of reproach," he put in quickly. "Please don't misunderstand. You would be in no way subject to censure if, after all this time, you should find yourself plagued by doubts . . ."

"Henry, dear, please sit down. No, not there. Here, near me. Now, then, I shall be as frank as you have been. I

want you to know that I have never for a moment
entertained the *slightest* doubts or the *thought* of another
attachment."

"Are you sure?"

"Perfectly sure," she said warmly.

He was much moved. He took her hand and lifted it to
his lips. For a moment neither of them spoke. Then
Henry, in a rush of affection, moved to take her in his
arms. She drew away, taking his hands from her
shoulders gently. "We mustn't, my dear," she whispered.
"Not quite yet."

"Why, what is it?" he asked, puzzled.

"You yourself pointed out the protracted length of
time since we last met. We need a little time to become
reacquainted, to reestablish the intimacy we once
enjoyed..." She lowered her eyes shyly.

He nodded understandingly. "Of course. You're quite
right," he agreed. "We've plenty of time."

Before he left, Edwina made it very clear that no
alteration of her feelings had occurred and that he was
welcome to call on her as frequently as was proper. As he
walked back to Thorne House, buffeted by an icy wind, he
told himself that he had every reason to feel that he was a
very happy man.

Although the weather continued brutally cold, the
calendar predicted an imminent spring. London was
rapidly filling with the returning members of the *ton*, and
the pace of social activities quickened. The silver tray on
the small table in the entryway of Thorne House filled
with calling cards each morning, some of which were from
young gentlemen paying court to Nell. Harry found
himself hanging about when they called. A more callow
collection of fools and fops he'd never seen. He could not
account for Nell's abominable taste in suitors. Of course,
he told himself, it was not his affair. If she found herself
entertained by such a circle of rackety court-cards, it was
entirely her affair.

As for himself, he was very well occupied. He spent two afternoons each week driving Miss Manning in the park. On fine mornings, he rode Caceres through the park, horse and rider quickly becoming the subjects of much admiring comment. In the evenings he attended dinner parties, appeared at the theater, dropped in at White's with Roddy, and in general lived the life of any London gentlemen. If the number of times each day he had to change his outfits was galling, if his leg pained him from the strain of the inadequate support from the cane, if he sometimes wondered what had possessed him to leave the tranquility of Cornwall for the superficiality of the life he was now living, no one—not even Roddy—knew. His poise, his grace, his ability to mingle in most situations without undue embarrassment in spite of his handicap was much admired by everyone he met. He was treated with courteous affection everywhere. He had no complaints. In fact, he had to admit that Nell's optimistic, romantic view of the polite world seemed to be more true than his. The only really troublesome matter was a vague and unnamed discontent. But he did not care to analyze the feeling or track down its source. He simply tried to cope with it.

Within a month of the time of Harry's interview with Edwina, the entire Thorné family received cards from the Mannings requesting the pleasure of their company at a rout-party to be held in honor of Lord Thorne's return. The evening promised to be the most exciting affair of the season, and everyone who received a card for it was much gratified. It was rumored that even the Prince had declared his intention to attend.

The week before the event was one of much flurried activity in the Thorne household. Seamstresses, hairdressers, milliners, valets, tailors, haberdashers and abigails hurried up and down the stairs all week, preparing for the great event. Anticipation charged the atmosphere and good spirits permeated the household.

Nell tried to rouse herself to a proper level of

excitement, but her spirits, like Lord Thorne's, were depressed. She, however, knew quite well the source of *her* depression. For one thing, she knew that the party would be a dreadful squeeze, and she was greatly concerned that Harry would find it difficult to manage the stairs and the crowded rooms with his inadequate cane. For another thing, she suspected that the party at the Mannings signified the official resumption of Edwina's betrothal to Lord Thorne, the man of the hour. Nell told herself that she was happy for him, but she could not fool the cold lump of despair (an omnipresent discomfort which had lodged itself somewhere in her chest) into believing her. No matter how much she scolded herself, the uncomfortable lump would not dissipate itself.

The evening arrived at last. The coach with the family coat of arms on its side stood waiting at the door, its panels polished to a lustrous glow and its brass lanterns gleaming. The family gathered in the library. The men, of course, were ready first, and passed the time waiting for the ladies by helping themselves to generous glasses of madeira. Amelia entered the library at only ten minutes past the appointed time and was rewarded for her promptness by receiving fulsome compliments from both gentlemen on her good looks and charming costume. Since she was well aware that her good looks had long since become a faded memory, and since her dress was the puce-satin-covered-with-black-lace that every woman past seventy was wont to wear, she did not take the compliments too seriously. But she *did* allow herself to be coaxed into taking a good swig of madeira and began the evening in a very mellow mood.

Nell and Sybil entered the room together and laughingly accepted expressions of admiration which the others lavished upon them. Although Lady Sybil's blue satin gown was cut so low across the bosom as to be considered shocking, its effect was somewhat mitigated by an overdress of sheer gauze threaded with silver. With her hair pulled back from her face and two great clumps

of crimped curls hanging over her ears in the very latest
mode, she looked dashing indeed.

But in Harry's eyes Nell was by far the loveliest
creature in the room. She wore the Venetian-red velvet
gown which Gwinnys had begged her to wear on the night
of Harry's arrival. It had long, demure sleeves and a
modestly high neckline, and Sybil had made a mocking
remark, when she'd met Nell in the hallway upstairs, to
the effect that Nell was turning into a bluestocking. But
high neck or not, the dress managed to be enticing just the
same, for the softness of the fabric outlined her slim
womanliness and the color brought a glow to her cheeks.
The unmistakable look of admiration in Harry's eyes
caused the color to deepen to a flush. If Nell were not so
fearful of the foreboding possibilities in the evening
ahead, she might truly have enjoyed the moment.

Just as Nell had feared, the Mannings' house was
thronged with visitors. It took the coachman the better
part of half an hour to maneuver the coach to the front
door, so great was the jam of traffic in front of the house.
Inside, the entryway and stairway were packed tightly
with people jostling their way to the dancing and
champagne above. Nell's heart failed her. How Harry was
to make his way up that stairway with only the aid of a
cane, she did not know.

As soon as they entered the hall, there was a stir of
welcome. Roddy was among the first to greet them, and
he joined their group quite as easily as if he were a member
of the family. Nell gratefully pulled at his arm and drew
him aside. Whispering to him of her concern for Harry's
possible predicament, she urged him to precede their
party up the stairs and to attempt to clear a passageway
through the press. "I wouldn't worry about old Harry,"
Roddy told her confidently. "There's no one better than
he in finding a way out of a fix. Getting up those stairs is
child's play when compared to some of the situations I've
seen him handle. I've seen him lead a whole platoon out of
ambush more than once."

Roddy proved to be right. Harry was leading his entire entourage through the crowd with a practiced, unobtrusive ease. With a handshake here and a tap on the shoulder there, he made his way through the teeming entryway without a stumble. Although progress up the stairs was slow, the going was no more impeded for Harry and his cane than for anyone else. With a smoothness Nell had not thought possible, they found themselves at the entrance to the ballroom without having suffered the least strain.

Harry was not the only man who was attracted to Nell's Venetian-red gown. Her dance card was filled with almost annoying rapidity. She had hoped that Harry might ask her to sit out at least *one* dance with him. He had been gallant enough to have done so on one previous occasion when he'd seen her sitting on the sidelines. But tonight, she caught not so much as a glimpse of him until suppertime. She had danced with a succession of bores, had been pressed into performing a waltz with Sir Nigel and had enjoyed only one dance—a Devonshire minuet with Roddy. At suppertime, she saw Harry with Edwina on his arm. Edwina's face had a rosy flush, and Nell thought, in despair, that the girl had never looked so lovely and so contented.

Edwina had every reason to feel contented. She had taken Harry into a little sitting-room and shut the door. "Mama has agreed that the time is now appropriate for us to set a wedding date," she'd told him, and she'd lifted her face to be kissed.

Harry had murmured the appropriate words and taken her into his arms. Two years before, such an embrace would have left him breathless. Edwina's expressive blue eyes, the lovely glow of color in her face, the softness of her hair against her cheek—he'd treasured the memory of these things through months of brutal battles and lonely marches, through weeks of feverish illness and dark despair. Why now, when she was his—a reality in his arms instead of an ungraspable dream—did he feel so...so unmoved?

The memory of another kiss flashed into his mind. He saw Nell's face, streaked with rain and tears, staring up at him. How strange that moment had been—he'd had no recollection of initiating it, but he'd found himself kissing her. A hunger had welled up in him and only the fierceness of the rain had brought him to his senses and kept him from crushing her in his arms. He'd let her go, but he'd been trembling and shaken.

What a time he'd chosen for these thoughts! Berating himself, he kissed his promised bride with as much warmth as he could muster and set about convincing her—and himself—of his delight at the news.

It was well after two when the Thorne carriage was called for and the family wearily climbed into it. As the coach rumbled over the cobblestones, the occupants were strangely silent. Charles had spent the entire evening at the card tables and was glumly attempting to calculate his losses. Sybil was concerned with the lack of comment on her hairstyle and was, in the darkness of the coach, attempting to reevaluate it in her tiny hand mirror. Amelia was dozing in the corner. Both Harry and Nell were absorbed in reflection. At last Harry looked up and spoke to them all. "I suppose you've surmised that I have an announcement to make to you," he began.

"Eh? Announcement?" Amelia mumbled, shaking herself awake.

Sybil dropped the mirror into her lap and clapped her hands. "Oh, Henry, *dear!*" she squealed. "She's *accepted* you!"

"Yes," Harry said quietly, "Miss Manning has agreed to marry me. A date has been set in June."

There was a chorus of congratulations, in the midst of which the coach drew up at the door. They alighted with an excitement equal to their boarding the coach earlier that evening, and they entered the hallway in noisy gaiety.

Beckwith, taking all the outer garments on his arm, joined the others in voicing his congratulations and managed, to Sybil's disgust, to pump his lordship's hand heartily.

After the others had fervently wished him joy and gone to bed, Nell lingered behind. "You haven't said a word, my dear," Harry remarked as he, too, headed for the stairway. "Don't *you* wish me happy?"

"You *know* I wish you happy," she said, coming to the foot of the stairway and looking up at him. "Aren't you glad, now, that you took my advice?"

"Yes, of course," he said shortly.

"And you see now that Miss Manning does not find you 'part of a man'?"

"Yes."

"And that all the plans you'd made before you went to Spain may still be realized? That you are accepted by the world just as before?"

"Yes, yes," he said, a touch of asperity in his voice, "you were in the right about everything. There! Are you satisfied now?"

The stairway was only dimly lit by a single candle in a wall sconce on the landing, and she had to peer into the gloom to make out his expression. But his face was shadowed. "What is it, Harry?" she asked, puzzled at his tone. "You *are* happy, are you not?"

There was a pause. "I *must* be happy," he said enigmatically, and he turned and climbed wearily up the stairs.

Chapter Fifteen

If HARRY'S WORDS had left Nell with doubts about his happiness in his betrothal, his subsequent actions dissipated those doubts completely. Lord Thorne's behavior toward his promised bride was more than exemplary. He was completely devoted. The story of their long-protracted courtship and its happy outcome was the talk of London, and many a dowager dripped sentimental tears over it, even after hearing the tale for the third time. The couple was much in demand, and they were forced to make a choice every evening from among dozens of invitations. They were much admired and fussed over, and Harry began to feel as if he were drowning in a sea of cloying sweetness.

The only outward sign of his distaste, however, was his suggestion to his betrothed, after a few weeks of constant

socializing, that Edwina attend some of her parties
without him from time to time. Understanding that it was
the strange way of men to prefer exclusively male
company occasionally, Edwina was sweetly agreeable.
Thus it was that, one evening in late March, Harry sat in
the library at Thorne House, bent over a chessboard with
only Roddy for company. They both had removed their
coats and neckerchiefs, and Harry had indulged himself
in the luxury of resting his weary leg on a hassock pulled
up before him. "Let's call it a draw," he said to Roddy
after studying the pieces that remained on the board with
a rather bored scrutiny.

"May as well," Roddy agreed. "You don't seem to have
your mind on the game anyway. You could easily have
taken my queen with your knight a few moves back."

Harry leaned back in his chair and stared at the ceiling.
"Too easy by half. It's no sport to win from a man who
leaves his queen so carelessly unprotected."

Roddy shrugged and busied himself with replacing the
beautifully carved chessmen in the velvet-lined chest
which housed them. "Nevertheless, old fellow, something
is on your mind. You've hardly spoken a dozen words
tonight."

"It's only that I'm deucedly tired. I'm unaccustomed to
the round of social engagements that seems to be required
of a prospective bridegroom. I don't see how Edwina
stands it. I'm worn to the bone."

"Oh, women thrive on such stuff," Roddy said with
assurance. "A woman can be prostrate with any
complaint from the headache to influenza, but the
moment someone suggests a party, she will fly from her
bed like a bird dog to a scent."

Harry chuckled. "And how have you become such an
authority on women, you mooncalf?"

"I'm an observer," Roddy grinned. "Merely an
observer. But you must admit that I'm a persistent and
astute one."

"I'll admit to only half of that. You, like all healthy

males, are a *persistent* observer, but very few of us are *astute* about the sex."

"Speak for yourself, Harry, old man. Which one of us was astute enough to avoid matrimony, eh?"

"The only reason you've avoided it so far," Harry rejoined, "is because you've never found a female who'd have you."

Roddy laughed, but he recognized the fact that Harry's quips lacked their usual spirit. Brushing his mustache with his index finger, he studied Harry closely. "Are you perhaps feeling some regret about the impending nuptials?" he asked.

Harry gave him a quick glance. "Of course not. Why do you ask?"

"I've heard that misgivings before the wedding are a quite commonplace symptom in males."

"I suppose they are," Harry said noncommittally.

"I didn't suppose that *you* would be inflicted with those misgivings, however. Your Miss Manning is a diamond."

"Yes, she is."

"A lady of the first stare. She never behaves in that silly, giggly way some girls have. She always appears just as she ought. Pretty as a picture and always says just the right thing."

Harry leaned forward and fixed his eyes on Roddy's face. "Do you think, perhaps," he ventured slowly, "that she is a bit *too* perfect?"

"*Too* perfect? I don't understand," Roddy said, brushing his index finger on his mustache again. "How can a woman be too perfect?"

Harry leaned back and stared thoughtfully ahead of him. "I don't know, quite. But don't you think it would become irritating to live with a woman whose hair was never tousled, whose temper was never unchecked, whose impulses were never spontaneous, whose words were never ill-considered?"

Roddy peered at Harry with sudden understanding. "Is that your impression of Miss Manning?"

Harry bit his lip guiltily. "No, no, of course not. I'm just offering a hypothesis."

"Well, it's a pretty silly hypothesis. There never was a woman in the *world* whose temper was never unchecked or whose words were never ill-considered. But if there were, I should snatch her up at once!"

Harry smiled, but Roddy noticed it was strained. "Would you indeed? I'd have thought you'd prefer your females a little wild and impulsive."

"Like your ward, Miss Belden?" Roddy grinned appreciatively. "Yes, now you mention it, I *would* like a girl like that."

Harry's laugh burst out. "Is there a type you would *not* like, you mushroom? By the way, may I remind you that Nell is not my ward?"

"Well, your niece then."

"She is not my niece. She is Charles's ward and not related to *me* at all."

"Good," Roddy said with a glint. "Then I need never find myself in the position of having to come to you for permission to pay my respects to her."

Harry turned to Roddy curiously. "Is there some seriousness behind that jest? Do you have designs in that direction?"

"Do you mean in regard to Miss Belden? Yes, indeed. I find her completely charming. You'd see it too, if you weren't so bemused by your Edwina. But Miss Belden has no eyes for me, I'm afraid, except as a friend. I think she's fixed her affections elsewhere."

"Do you?" Harry asked, elaborately casual. "And where do you think she has fixed them?"

"On you," Roddy suggested, after a slight hesitation.

Harry looked away quickly. "Rubbish! She regards me as an uncle . . . or an older brother . . ."

"Does she? Are you certain?"

"Of course. Just as I'm certain that I regard *her* as a delightful little sister." The words were barely out of his mouth when the recollection of a kiss again flashed across his mind. Sister, indeed! He shifted in his chair uncomfortably.

Roddy was observing him shrewdly. "Yes, of course," he said agreeably, rubbing his mustache with his finger in that irritating way of his. "How else can you regard her, when you're pledged to Edwina so irrevocably?"

"You're hinting at something quite nonsensical," Harry said irritably. "You sound like a gabbling old busybody. If this is the extent of your conversational talents, let's set up the chessboard again."

But Roddy's conversation was not so easily put out of Harry's mind. He knew that his feelings for Nell were far from brotherly. He lay awake well into the night wondering why he'd found it necessary to try to convince Roddy that Nell was like a sister to him. Was he ashamed of his feelings for her? And if so, why? Carefully and dispassionately analyzing the situation, he reasoned that there was something in his attachment to the girl that made him feel unfaithful to Edwina. But the only way *that* could make sense would be if he loved *Nell* ... !

Suddenly it all seemed blindingly clear. What a fool he'd been! He'd been in an emotional turmoil ever since he'd laid eyes on the girl in her bedroom at Thorndene as she'd stood staring at a ghost, her nightcap askew and her eyes sparkling with intrepid amusement. Only a complete gudgeon would have taken so long to diagnose the trouble. What he'd felt for Edwina before he'd gone to the Peninsula was a boyish fantasy compared to the breadth and depth of what he now felt. Love had come to him at a time of personal suffering and bitter loneliness, and it had been unrecognizable because it had been neither romantic nor particularly soothing. It had *hurt*, and it had mixed itself up with all his other pains.

Nell was lovely, but, objectively speaking, Edwina was more beautiful. Edwina was more gentle, more steadfast, more serene. Edwina would never have entertained a ghost in her bedroom, nor asked rude questions about a man's private feelings. She would neither have nagged him nor quarreled, nor kissed him when she knew he was promised to another (out on the cliffs in a driving rain). And she would never have broken three betrothals. She would not break even *one*. Edwina was sensible and thoughtful and fair and fine. *And he didn't want her at all.* He wanted the stubborn, rude, impulsive, foolish little chit who'd pushed and coaxed and irritated and cajoled and *dared* him back to life when he'd felt almost dead.

Good God, what had he done? To prove to Nell that he had the courage to face the world, he'd tied himself to Edwina in a betrothal he no longer wanted. And, as Roddy had put it, a betrothal was an irrevocable pledge. Ladies, of course, had the right to change their minds, and if they were capricious (as Nell had evidently been in the past) they cried off carelessly and frequently. But a gentleman had no such privilege. He could *never* cry off.

Harry tossed fitfully on the pillow to relieve the feeling of imprisonment which overwhelmed him. He shut his eyes and urged sleep to come, but, like a willful girl, it eluded him. Surrendering at last to sleeplessness and utter dejection, he lay staring up into the darkness. "Oh, Nell," he muttered miserably, "what a mull we've made of it, between the two of us!"

Hoping to avoid seeing Nell until the shock of his new discovery had been subdued into resignation, he came down to breakfast an hour earlier than usual, and of course came face to face with her. He reddened, mumbled an unintelligible greeting and sat down. Quickly he occupied himself in reading several innocuous messages with avid attention. Nell offered him tea, which he accepted with a grunt and without meeting her eyes. When at last he looked up from the note which he'd reread three times without understanding, he found her looking at him curiously. "Is something amiss?" she asked. "You seem a trifle out of curl."

"I'm fine, perfectly fine. Will you be good enough to

pour a cup of tea for me?" he asked, looking quickly down at his letter.

"Of course, if you wish it, although you've barely touched the tea you have."

Harry had forgotten that he'd already accepted a cup from her, and he stared at the cup in front of him embarrassedly. "Oh, yes. Well, it's probably cold," he said awkwardly.

She handed him a fresh cup, and he took a hasty gulp. Since it had just been poured, it was quite hot and scalded his tongue. "Aah!" he gasped helplessly, setting the cup down precipitously and sloshing the steaming liquid over his hand, causing another uncomfortable sting. "Damnation!" he muttered, his ears reddening.

"Are you *sure* you're quite up to snuff today?" Nell asked in some amusement. "You do seem to be in an odd humor."

"There's nothing at all wrong with my humor," Harry growled irritably, "except for the fact that I don't enjoy an inquisition at the breakfast table."

"An *inquisition!*" Nell repeated, half astounded and half offended. "Really, Harry, of all the unjust remarks! I was only showing a mild concern—"

"I don't need your concern, thank you," he muttered, feeling very foolish.

"Very well, then, I shall not question you further. I certainly didn't intend to cause you to take a pet for no reason." And they lapsed into silence.

As soon as Harry felt he could take his leave without seeming abrupt, he rose from the table. Nell looked up from her teacup. "I was wondering, Harry, if you and Miss Manning plan to attend the Caldicott masquerade this evening?"

"We most certainly do *not*," he answered curtly. "Why do you ask?"

The fact of the matter was that Sybil had importuned Nell to accompany her to the affair, but Nell had been reluctant to agree. Henrietta Caldicott's reputation was

unsavory, and her parties always seemed more than a
little disreputable. If she could have enlisted the company
of Harry and Miss Manning, however, Nell felt that she
could, in good conscience, make an appearance; otherwise, she intended to refuse. In answer to Harry's
question, she launched into an explanation. "Sybil has
asked me to accompany her, and I was wondering—"

But Harry, irritable and impatient to be gone, did not
let her finish. "You needn't have wondered. Anyone with
sense should realize that a masquerade at the Caldicott
ménage is bound to become a boisterous rout. But why do
you bother to ask me? Surely you have no need for my
permission. If you and my aunt are determined to amuse
yourselves at such unsavory gatherings, it is not my place
to prevent you. I will only add that, if you were hoping for
Miss Manning's and my company to add a touch of
respectability to your outing, you were fair and far off! It's
the very *last* place I would dream of taking a lady of her
refinement!" And with that he slammed out of the room.

Nell stared at the door openmouthed. She had no idea
what she'd said or done to cause such a violent reaction
from him. The blood rushed to her cheeks as his last
words echoed in her ears. Miss Manning was a lady of
refinement, he'd seemed to say, and *she* was *not*! How
dared he speak so to her! The more she reviewed his
words, the more furious she became. As if she needed *his*
presence to achieve respectability! She'd had no desire to
attend the masquerade, but now her feelings changed. She
sprang up from her chair with her eyes blazing and
stormed into Sybil's room to inform that surprised lady
that she would be delighted to join her that evening and to
ask for assistance in contriving to find a suitable costume
for the occasion.

A costume could not be devised in time, and Nell
appeared at Mrs. Caldicott's party in a simple hooded
domino. To her chagrin, she could recognize not one of
her acquaintance among the roisterers who thronged the

rooms. Lady Sybil had left her side almost immediately upon entering, and Nell felt a bit frightened and quite alone. The dancing was already in full swing, and the attitudes of the dancers—their too intimate closeness and their raucous laughter—gave ample evidence that Harry had been right in his assessment of the quality of the evening. She pulled her hood as far over her face as she could and retired into a corner where she hoped she would be unnoticed until Sybil was ready to return home.

Harry was spending the evening in the very opposite kind of company. The Mannings were giving a dinner to present him to an elderly aunt and several other relations. The conversation was at best insipid, but because the aunt was somewhat deaf, almost every remark had to be repeated into her ear trumpet. Insipid remarks, when repeated, become inane, and Harry was feeling very bored indeed. His mind began to wander, and he found himself remembering with disturbing clarity his diatribe of the morning. He could see Nell's face looking up at him in pained astonishment as he berated her for her plans. That he had grossly overreacted was apparent. He didn't like the idea of her attending such a party, but he needn't have spoken so rudely. He began to itch to make amends.

It didn't occur to him that Nell would attend the Caldicott masquerade in spite of his objections, and he hoped that he would return home early enough to see her before she retired for the night. He was therefore taken by surprise when, after leaving the Mannings so early that some eyebrows were raised, he learned from Beckwith that Miss Belden had indeed accompanied Lady Sybil to the masquerade. The news caused his temper to flare again, and he stormed out of the house and into his carriage with his fists clenched and his mood chaotic.

He arrived at Mrs. Caldicott's residence with his temper unreconciled. The fact that he didn't immediately see Nell infuriated him even more. Before he could begin his search for her, his presence was noted with jubilant enthusiasm by the hostess, who came rushing to his side.

"My lord!" she cooed, "What an *honor*! I had no *idea*, when I sent you a card, that you would deign to attend. You have quite *made* my evening, I assure you! May I ask your indulgence for a few minutes and make you known to some of my friends?"

"Thank you, ma'am, but I've come merely to escort Lady Sybil and Miss Belden home. If you but tell me where I may find them, I shall not take up your time."

Mrs. Caldicott, chewing her underlip in vexation, said that she hadn't seen Miss Belden, but she led the way to a side room where she thought his aunt might be taking a bite of supper. In the room was a long, well-laden table surrounded by noisy, gluttonous merrymakers. There he found his aunt, her mask dangling from one ear and her cheeks flushed with high color from an overabundance of wine. Controlling his voice with heroic effort, he said softly, "Good evening, Sybil. I've come to take you home. Where's Nell?"

She waved him off airily. "Don' wish to go home jus' yet, dear boy," she said woozily. "Can't go home wi' you in any case—I've brought m' own carriage."

Not trusting himself to say another word, he took her firmly by the arm and, ignoring her objections, propelled her firmly to the hallway. There he instructed a butler to call her carriage and see to it that she was conveyed home. Then he returned to the ballroom to continue his search for Nell.

To his dismay, he found her in a curtained alcove, struggling in the arms of a masked gallant in the costume of a Venetian gondolier. "Let me go!" she was crying breathlessly. "If I would not *dance* with you, you cannot expect me to permit *this*!"

The would-be beau did not answer. He suddenly found that both his arms were pinned behind his back in an iron grip. "I am quite tempted," Harry muttered into the fellow's ear, "to tip you a settler you won't soon forget. But it's your good fortune that I've no wish to kick up a dust in this place. I advise you, however, to take yourself off before I change my mind." He released the fellow, who took one quick look over his shoulder to evaluate the man who stood glowering over him, and ran quickly out.

"Oh, H-Harry," Nell breathed, attempting awkwardly to compose her hair and adjust her mask, "how can I th-thank—?"

"Never mind!" he muttered tightly. "Just take my arm. We'll say goodnight to your hostess and leave."

He uttered not another word until they were seated in his carriage and on their way home. Even then, it was she who broke the silence. She was eager to express to him her intense gratitude for his rescue, but before she opened her mouth to speak, she glanced covertly at his face. He appeared tight-lipped and strained, and she suddenly realized the extent of his anger. "I don't know why you should be so furious," she said at last, looking down at her hands which were demurely folded in her lap. "I did not *ask* you to come to rescue me."

He fixed her with a look of utter disdain. "And what would you have done if I hadn't come?" he sneered.

She lifted her chin. "I could have managed him," she declared.

"No doubt you could have," he said in scornful agreement. "Your behavior tonight convinces me that you've endured *many* such experiences."

Nell's feelings of gratitude dissolved instantly. "Yes, I have!" she said belligerently. "*Most* women have. But you needn't look so shocked. I don't suppose your so-perfect Miss Manning has ever found herself in such a fix. She has too much *refinement* to be thus accosted."

Harry turned away from her in disgust. "You are quite right. And she has better sense than to permit herself to be taken to a secluded alcove where such scenes are more likely to occur."

Nell sputtered in indignation. "I did *n-not* permit myself to be *taken* there!" she cried in vehement denial. "I had gone there to *hide* from him. But the wretch followed me."

"Oh, I see," Harry said, some of the wind taken out of his sails. "I beg your pardon. Nevertheless, you could have avoided the entire situation had you refrained from attending in the first place. After all, I *did* warn you—"

"I don't care to discuss this any further, my lord," Nell said coldly. "Please accept my gratitude for coming to my rescue. I suppose you meant well. But I shall be a great deal *more* grateful if, in the future, you refrain from meddling in my affairs. I can handle them quite well without you." With that, she turned to stare out the window, and they did not exchange another word.

When they entered the house, Nell, her head proudly erect, made straight for the stairway. Harry, standing at the foot, looked up at her retreating back and found that all his anger had melted away. "Nell—!" he called after her, not knowing quite what he wanted to say, but instinctively attempting to end the estrangement between them. But Nell did not turn, and he couldn't tell if she had not heard or she'd chosen not to answer.

Nell marched up the stairs without a backward glance and went straight to her room. Gwinnys was waiting up for her, but Nell, on the verge of tears, told her in a choked voice that she would not be needed and urged her to the door. "But won't 'ee need some help wi' your buttons?" Gwinnys asked, looking over her shoulder at her mistress' troubled face with sympathetic anxiety.

"I'll manage them myself. Goodnight, Gwinnys," Nell told her and shut the door with finality.

Assured of her privacy, Nell sat down at her dressing table and opened her jewelry box. From a back corner she withdrew a little wooden box and opened it. There, resting on a bed of padded satin, was a long-shafted key on a silver chain. It was the key to the entrance of a secret passageway. Nell looked at it with a tremulous sigh. Not for the first time did she wish fervently that she had never discovered Harry's identity. If she had let matters rest, they might still be living happily in Cornwall, with Harry making nightly ghost-visits to her room.

She removed the key from the box and fondled it affectionately. Those early weeks in Cornwall had been the happiest time she had had since her childhood. Remembering the lighthearted, diverting, titillating relationship that had existed for a few weeks between a girl and a ghost, she felt a painful homesickness for a place which had been her home for less than two months. With the key clutched in her hand, she threw herself across the bed. Perhaps, with that talisman in her hand, she might return to that time and place in her dreams.

Chapter Sixteen

THE NELL WHO appeared at breakfast late the next morning was a different girl from the one who had returned from Cornwall. When she'd come back, she had behaved instinctively in a manner which she felt would please Harry. She had been modest, sensible, restrained and mannerly. Now, her eyes sparkling militantly, she seemed to revert to the outrageous, discreditable girl she used to be. She embarked on a program of activity which seemed to be calculated to cause dissention and perplexity among the family.

First, she began to flirt outrageously with all the young men of her acquaintance, with the result that the door knocker was never still. Beaux of all descriptions came calling to escort her riding, to bring her messages or posies, to leave a card or to accompany her to one or another of the various festivities which, a few days before, she would have scorned to attend. Among the beaux she was evidently encouraging was one whom her guardians were delighted to see—Sir Nigel Lewis was among her most frequent escorts and had evidently been persuaded to resume his courtship.

Another change Nell instituted in her life was the abandonment of what her godmother had called her "Cornish prudery." She took to wearing the most dashing costumes, especially a particularly shocking riding ensemble of a very military cut, with epaulets and brass buttons. The costume caused many respectable eyebrows to elevate when she appeared in the park, and the style was much copied by the younger, more daring ladies of the *ton* and a few of the demimonde. Nell wore her riding costume topped by a high-crowned hat with a curly brim and set off with an ostrich plume which was pinned to the side and fluttered excitingly behind as she rode. The hat was worn at a very rakish angle and looked quite fetching perched atop Nell's chestnut curls.

Harry, when he saw it for the first time, was torn between an impulse to laugh and a desire to tell her how charming she looked. He did neither, but when Edwina later whispered to him that the habit and its shocking hat made his young relation look rather fast, Harry changed his mind. Thinking to do Nell a service, he repeated Edwina's comment to her. Instead of being grateful, Nell turned on him furiously and declared that for one thing she did *not* relish being discussed behind her back, and that for another she was quite capable of evaluating her own apparel, thank you! From then on, Harry was aware that she flaunted the riding habit and its controversial hat before his eyes on many more occasions than seemed warranted.

Her behavior, too, became a matter of gossip and concern. She challenged Tubby Reynolds to another race, and Harry learned that bets were being laid at all the gambling clubs. She was heard to say something quite rude to the Princess Esterhazy, and although that spirited lady laughed heartily, those who overheard it were quite shocked. At the Gordon's ball, she pushed Thaddeus Wickenham into a potted palm, and although there were many who declared that he had molested her and had therefore deserved it, others murmured that she had probably encouraged his attentions in the first place. All this gossip became embarrassing to Harry, whose affianced bride was the offspring of a very respectable family, members of which were beginning to feel that Nell's antics reflected discredit upon *them*.

The day appointed for Nell's race with Tubby was fast approaching, and interest in it ran high. Although curricle races were all the rage, it was not often that a female participated in such competitions. Nell was not the only young lady who could handle the ribbons, but most of those who *could* knew that indulgence in such sport was not at all seemly for well-born, well-nurtured females. Edwina, who had found herself enduring several conversations in which Miss Belden's forthcoming adventure was the primary subject of discussion, felt impelled to speak to her betrothed about the matter. One afternoon, when they were returning from a ride, she broached the subject. "Henry, my dear," she ventured, "I'm very much afraid that the race your Miss Belden has proposed is a matter to which you must give your attention. Mama says that if Miss Belden persists in this scandalous conduct, it cannot help but reflect badly upon *us*. Can't you stop her?"

Harry, who had been himself quite irked at Nell, felt an inexplicable resentment at Edwina's interference. Keeping his eyes on the horses he was handling, and with what had become his customary restraint, he said quietly that the matter was not his affair. "Miss Belden is not a relation of *mine*, you know," he reminded his betrothed, "but of my aunt and uncle. She is *their* ward, and her behavior must be their concern. I would be merely interfering if I took it upon myself to offer criticism or chastizement."

"I honor your scruples, my dear," Edwina said, her expressive, blue eyes smiling up at him approvingly, "but you are too nice in your feelings. Remember that you are the head of the family. She *is* a member of the family, if only by adoption, and you are quite within your rights to exercise control over her."

Harry was beginning to understand that Edwina's serene manner came from her unshakable conviction that she had only to smile into someone's eyes to get her own way. She had never in her life needed to raise her voice, to pout, or to stamp her graceful little foot in vexation. From the time she was a little girl, her regal air and eloquent eyes had made the people surrounding her her slaves. And now she looked at him with the same expectation of having her way. He was expected to be another slave in her entourage.

He could almost feel a slave collar tightening about his neck. Yet there seemed to be no way to fight back. Edwina's manner was so calm, so assured, so reasonable. She never made demands, only requests. She never insisted. How could one fight with a *paragon*? If only she would once lose her temper, once say something rash, once do something impulsive. The prospect of spending his lifetime harnessed to a pattern-card of perfection was becoming more and more galling. He whipped up the horses to vent his rising spleen and said brusquely, "I do not choose to exercise control over my family. I am not anyone's master. I find it difficult enough to master myself."

Edwina protested with a little laugh. "Oh, Henry, really! One would think I had asked you to *horsewhip* the girl. I only want you to *speak* to her." She placed a gloved hand gently on his arm. "After all, you cannot like *our* being sullied with such gossip."

"How can *we* be affected by it?" Henry demanded.

"The reputation of the entire family can be affected," Edwina insisted calmly, "when one of the members appears so often and so shockingly on everyone's tongue."

"Balderdash!" Henry's jaw clenched and a muscle in his cheek twitched. In a kind of last-ditch rebellion, he said irritably, "Your family's reputation is not on such flimsy ground that a distant association with a headstrong girl will cause it to collapse. And as for *my* reputation, I don't care a jot what the damned prattle-boxes say of me!"

Miss Manning, not being a fool, did not fail to observe his irritation and wisely let the matter drop. She had little liking for Miss Belden and the rest of Lord Thorne's rackety family, but *he* was a rich prize. She would not let him slip through her fingers for so little cause. So she folded her hands in her lap and remained silent.

Harry, however, could not shake off his irritation so easily. Having been prevented from venting it on Edwina by her unshakable ability to avoid quarrels, his ire found another target—Nell herself. The irksome girl was behaving in an exasperating, provoking, vexatious manner, and he had an irresistible urge to wring her neck. He stormed into the house intent on carrying out the urge, but learned from Beckwith that she was out and not expected back until late. Even the fact that she had been escorted by his own friend, Sir Roderick, did little to ease his frustration. Fortunately, Lady Sybil was at home. There, at least, was *someone* on whom he could vent his spleen.

Poor Lady Sybil had to endure a most difficult half-hour. Lord Thorne told her without roundaboutation what he thought of her manners, her morals, her taste, her finances and her ability to raise a daughter. He informed her that he would hold her personally responsible if Nell so much as *left the house* on the day of the race, and that, if Nell *did* participate in so inappropriate and vulgar an activity, he would see to it that they *both* were confined to their rooms for a month! With that, he marched awkwardly out of the room and locked himself in the library for the rest of the day.

On her return, Nell found Sybil waiting for her in her bedroom. Sybil had dismissed Gwinnys and was pacing nervously between the fireplace and the window when Nell entered. The girl took one look at her godmother and knew something was amiss. "Heavens, Sybil, what's wrong? You look ghastly!"

"And well I might," Sybil snapped. "You've gone too far, you ninny. Lord Thorne is furious with you!"

"Why?" asked Nell in surprise. "What have I done?"

"What have you *done*?" Sybil repeated furiously. "Surely you must be aware of what you've done. You've been behaving like a veritable hoyden. You have all of London gossiping about you. Your clothes, your flirtations, your wild races—"

"What has all this to do with Lord Thorne?" Nell cut in coldly.

"It has a great deal to do with him. We are his *family*!"

"*You* may be his family. I am not," Nell declared with icy dignity.

"That is nothing but a sophistry. I do not care to quibble over mere terminology. Whether you consider yourself part of his family or not, the fact remains that you live on his largesse," Sybil stated bluntly.

Nell whitened. "What do you mean? It is you and Charles who are my guardians! You don't mean—"

"That, too, is a mere quibble. If Charles and I live on his indulgence, and you live on *ours*, it is all the same in the end, is it not? Besides, we haven't paid *your* bills since your return from Cornwall. We pass them on directly to the Earl's man of business who has set up a separate account for you. Henry ordered the arrangement."

"I see," Nell said, stunned. "Of course. I don't know why I didn't think of this before." She sank onto her bed and stared across the room at her godmother. "What does he want me to do?"

"The answer should be obvious to you. He wishes you to cancel the race with Tubby Reynolds, of course."

"What nonsense," Nell muttered. "Why should he kick up a dust over so silly a matter? What difference can my racing make to *him*?"

"Do you think a man of his consequence enjoys having a member of his household engage in so indiscreet a display?"

"Indiscreet?" She put her hand to her forehead, for her head was whirling in confusion. "But why? It's only to be a short dash through the park in the early morning when most of London is still abed."

"Half of London plans to *be* there, you goose! The affair is talked of everywhere. Everyone knows you to be wild and flirtatious. Do you think that Henry can abide having someone in his own family who behaves in so vulgar and wanton a fashion?"

Nell's eyes widened in dismay. "*Vulgar and wanton?* He couldn't think—! Did *he* say that?" she asked, a tremor in her voice.

"His very words," Sybil answered unfeelingly.

Nell shuddered, closing her eyes in pain. There was a long silence. White-lipped, Nell sat at the foot of her bed staring at the fingers clenched in her lap. After a while, she looked up at her aunt with unseeing eyes. "Go to bed, Sybil," she said flatly. "You need have no further concern for my behavior. I shall not race Tubby."

Sybil sighed and hurried to Nell's side, kissing her cheek in relief. "That's my good girl," she murmured. "I *knew* you would be reasonable. Now, if you can only avoid getting into any other scrapes, we shall all be easy again."

Nell sat unmoving long after Sybil had gone. The clock striking midnight seemed to rouse her. Moving like a somnambulist, she went out of her room and down the hall to Lord Thorne's bedroom. Heedless of the hour, she knocked at his door.

"Come in, Beckwith," he said.

She opened the door and went in. The room was dark, lit only by the glowing embers of the fire dying in the grate and the moonlight spilling in through the uncurtained window. Harry, wearing a long dressing gown, had evidently been unable to sleep and had been gazing out of the window. He turned at the sound of the knock and stood leaning against the window-frame, peering into the shadows at the doorway.

"It is not Beckwith," Nell said in a low, rigidly controlled voice.

"Nell?" Harry asked, puzzled. "What is it?"

"I have something to say to you."

"This is a strange hour and a strange place to hold a conversation. Should you not wait until morning?"

"I want to tell you now."

"Very well." He reached for his crutch, which had been propped against the wall near him, and swung across the room to his nightstand, where he struck a match and lit a candle. He held it up and looked across the room at her. "Please sit down," he said politely, motioning her to an easy chair near the fire.

"No, thank you. This won't take long." Irrelevantly, she added, "You are using your crutch, I see."

"Yes," he said wryly, "but only in the privacy of my room."

Nell nodded but said nothing. Harry crossed the room with the candle and was able to see her more clearly. He noted that her lips were pale and her eyes glittered with some suppressed emotion. "What is it, Nell?" he asked in some anxiety, setting the candle on the mantelpiece.

"I've come to tell you that I shall obey your wishes and cancel the curricle race—"

"I'm glad of that," he said, eyeing her uneasily. "You'll be glad, too, when you've had time to reflect on it calmly."

"I shall never be glad," she said coldly. "I am merely obeying the commands of the man who provides for my support. I can in good conscience do no less."

"What?" Harry asked in bewilderment. "I don't

understand you. What on earth is this all about?"

"It is quite plain. I reside here and take my meals under your roof and buy my frippery clothing and everything else I need all at your expense. I did not think about it before, but—"

"You needn't think about it now," he told her shortly. "It has nothing to do with—"

"It has *everything* to do with it! The man who pays the piper calls the tune—is that not how the old expression is worded?"

"Nell, you become offensive! I never gave a *thought* to such matters!"

"Of course I become offensive. It is to be *expected* of such a vulgar, wanton creature as I!"

"Nell!" he cried, appalled.

"Why are you so astounded? That is how you yourself described me, is it not?"

"You're mad! I *never*—!"

"You said I was wild, flirtatious, vulgar and wanton. I have it on excellent authority."

He grasped her shoulders and shook her furiously. "*Stop it!* You're behaving like a fool!" His crutch toppled unheeded to the floor. With his hands grasping her shoulders, they glared at each other angrily until two tears rolled down Nell's cheeks and her whole body began to tremble. With a groan, he pulled her into his arms. She clung to him, sobbing uncontrollably. With his lips against her hair, he murmured brokenly, "Oh, Nell, surely you know—! If only I could tell you—!"

When her sobs had subsided, he tried to let her go, but for an unwitting moment, she hung on to him desperately. Then, with a gasp of shame, she withdrew her arms from around him. He knelt awkwardly, picked up his crutch and swung himself back to the window, turning to stare out at the moonlit roofs below. She watched silently as he stood framed in the window, silhouetted in silver. Then she walked softly to the door. "It's quite clear that I must find a way to leave this house," she said dully.

His silence signified his reluctant agreement.

She nodded unseen. "That's what I came to tell you. I've decided to marry Nigel after all."

"No!" His voice was gruff. "I won't allow it. I know you must marry one day—I even realize that your eventual marriage is *a consummation devoutly to be wished.* But not yet. And not to him."

"That is not for you to say," she reminded him gently, and she quietly left the room.

He stood staring out of the window until long after the moon had disappeared. Eventually, in the darkest part of the night, just before dawn, he gave up his senseless vigil and went to bed.

Chapter Seventeen

NELL'S WITHDRAWAL FROM the race would have caused
great comment had not the news of her second betrothal
to Nigel (and her fourth betrothal in less than a year)
superceded it. There was much material for gossip in the
liaison. For one thing, Nigel had quarreled with his
mother over it, and Lady Imogen Lewis had let it be
known that she thoroughly disapproved of the match.
For another, Miss Belden had seemed to turn over a new
leaf, and everyone wondered how long it would be before
she would break loose and perpetrate some new outrage.
When Edwina repeated this nonsense to Lord Thorne, he
merely said in his driest tone that he hoped she would
commit her outrage very soon, since she was being
maligned in any case.

But Nell committed no outrage. She accompanied

Nigel meekly to the opera, the theater and the few social gatherings to which they were invited. She behaved and dressed modestly and held her tongue, even when sorely pressed to utter something sharp. Nigel was very pleased with her, and with himself for what he thought of as his success at taming her to the bridle.

Nell and Harry did not see each other except when occasionally passing on the stairs or meeting awkwardly in the breakfast room. But Harry could not help but note her pallor, her lack of sparkle and her air of hopeless passivity. Helpless to do anything to alleviate her plight, he grew daily more embittered and unhappy. One evening, having joined Roddy at White's, he left the gaming table for a breath of air near one of the open windows. While standing there, he overhead Nigel discussing his betrothed with a crony whose voice Harry didn't recognize. "It's just as I've always said," Nigel was boasting. "Women must be treated exactly as one would a nervous thoroughbred. One has to know when to let her run wild and when to rein her in. When she's skittish, give her a little rope, but when the time is right, pull her back with a firm hand. That's what the she-devils need—a firm hand. Look at my Nell now. Completely broken to the bridle. She's as docile as any sweet goer in my stable."

Harry clenched his hands until the knuckles showed white. He would have liked to murder the man with his bare fists. To think of Nell married to that damnably arrogant scoundrel made him physically sick. He remained at the window until he'd regained his self-control, but when he returned to the table he could no longer concentrate on the cards.

Roddy noticed his agitation and suggested that they depart early. The two friends walked silently down St. James Street, Roddy waiting patiently for Harry to reveal what was on his mind. He did not have long to wait.

"Do you remember, Roddy, making a remark—some time ago—that, if she'd have you, you'd snatch up a girl like Nell? You called her a 'regular out-and-outer.'"

"Yes, of course I remember. And so she is," Roddy said with enthusiasm, but at the same time keeping a wary eye on his friend's face. "Why?"

"If you still feel that way, why don't you make her an offer?" Harry suggested, a weariness in his voice revealing the effort it had cost him to say those words.

Roddy looked at him suspiciously. "This is a queer start. Are you up to something smoky?"

"Not at all," Harry assured him. "I've never been more in earnest."

"But the girl's betrothed!"

"I know. That's just it. I can't stand by and let her wed that...that bumptious *maw-worm*!"

Roddy nodded with sudden understanding and fingered his mustache thoughtfully. "I won't say that I don't agree with you, but what on earth has chanced to put you on your high ropes so suddenly?"

"I overheard Sir Nigel tonight, conversing about his bride-to-be. The damned blackguard actually bragged about breaking her to the bridle, as if *my Nell* were nothing more than a mare in his stable."

"*Your* Nell, eh?"

Harry shot a quick, guilty glance at Roddy's face. "A slip of the tongue," he admitted ruefully. "My desires triumphed over the truth, I'm afraid. But the truth is that she can never be *my* Nell..."

Roddy sighed. "It's bellows to mend with you, eh? I guessed as much."

"I thought you had. But it doesn't bear speaking of. I'm no skirter-jilter."

"Damned shame," Roddy said compassionately.

"Nevertheless, I'll not permit that...that court-card to take her!" Harry said with vehemence.

"Not much you can do about it, I'm afraid."

"No," Harry agreed, "but *you* can. Surely she'd prefer *you* to that loose fish."

"Thank you for the compliment," Roddy said with an ironic bow. "It's flattering to learn how well you think of me."

Harry laughed shortly. "It's not necessary for me to flatter you for this purpose. I'm not recommending you for the Light Bobs or a cavalry commission. Besides, you *know* Nell likes you."

"I had hoped, when I married," Roddy said wistfully, "to find someone who *loves* me a little. Don't you think that someone, somewhere, might—?"

"No, I don't," Harry mocked. "How can you dream of another girl when you might have Nell?"

"Stupid of me," Roddy admitted, his lip curled in wry amusement. "Although it *is* possible, you know, that someone might inexplicably prefer another female to wed."

"No, not if he had any sense," Harry smiled, indulging in the foolishness a little longer. It lifted his spirits to admit so openly that he was besotted over Nell. For the moment at least, he could reveal the secret he'd repressed so painfully and for so long a time.

They walked along companionably for several minutes, but then Harry grew serious again. "You *must* do this, Roddy. We can't let her ruin her life."

"I'll try, old boy, I'll try," Roddy promised, "but I can't guarantee success. It's the lady who must make the final decision."

It took a great deal of pluck on Roddy's part—and much urging from Harry—to bring Roddy to the doorway of Thorne House, but, a few days later, he arrived at mid-morning and was informed by Beckwith that Miss Belden was at home. He found her in the sitting room, seated at a writing desk and frowning down at a blotted, criss-crossed sheet of paper while nibbling thoughtfully at the top of her pen. She roused herself at his cough, and her face broke into a warm smile. "Roddy!

Where have you been hiding these last few days?" she greeted him eagerly. "Do sit down."

"I am disturbing you, I'm afraid. Am I keeping you from your writing?"

"Oh, bother my writing. I was trying to compose a letter to Nigel's mother. He wants me to invite Lady Imogen to tea so that we may come to terms. But I *know* that, no matter how I phrase the note, she will refuse me. It's nothing but a waste of time. I'm relieved to have an excuse to give it up." She tossed the pen aside, left the desk and seated herself on a small sofa.

Roddy sat down on the edge of a chair opposite her and studied her closely. "You haven't the look of a happy bride, my dear," he said sympathetically. "Is it Nigel's mother who causes you to look so wan?"

Nell made a face at him. "Need you be so frank? If you intend to spend the morning telling me I'm not in my best looks, I shall make this a very short interview."

"Well, even when not in your best looks, you're the prettiest sight in the world," Roddy grinned.

"That's much better," Nell acknowledged, grinning back at him. "Although you need not have gone so far as the whole world. The environs of London would have done quite well enough."

Roddy shook his head. "There is no pleasing you, I'm afraid. This does not augur well for my mission."

"Mission? You have a mission?" she asked interestedly. "I thought this was purely a social call."

"Oh, no, my dear, I have a most serious purpose. It has a bearing on the very direction of your life."

"My *life*?" Nell asked, more amused than impressed. "That is serious indeed."

Roddy sighed. "I *knew* I'd do this badly. You're laughing already, and I haven't even told you why I've come."

"Then perhaps you should tell me without all this preamble," she suggested.

"Very well, if you insist. I've come to ask you to marry me, Nell."

She gurgled. "I don't know what sort of prank this is, but you *are* doing it badly. You should be down on one knee, you know, making me a long speech; first you must tell me of your high regard for me, and then you must list my many virtues—"

"Dash it, must I?" he asked in mock horror.

"But of course!"

"No. If I did that, you would *surely* laugh, and I mean this very seriously, Nell."

She took a quick look at his face and her smile vanished. "You can't be serious. You know that I'm betrothed—"

"Yes, I know. But you aren't yet married. It's not too late to change your mind. You've done it before."

She looked at him in complete confusion. "I don't understand this at all, Roddy. Are you trying to pretend that you *care* for me?"

"It's no pretense. I *do* care for you," he said earnestly.

"What humbug! You've never shown me the least regard—at least not in *that* way. You must not confuse your feelings, Roddy. I suppose you care for me as a friend—"

"A very *good* friend," he insisted.

"A good friend, then. But surely you realize that you've no regard for me in any other way. What caused you to make such an impulsive gesture?"

"Really, Nell, it was not a mere gesture. You must stop suspecting that this is some sort of a hum. I'm completely in earnest. I most urgently desire that you accept my offer of marriage."

"But *why*?"

"Why? What a strange question. Why does *any* man ask a woman to wed him?"

"Because he *loves* her, you idiot," she chided. "You are not going to pretend that you love me, are you?"

"Well, you're not going to pretend that you love that Lewis fellow, yet you agreed to marry *him*," he countered.

She paled. "That is entirely different," she said stiffly.

He leaned forward and grasped both her hands in his. "You mustn't go ahead with it, Nell. He's . . . not worthy of you. You can't make me believe that you'd not be happier with me!"

Nell's eyes misted over, and she lowered her head. "It is most kind of you, Roddy, to show this concern for me. I am . . . very touched. But I would *not* be happier with you. I'd be miserable, for I would know that I had kept you from finding real happiness—the happiness you truly deserve. One day soon, you will *love* someone . . . someone not at all like a good friend . . ." Her voice trailed off in a small sniffle.

He released one of her hands and reached for a handkerchief, which he handed to her unceremoniously. She sniffed into it briefly and then looked up with a smile. "There. I've quite recovered. May we return to being good friends now?"

"Confound it, Nell, how can I be a friend to you if I meekly accept your refusal and permit you to proceed with your plans to marry a man who is certain to make you miserable?"

She withdrew her hand from his grasp and said with quiet dignity, "You have no choice, Roddy. I am quite capable of making decisions in regard to my own future."

"But . . . what if this decision is a dreadful mistake—?"

She jumped up angrily. "I cannot permit you to say such things to me. Nigel is my affianced husband, and I cannot allow you to disparage him to me. Nor can I entertain any discussion of marriage behind his back."

"Very well, my dear," he sighed dejectedly, "you've no need to comb my hair. I didn't really expect this scheme to succeeed, anyway."

They sat in silence for a moment until Nell, moved by Roddy's worried frown, patted his hand comfortingly. "You needn't look so blue-deviled. I *do* appreciate your solicitude. But you see, I am quite prepared to accept the shortcomings as well as the benefits of married life. I shall brush through well enough, never fear."

"Perhaps," Roddy said dubiously, "but I very much doubt that your assurances will be at all convincing to—" He cut himself short and looked away awkwardly.

"To whom?" Nell asked, arrested.

"No one," Roddy said quickly, jumping to his feet. "I'm sorry. I don't know what I'm saying. Please excuse me, Nell, for leaving so abruptly. It isn't every day that a man's offer of marriage is rejected. I need a little time alone, to recover—"

Nell was not fooled by his prattle. "Did Harry send you?" she demanded.

Roddy faced her with a look of injured innocence. "*Harry*? How can you suggest such a—"

"*Roddy!*" Nell interrupted threateningly.

He met her eye obstinately for a brief moment, but the firm challenge in her expression caused his defenses to crumble. He sank back into his chair and shrugged helplessly. "He didn't *send* me, Nell. I *wanted* to come. Truly."

"But he knows of this?"

"We...discussed the matter, you might say."

"I might say a great deal more, I suspect," she said with heavy sarcasm. "I believe I might say that this was *his* idea, was it not?"

Roddy lowered his eyes and said nothing.

"Of course it was! I might have known. Who else would take it upon himself to maneuver other people's lives like this? As if we were pieces on a chessboard! How *dared* he? How *dared* he meddle in our lives this way?"

"He dared because he is troubled. You *must* realize that he only wants to see you happy."

"That's not true. Not *at all* true!"

"I tell you it *is*. You may take my word on it," Roddy declared loyally.

"If it were true, he would be here *himself* to offer for me—not taking advantage of his friend!" she said wrathfully.

Roddy regarded her reproachfully. "You know he

couldn't do that...in his position."

"Of course he couldn't," she said, pacing up and down resentfully. "He's safely rivetted to his so-perfect Edwina!"

"Yes, the poor fellow..." Roddy ventured carefully.

"Poor fellow? Why 'poor fellow'?" she demanded, turning on him. "He's won the lady he's always dreamed of winning, hasn't he? *I* would call him a very *lucky* fellow!"

"Come now, Nell, don't play coy. You surely have noticed that he's long since awakened from that dream."

Nell stiffened, her breath caught in her throat. "I do not *play coy*," she managed. "What is it that you're suggesting?"

Roddy shifted in his chair guiltily. "Nothing, nothing. I've gone too far. I'm quite out of my depth."

But Nell could not be stopped. "You're suggesting, are you not, that Harry's feelings for Edwina have changed? That, my friend, is utter nonsense."

Roddy glanced up at her. "Are you sure of that?"

"Quite sure."

"What makes you so certain?"

"Because he is still betrothed to her. If his feelings were no longer engaged, he would have severed the connection. Just as I have done on more than one occasion."

"But...what are you saying?" Roddy asked in sincere confusion. "No gentleman may cry off as ladies do. You must be aware that it just isn't done."

"What a simpleton you are," Nell mocked, turning her back on him and striding across the room to the fireplace. "It's done all the time."

Roddy was shocked. "Surely you're mistaken! I've never heard—"

"Of course you've never heard. It must always *seem* as if the lady had done it."

Fascinated, he followed her across the room. "But...but how is it contrived?"

Nell, suddenly noting the intense interest on his face,

was struck with guilt and misgivings. What was she *doing*? It was almost as if she were plotting to encourage Harry to break with Miss Manning. What a horrible, scheming wretch she was becoming. She turned away from Roddy in shame. "Never mind, Roddy. This entire subject is quite unseemly. I apologize for having entered into it. Neither Harry nor I has the right to interfere in each other's life. Nor have we the right to involve you."

Sensing that she was dismissing him, Roddy reluctantly retreated. "But... what am I to say to him?" he asked plaintively, half to himself.

"To Harry?" She spoke with a new and adamant authority. "You are to say *nothing*, Roddy, do you hear? Nothing at all!"

"But I must tell him *something*! He's completely *beside* himself!"

"You exaggerate the extent of his concern."

"You are quite wrong, Nell," Roddy said on a sudden impulse. "He loves you."

Her eyes rested on his face for a moment, but then she shook her head. "I have sometimes thought... It has sometimes seemed... But it is not so," she said with a tremulous inflexibility. "He is fond of me, I think, but love is made of... of stronger stuff."

"You are mistaken, my girl," Roddy said sadly. "You underestimate the strength of his feelings and his sense of honor." He followed her to the door. "It will go hard with him when he learns that you intend to proceed with your wedding plans," he added in a last, hopeless attempt to save the situation.

"He will learn to accept it, as we *all* must," Nell said in a tone of mature womanliness he had not heard in her voice before.

He stared at her with new respect. "You're a surprising young lady, Nell. I had no idea you had such ... such *steel* in you."

A reluctant laugh escaped her. "Steel? Does it indeed seem so to you? To me, my innards seem completely composed of quivering, cowardly, quaking *mush*!"

*   *   *

Roddy's innards felt a bit like mush when he faced Harry on his return. Harry turned ashen when he reported that Nell had refused him. "I don't understand it," Harry said wretchedly. "She *cannot* prefer that cur to you!"

"She says that I deserve a wife who loves me," Roddy explained briefly. "*She* does not."

And that was all Harry could extract from him.

Chapter Eighteen

NELL'S "INNARDS" PROVED less and less like steel as the day of her wedding approached. She had long ago had the measure of Nigel's character, and she therefore had little expectation that she would find contentment as his wife. The most she could hope for was that his interest in her companionship would dwindle with time and that he would "go his own way," as Sybil had suggested so long ago. Perhaps Sybil had been right about married life (it was certainly true of Sybil's own—she and Charles often passed entire days without coming face to face with each other), but Nell was not finding it to be true during the courtship. Nigel was everlastingly under foot, and his omnipresence set Nell's insides quivering more and more as the days went by.

With Nell's nuptials scheduled for late May and

Harry's for mid-June, the Thorne household buzzed with wedding plans. Sybil dreamed excitedly of arranging an elaborate reception for her ward, and she decided to approach Henry to discuss financing the affair. With great trepidation, she told him her plans. He responded in a tone so brusque that she would have considered it positively churlish except that he actually agreed to all her suggestions. He gave her permission to spend whatever she deemed necessary and to send the bills to him. To her, this signified that she had free reign, and she embarked on a program of spending that filled her ostentatious soul with delight.

Soon the deliveries began. Tradesmen knocked at the back door several times a day delivering cases of champagne, polished wooden boxes filled with gold plate, barrels of monogramed Worcester Royal porcelain, crystal glasses, table linens, candles by the hundreds and the candlesticks to hold them, engraved invitations, rolls of red carpet, potted palms and dozens of other articles and accoutrements Sybil considered "necessary" for the occasion.

In addition, Nell was forced to endure a number of fittings for a wedding gown and headdress worthy of a royal princess. Sybil hoped that these grandiose preparations would dispel the look of misery which (Aunt Amelia pointed out to her worriedly) lurked deep in Nell's eyes. She and Charles had much to gain from the alliance between Nell and Nigel, and Sybil didn't want anything to interfere again. She therefore tried to coax Nell into a bridal glow by urging her to take part in the preparations, but her attempts met with no success. In fact, they had the opposite effect. Nell's inner quakings and tremblings were rapidly degenerating into a sick terror.

Another person who viewed the wedding preparations with disapproval was Edwina Manning. As the news spread about the size and magnificence of the reception Sybil was planning, Edwina sensed that the interest in her *own* reception was declining. Her mother had planned a modest celebration to follow the wedding ceremony, with only the family and one hundred carefully selected guests in attendance. Edwina's gown was being made by the family dressmaker, not a French modiste, as Nell's was. The wedding cake was to be only three tiers high and baked by the family's cook instead of the six-tiered tower that Sybil had ordered for Nell, to be baked by a French chef whose icing designs were internationally renowned.

Edwina was quite aware of the gossips making whispered comparisons behind their fans, all derogatory to her, but she ignored the whispers and went about her business with the appearance of complete composure. It was only to Henry that she revealed her conviction that Lady Sybil was passing the bounds of good taste and moving into the area of vulgar ostentation. But the only response she was able to elicit from his lordship was a stony silence.

There was, however, one benificent result of Sybil's wedding plans—the effect they had on Lady Imogen. Nigel's mother, impressed by the grandeur of the elaborate preparations in progress, determined to forget Nell's former transgressions and take Nigel's affianced bride to her bosom. To indicate to society that she had changed her mind and now looked upon the match with approbation, she sent out cards to one hundred persons inviting them to a lavish dinner party in honor of her future daughter-in-law.

If Lady Imogen's past dinner parties had been a trial to Nell, this one was far worse an ordeal. The guests had been selected from among the most pompous, insipid and irritating of London society. Every one of them seemed to her to be overweening and overdressed. They minced through the rooms with magisterial self-consciousness and spoke to her with condescending self-importance. Yet Nigel escorted her into the enormous dining room beaming with satisfaction and pride. He seemed truly to be enjoying himself. It didn't take long for her to realize why—*he was one of them*!

The dinner seemed interminable. She was seated at Nigel's right, but he spent most of the evening conversing with the bejeweled dowager on his left. The gentleman on *her* left was an absent-minded octogenarian whose movements were so slow and stiff that she was convinced he feared his bones would crack if he tried to turn or bend. When she spoke to him, he leaned toward her without turning his head. Sometimes, in his efforts to speak to her, he leaned so far over that she expected momentarily he would topple over into her lap.

After dinner, the guests were ushered into a large music room where seats had been placed in neat rows. Lady Imogen had engaged for the evening's entertainment an Italian soprano whom she had secured at great expense. Although Nell was grateful for the improvement of the entertainment over the amateurishness of the last dinner party she'd attended here, the singing was not of a quality to soothe either a savage breast or Nell's rapidly developing headache. The soprano was short, stout and shrill, and instead of singing some of the beautiful songs of her own country, she chose to entertain the guests with ballads and folk-songs of England. Her command of the language was very limited, and Nell found herself hard-pressed to keep from laughing at her rendition of "The Cuckoo Song," ("Well-a sings-a da cuccu," she warbled) and a little ditty Nell had never heard before about a "leetla feench." She cast an amused glance Nigel during the "little finch" song, but his response was a quelling frown.

By the time the evening had ended, Nell's smile had become strained and false, and her head ached with the fatigue brought on by the excess of formality which she'd had to endure. When she could at last take her leave of her hostess, Lady Imogen thrust a huge floral arrangement (one of several which had decorated the music room earlier in the evening) into her arms as a sign of her approval of Nell's behavior during the party and offered her cheek for Nell to kiss. It was with a weary sigh of relief that Nell climbed into the carriage and deposited the enormous floral offering on her lap.

But her ordeal had not yet ended. Nigel climbed in after her and took his place beside her simply oozing with self-satisfied complacency. "It was a splendid evening Mama gave for you, was it not?" he asked smugly.

"Didn't you find it just the least bit stiff?" Nell asked in a mild attempt at honesty.

"Stiff? Not at all. Mama's galas are never stiff. It is acknowledged throughout London that she is the most gracious of hostesses."

Nell made no answer. She did not wish to be churlish, and she was quite sensible of the fact that Lady Imogen had put herself to great effort on her behalf.

"It was most condescending of Lord Pickersleigh to attend, I think," Nigel continued proudly. "Mama says he almost never leaves his rooms these days, and she was quite overcome when he agreed to attend."

Nell had no inkling of who Lord Pickersleigh was, and, not wishing to put Nigel to the task of describing him, she merely murmured, "Indeed?"

"And of course Mr. Leslie and the Milbankes—one doesn't see *their* like at ordinary dinners, you know."

Since Mr. Leslie had been the elderly gentleman on Nell's left, she could not refrain from muttering, "Let us hope not!"

Nigel stiffened. "What was that?" he asked. "Are you suggesting that you were not pleased with Mama's guests?"

"It is not my place to be pleased or displeased. Your mother has the right to ask whomever she likes to dine with her."

"Indeed she does, but I hoped you would show a proper regard for the honor conferred upon you this evening."

"Oh, but I *do* feel honored," Nell declared irrepressibly. "Especially by Mr. Leslie. Mr. Leslie conferred upon me the honor of almost toppling into my lap!"

Nigel was not amused. "It's well that Mama did not hear you say that. She disapproves of levity in females, and I heartily agree. As my wife, I sincerely hope, my dear, that you will refrain from indulging in your unfortunate proclivity to flippancy."

"May I sometimes dare to *giggle*? It would be very softly, of course, and only in the privacy of my dressing-room."

He glared at her and then turned away in pique. "I daresay I should be grateful," he said grudgingly, "that you had the good sense to refrain from ridiculing Mama's guests while you were in her house."

"If not the good sense, at least the good manners," Nell said placatingly.

He accepted her peace offering with relief. "Yes, you behaved very well. Mama was quite pleased with you. She told me so."

"How *good* of her," Nell said, unable to keep the edge of sarcasm from creeping into her voice.

"*I* think so. It is not easy for a lady in Mama's position in society to overlook the past transgressions of a prospective daughter-in-law, especially when those transgressions have been so widely reported. I hope you appreciate the extent of her condescension."

Nell's fingers curled into fists. She had had quite enough condescension for one evening. "Oh?" she asked with dangerous sweetness. "Have my 'transgressions' been so enormous that they require such very great condescension?"

Nigel failed to notice the warning signals darting from her eyes. "Well, you can hardly expect her to approve of a girl whose been a jilt—"

"A *jilt*?" Nell put in softly.

Nigel, warming to this theme and eager to have Nell understand how much his mother (in her largeness of heart) had had to forgive, ignored the interruption. "—And who rode through the park in a costume which everyone described as brazen—"

"Brazen! Do go on," she urged, her eyes glittering ominously.

"—And whose style is described by respectable matrons as positively fast—"

"A fast and brazen jilt, am I?" she asked icily. "I'm surprised that you managed to convince her to accept me into the family at all!"

"Now, don't fly into a pucker, my dear," Nigel said pompously, completely confident that he had made his point. "All that is in the past. I've assured Mama that you've been properly broken to the bridle at last."

"Broken to the bridle!" Nell flared. "Like all the *other* horses in your stable?"

Nigel was startled. "Come now, don't take a pet. Look, we've arrived at Thorne House. We can't permit the footman to hear us wrangling. Besides, you don't wish to turn stiff-rumped after such a fine evening, do you?"

"Stiff-rumped? Is that *more* of your stable talk?" she asked furiously.

Nigel realized he was blundering badly. "Hang it, Nell, it's only a manner of speaking—"

"Well, then, *in a manner of speaking*, I'd like you to know that *this* horse is not quite broken yet! This *prime bit o' blood* has *some* spirit still!"

The footman had lowered the step and stood waiting for Sir Nigel to open the carriage door. Beckwith, who had opened the front door of the house and was awaiting Miss Belden's appearance with a puzzled frown, started down the front steps. "Here comes Beckwith," Nigel said hastily. "Best to drop this for tonight. You'll feel more the thing in the morning."

But Nell, her eyes blazing, would not be stopped. "Oh, no! This little mare is about to *break loose*! One little hurdle, and she can run free."

"Hurdle? What do you mean?"

"I mean our betrothal. I'm about to break it again!"

Nigel sneered. "You're jesting. You made this mistake once before and regretted it. You can't be such a fool as to do it again."

"Can't I? Well, perhaps *this* will convince you—!" And, just as Beckwith opened the carriage door, she lifted her lapful of flowers and dropped them on his head.

Nigel gasped and sputtered in astonishment. Nell patted his head soothingly. "Don't fall into the dismals because one little horse has bolted, Sir Nigel. Even the *best* of trainers fails with one or two. Good-bye."

She offered her hand to the goggled-eyed Beckwith and gracefully stepped down. Then, smiling with angelic innocence, she turned back to the stupified, open-mouthed Nigel. He sat frozen amidst the hawthorn blossoms and rosebuds that clung to his hair and shoulders, and the larkspur and peony blooms that had fallen all about him. A large, wet leaf had stuck to his nose, and a sprig of lily-of-the-valley hung from behind an ear. "By the way, Nigel, please remember to thank your Mama for giving me those lovely flowers," she said sweetly. "I've never enjoyed a bouquet more."

Chapter Nineteen

SOMETHING ABOUT BECKWITH'S expression as he bumbled about the breakfast buffet the following morning made Sybil decidedly nervous. "What's wrong with you, Beckwith?" she asked suspiciously. "You've rearranged those cups three times. And you *still* haven't brought me those biscuits which I've asked for twice. Haven't I asked twice, Charles?"

Charles, absorbed in buttering his toast with the intense care required to ensure that the entire surface would be evenly coated, merely shrugged.

"Sorry, m'lady," Beckwith mumbled, ambling over with the biscuits with an irritating, dilly-dallying shuffle.

"Something's amiss, I can tell," Sybil declared, her eyes narrowed. "Why are you hanging about in this way? You know we don't require your services at breakfast."

"I only want to see to the tea things, m'lady," Beckwith said, ambling back to the buffet. "We don't want Lady Amelia to go into one o' her takings because the tea ain't brewed proper."

"Hasn't Amelia been down *yet?*" asked Sybil in amazement. "It's well after ten!"

"No, m'lady, not yet."

"Don't recall her ever coming down this late before," Charles remarked. "And I don't recollect that Beckwith's ever fussed so about the tea, either."

"That's quite true, Charles," Sybil agreed. "There's something havey-cavey in the air this morning. Out with it, Beckwith!"

The butler, who knew a great deal more than he intended to reveal, had hoped to be able to observe at first hand the cyclone which he knew was about to strike, but he realized that he'd run out of excuses to remain. "I've finished," he muttered, edging reluctantly to the door. "I'm just goin'."

He was about to close the door behind him when a nervous Lady Amelia made her appearance. "May I serve you y'r tea, m'lady?" Beckwith asked her eagerly, holding the door for her.

"No, thank you, Beckwith. We won't be needing you," she answered, dismissing him and carefully shutting the door. "Good morning, Sybil, and you, too, Charles."

"*There* you are, Amelia," Sybil greeted her curtly. "How is it you're so late this morning? And, by the way, where is Nell?"

"I'll tell you in a moment. Only let me pour myself a cup of tea first, if you please."

"Tell me *what?*" Sybil cried impatiently. "I *knew* something was amiss, I knew it! There's an *air* about the house this morning like... like impending *doom!*"

"No need to enact a Cheltenham tragedy," Amelia said bracingly and carried her cup to the table. The fact that her cup trembled enough to cause some tea to slosh over into the saucer was not lost on Sybil.

"Then get *on* with it," she urged tensely.

Amelia took a heartening sip of her indispensable brew and sat back in her chair. "I have a letter for you, my dear," she said to Sybil in a voice that seemed to underscore the importance of her otherwise innocuous words. She pulled from her sleeve a folded sheet of notepaper and handed it across the table.

"What is it?" Sybil asked, looking at the letter as if it were a snake about to bite. "Who sent—?"

But before she could finish her question, the door opened, and Beckwith, his face flushed with anticipation, entered. "Lady Imogen Lewis to see you, m'lady," he told Sybil with ill-suppressed glee.

Sybil, her eyes fixed on her letter, waved him aside. "Tell her I'll see her in a few minutes. Make her comfortable in the—"

"There is nowhere in this *house* where I'd be comfortable," came a caustic voice from the doorway, "and you may as well face the fact, Sybil Thorne, that I *won't* be put off!"

"Why, Imogen, what a surprise—!" Charles murmured embarrassedly, standing up in awkward haste. "Do come in."

"I *am* in," Lady Imogen said coldly.

"Won't you sit down?" Sybil asked with a forced smile. "We were just—"

"No, I won't sit down! Nor will I ever set foot in this house again after I've had my say. What do you mean, ma'am, and you too, my lord, by permitting your ward to *jilt my son again?*"

Charles gasped and fell back into his chair. Sybil, with a chagrined *"What?"* could only stare at her guest in dismay. "What are you *saying?*"

"Are you trying to pretend you know nothing of this?" Lady Imogen demanded.

Sybill shook her head, completely confounded. "No, *nothing!*" she gasped breathlessly. "I've not heard a *word—!*"

"Then let me be the first to tell you," Lady Imogen said flatly. "Your ward, a foolish chit whose disreputable behavior and shocking callousness reflect no credit on those who reared her, had the temerity and the singular lack of judgment to announce to my son last evening, in the rudest, most tasteless way, that their betrothal was at an end. And this was done immediately following a magnificent dinner party which had signified to the very *cream* of English society my approval of the match!"

There was a moment of silence while the others tried to digest the import of Lady Imogen's flood of words. Charles, who understood only that his ward had been maligned, felt that it behooved him to come to her defense. "I think I must take exception, Lady Imogen, to the way you speak of our little Nell. I cannot permit—"

"Oh, be still, Charles!" Sybil interrupted brusquely. "If what Lady Imogen says is true, I shall speak of our little Nell in terms a great deal *worse*! Lady Imogen, you must be mistaken. Nell has been most docile and tractable since the understanding with Nigel was reached. I can't *believe* she could have changed so abruptly."

"I am *not* mistaken," Imogen stated. "The little wretch has destroyed *everything*. When word of this leaks out, she will not only have wrecked her own reputation beyond redemption, but she'll have made my son and me the laughingstocks of England." Suddenly her lips began to quiver and her face took on an expression of pathetic self-pity. "I don't know how I shall be able to hold up my head!"

"Don't say so," Sybil said, jumping up and running to Lady Imogen's side. "Here, sit down, please! Not a *word* of this will leave this room. It's all been some sort of terrible mistake. A lover's quarrel, no doubt. We'll talk to Nell and bring her round, and everything will go on just as we've planned."

Lady Imogen allowed herself to be seated, but she would not otherwise be placated. "You're a fool, Sybil

Thorne, if you think this can ever be patched up. Nigel is beside himself with rage. He won't have her name mentioned in his hearing!"

"Oh, dear," Sybil said in some discouragement. She paced about behind Lady Imogen's chair thoughtfully. "But surely *you*, Lady Imogen, could convince him to relent, if you truly put your mind to it."

"Do you imagine that I would do anything to encourage my only son to shackle himself to that . . . that . . . wayward, skittish, shatterbrained *minx*?"

"But I tell you she's changed! We haven't heard *her* side of this. I'm certain she can explain everything to your satisfaction. Be reasonable, Lady Imogen. Would you not like to have this incident buried? Would you not like to be able to go on as before, with no need for embarrassment or shame? Let me send for Nell. I know she can put all this right."

She bent over Lady Imogen breathlessly. Imogen looked at Sybil with speculative eyes and then nodded almost imperceptibly. Sybil, with a sigh of relief, reached across the table to the little silver bell near her place and rang it. Beckwith, who had never left the room, stepped forward. "Yes, m'lady?"

Sybil started. "*Oh!* Good *heavens*, have you been standing there *all this time*? Beckwith, you try my patience beyond *endurance*! But never mind that now. Find Miss Belden and tell her to come here at once!"

Beckwith shook his head. "She's not at home, m'lady."

"Not at home? But where can she have gone so early?" Amelia coughed gently. "Sybil, dear—"

Sybil waved her off impatiently. "Not *now*, Amelia, please! Can't you see that I've a crisis on my hands? Well, Beckwith, where has the girl gone?"

Beckwith shrugged. Amelia tried again to attract Sybil's attention. "She's *left*, Sybil. The *letter*, remember?"

"Letter? Oh, good *God*!" She looked down at the letter

still clutched in her hand. "Has *this* anything to do with—?" She ripped open the seal and her eyes flew over the words.

In the silence, Amelia turned to Imogen. "May I offer you a cup of tea? There is nothing more soothing—"

Before she could finish, Sybil let forth a piercing wail and tottered to the nearest chair. The door burst open and Harry, with Roddy close behind, came hurrying into the room. The two men, still in their riding clothes, had just returned from a brisk canter through the park. "Good lord, Sybil," Harry exclaimed in alarm, "what's the cause of this to-do?"

"Disaster!" she announced in a voice quivering with passion. "Complete disaster! I am about to have an attack of *apoplexy*!" And she fell back against the chair with a groan and shut her eyes.

"Here," Amelia suggested promptly, "have a cup of tea. It will do you good." She placed a cup in front of her stricken niece, but Sybil opened her eyes, glared at Amelia venomously, groaned and shut them again.

Harry and Roddy exchanged looks of complete perplexity. When Harry turned back to the table, he found himself face to face with a tall, angry dowager who had risen from her chair and now stared at him in frozen-faced disdain. "I am Lady Imogen Lewis," she said awesomely, "and it seems to be my place to bring information to this household which, were this a house at all well run, you would have ascertained without my intervention. I regret to have to inform you, Lord Thorne, that your Miss Belden has terminated her betrothal to my son—and for the second time!"

Harry stared at the dowager in fascination. "Has she indeed?" he asked with admirable restraint, trying to ignore the choked sound emitted by Roddy.

"So I've said," the dowager continued. "The wretched girl has jilted my son, ruined my social standing and made a shambles of the reputations of your family and mine. As head of this family, Lord Thorne, you must bear the brunt of the responsibility for what that heedless and heartless wretch has done."

Harry, delighted beyond measure by the news, was hard pressed to keep from breaking into a wide grin. "I regret ma'am, that you should be put to any... er...inconvenience because of this rather precipitous conclusion to the relationship between Miss Belden and your son," he said with elaborate formality. "You will, however, wish to hurry home to console your son in his disappointment, so we will not try to detain you."

"*Henry!*" Sybil cried, dismayed.

Lady Imogen could scarcely believe her ears. "See here, young man, are you suggesting that my presence here is *de trop*?" she asked, her neck growing mottled with rage. "I have no intention of taking my leave until I am satisfied that this matter will be dealt with in proper fashion! And as for offering my son *consolation*, I'll have you know that I haven't the slightest reason to do so! He is rather to be congratulated! Yes, *congratulated* for having escaped so dire a fate as to be riveted to that—"

"In that case," Harry interrupted smoothly, "we need not express any regrets at all."

A choked sound of laughter came from Roddy, and Harry's lips twitched. Lady Imogen, realizing that she'd been bested in an exchange, became even more mottled. "Lord Thorne," she said indignantly, "it seems to me that you cannot be fully aware of the extent of Miss Belden's iniquities. Not only did she jilt my son, and for the second time, but she did it in the most humiliating way. He told me that she *threw something at him*!"

Sybil groaned and clutched at her breast. "I shall certainly have a seizure!" she wailed.

Harry heard Roddy choke again, and he himself had great difficulty in keeping his countenance. "Did she in...indeed?" he managed to ask politely.

"She most certainly did! It is fortunate that Nigel was not *injured*!" Lady Imogen said dramatically. "He was quite overcome by the incident, I can assure you."

"Quite overcome?" Harry murmured, enthralled. "How unfortunate. What was it she threw at him?"

"I couldn't say, my lord, for poor Nigel could barely speak coherently! It was all I could do to obtain the salient facts last evening. He had not emerged from his room this morning when I left the house."

"'Twas a bunch of *flowers*," Beckwith volunteered, grinning.

"Beckwith!" Sybil cried furiously *"Will you remove yourself from this room?"*

But Harry turned to Beckwith with an incredulous stare. "Flowers?" he asked choking.

Beckwith nodded. "Nothin' but a bunch of flowers. She dumped 'em on his head. I seen 'er do it!"

Sybil, with a helpless wail, dropped her head forward and covered her face with shaking hands. Roddy, no longer able to restrain himself, broke into a hearty laugh. Charles also guffawed. "Flowers? I say!" he chortled, slapping his knee gleefully. "The chit can't have inflicted much of an injury with a handful of *posies*."

Lady Imogen, offended beyond words by the apparent lack of seriousness with which her news was being received, drew herself up proudly. "It was more than a handful of posies, Lord Charles," she declared roundly. "It must have been the bouquet I bestowed upon her, and it was a *very large bouquet indeed*!"

This proved too much even for Harry's self-control, and he turned his face to the nearest wall, his shoulders heaving. Lady Imogen stared at his back icily. When at length he regained his breath, he turned back to face her, his expression appropriately calm except for the laughter that still danced in his eyes. "I beg your pardon, Lady Imogen," he said with a slight tinge of breathlessness in his voice, "but I trust this discussion is now at an end."

"Good!" said Amelia. "Now, perhaps, we can all have some tea."

"Aaaah!" screamed Sybil, as if poor Amelia's remark were the last straw.

"Must you keep offering us tea, ma'am?" Lady Imogen asked in disgust. Then turning back to Harry, she said, still undaunted, "You have not yet informed me of what you intend to do to see that Miss Belden is taken properly to task for her outrageous and reprehensible behavior."

"Our intentions in regard to Miss Belden are, Lady Imogen, entirely *our* affair. May I wish you a good day? Beckwith will show you to your carriage."

When Lady Imogen had been led out of the room, Roddy ran up to Harry and the two men pounded each other joyfully on their backs, laughing and shouting at once. "She cried off! I *told* you she was an out-and-outer!" Roddy cheered.

"An armload of flowers!" Harry crowed. "Dumped 'em right on his head, by God! I wish I'd been there to see his face!"

"Have you both lost your *minds*?" Sybil cried. "How can you stand there laughing like loobies? We have invited *hundreds* of people to a *wedding*! What do you suggest we do about *them*?"

"Tell them not to come," Harry said, grinning.

"And what about the things I've purchased for this affair? Do you realize that I've filled this house with dishes, glasses, gold plate, hundreds of bottles of champagne and I-don't-know-what?"

"Send it back," Harry said promptly, still grinning at Roddy in intense relief. "Throw it out! Give it away to the poor!"

Sybil, pushed beyond endurance, rose from her chair and tottered over to them. She placed herself directly before her nephew and spoke in trembling wrath. "So, this is all an enormous *jest*, is it? We shall be made ridiculous before the entire world, we shall have to notify half of London that there will be no wedding, we have lost the opportunity to benefit from the Lewis' wealth, and we shall probably be left without a friend to stand by us in the ordeal! It is all most amusing! Very droll! Completely hilarious! Very well, my lord, read *this*! If you find it humorous, perhaps I'll be able to laugh with you."

Harry, with a sudden frown, took the letter she thrust at him. "What *is* this?"

"It's a letter from the very same young lady whose antics you seem to find so entertaining. She's *run away*! *Now* let us hear you laugh!"

Chapter Twenty

HARRY HOBBLED ACROSS to the window and, turning his back on the assemblage, eagerly read the letter.

Dear Sybil, she had written. *By the time my dear Amelia delivers this letter to you, I shall be gone from this house for good. I know this will be a blow to you, and I am most unhappy to have to cause you pain. You and Charles made a home for me when I was left alone in the world, and for that you will always have my most sincere gratitude and devotion, but, in one matter, I cannot find the will to oblige you. You will have guessed that I am speaking of my betrothal. I realized tonight that I could never, under any circumstances, endure being wed to Nigel. We are completely unsuited. I appreciate deeply the effort you have made to give me a memorable wedding day, but even you will admit that one such day could not make bearable a lifetime of unhappiness, and unhappiness would be my future if I married him.*

The fact that I have run away will seem to you most cowardly. It is with deep regret that I leave you to face without me the chaos, the confusion and the gossip which will follow the cancellation of a wedding such as the one you have been planning. Please believe that I had no choice. I have strong personal reasons—having nothing to do with Nigel or the wedding—for my conviction that Thorne House is no longer the proper residence for me.

Amelia will support me in my claim that I shall manage quite well in the new life to which I go. There is not the slightest need for you and Charles—nor anyone else in the family—to feel the least concern for my health and safety. I hope you don't mind that I'm taking Gwinnys with me— she refuses to stay behind. With the warmest good wishes for your future happiness, I am and will always remain, your loving Nell.

Harry reread the letter several times, but the repetitions did not reveal any more than the first perusal. She was gone, and he knew why. The spirit of hilarity that her severed relationship with Sir Nigel had induced now evaporated completely. He looked up from the missive in his hand, his face tense and strained. "When did you get this?" he asked Sybil.

"Just before you came in. Amelia handed it to me."

"Did you see her leave, Amelia? When did she go?"

"I saw her off very early this morning," Amelia said calmly.

"Why did you permit her to do it, you noddy?" Sybil demanded. "Have you no sense of responsibility to this family?"

"She convinced me of the necessity of her action," Amelia replied.

"The only necessity that I can see is that she wanted to escape from facing the repercussions of her inexcusable behavior," Sybil declared.

"She says here," Harry interfered firmly, "that she had

pressing private reasons. I accept the truth of that statement, and so must you, Sybil."

"And is that all you have to say?" Sybil asked incredulously. "Are you not going to find out where she's gone? Have you no concern for her welfare?"

Amelia snorted. "Do *you* have any concern? You sent her off to Cornwall last year and never made the least inquiry to learn if she'd arrived. You never even let the caretakers know she was coming! You never sent for her to return. You pushed her into a betrothal she didn't want simply to feather your own nest. How do you account for this sudden concern *now*?"

"I do not have to account to *you*, Amelia, for anything I do!" Sybil said furiously. "I'll thank you not to interfere in what is not your affair. Nell is my ward, and I *do* care for her, whatever you may think. And if you were truly as concerned as you pretend, you would tell us where she's gone—for obviously she's told you—so that Henry can follow her and bring her home."

"She doesn't want to be followed. And she did *not* tell me where she went," Amelia said, reaching for the teapot. "Does *anyone* want a cup of tea?"

Harry took the chair next to his great-aunt and smiled affectionately at her. "Are you sure she gave you no clue as to her destination, Amelia? I won't follow her, if she doesn't wish it, but you can understand that we must be assured that she has adequate means, proper surroundings and all that a young lady needs."

"She left something for you, Henry, that she said will reassure you," Amelia told him with an answering smile. From her sleeve she withdrew a small wooden box and handed it to him. Harry opened it eagerly. Inside, lying on its bed of padded satin was a long-shafted key on a silver chain.

"What's that?" Roddy asked curiously.

Harry held up the key, a strange half-smile on his face.

"A key? Does *that* reassure you?" Sybil asked curiously.

"Yes, it does," Harry answered, keeping his eyes, which seemed to glitter with an unusual intensity, fixed on the key dangling from his fingers.

"Well, aren't you going to explain?" Sybil demanded.

"No." he said shortly.

"*That* is the outside of enough!" she cried, jumping to her feet. "After all I've been through this morning, one would think you'd have the kindness to tell me what's going on!"

Charles, who'd been listening to the goings-on without much comprehension, nevertheless understood that his wife was prying. "Take a damper, Sybil," he said firmly, his good breeding asserting itself in the purposeful way he rose from his chair. "It's time you went to your room for a bit of repose. We've had enough theatrics for one morning." He helped her from her chair and drew her inexorably from the room.

Amelia rose to follow. "If no one wants tea, I think I shall go, too. See you later, dear boy," she said, patting him affectionately on the shoulder as she passed.

Only Roddy was left in the room. His eyes were fixed on Harry, his brow wrinkled in puzzled concentration. "Does that key give you a clue to Nell's whereabouts?"

Harry swung the key idly. "Yes, it does."

"And will you go after her and bring her back?"

"No," Harry said thoughtfully. "At least . . . not yet."

"Not yet? Oh, I *see*," Roddy said with a dawning smile.

Harry cast him a quick glance. "*What* do you see, Roddy?"

"It's quite obvious—you're going to wait until you're free from *your* entanglements."

Harry smiled wryly. "You seem to have been reading my mind. But the girl has left me with a knotty problem. How can a man of honor extricate himself from an entanglement like mine?"

"I don't know, although Nell once suggested . . ." Roddy stopped himself awkwardly.

"What did she suggest?" Harry asked hopefully.

Roddy shook his head in self-disgust. "Nothing, really. I should not have mentioned it."

"But you did. Go on, please."

"She only said that gentlemen cry off all the time."

"Did she say that? How odd! I've never heard of such things."

"So I said to her. But she would only say that one does not hear of a gentleman crying off because it is made to look as if the *lady* had done it."

"Ridiculous! The only way *that* can be done is by mutual consent, when *both* parties wish to terminate the betrothal. However, I suppose a gentleman could *encourage* a lady to...to..." and his voice trailed off as his eyes seemed to light up with an idea.

"To *what*, Harry?" Roddy asked eagerly.

"Just let me think..."

As Roddy watched, Harry sat lost in thought, his eyes fixed on the key which he absently continued to swing from its chain in a shaft of sunlight streaming in from the window. After a while, Harry's lips curled in a tiny smile, and his eyes gleamed with amusement. "Have you thought of something?" Roddy inquired hopefully.

"Perhaps..." Harry said slowly, his smile broadening. "I think...yes, I *believe* something may be contrived..."

It was not long afterward that Lord Thorne began to stumble. At first it occurred only in public places, like the crowded stairway leading to the boxes at the King's Theater, when the cause might be laid to the carelessness of the passers-by. The incidents tended to be a bit embarrassing for Lord Thorne and his party, for the passers-by always showed a great deal of concern. Lord Thorne had to give repeated assurance that he was indeed quite all right, and people tended to gather and gawk. These little scenes were usually unremarkable, and Lord Thorne and his party were soon able to put them out of their minds.

But when he stumbled in a dining room or at a private

party, the incidents tended to be more embarrassing. Edwina, who was usually at his side, would have to support him until he'd regained his balance. He would always apologize profusely, thus drawing more attention to the incident than Edwina thought necessary. Once, when he stumbled, and she bent quickly to support him, he inadvertently moved the tip of his cane on the hem of her skirt. When she straightened, the hem ripped away from the skirt, leaving a great gaping hole in the bottom of her dress. Although she was very gracious in her insistence that it was a mere nothing, it was plain that her evening had been somewhat spoiled.

After the third such incident in as many days, Edwina decided that it was necessary to speak to Henry about the matter. "I would rather die than have you believe these incidents disturb me in the *least*," she told him earnestly. "It is only my apprehension for your safety that makes me speak of the matter at all. You see, you had not seemed to have this difficulty before. You always seemed to manage so perfectly, one was hardly aware ... that is, I could not help but wonder if perhaps you are not well ..."

"It's this inadequate cane," Henry said bluntly. "It's damnably difficult to manage and always has been. It was only vanity that made me take to it. If I'd used my crutch, none of this would have happened."

"Then you must return to the use of the crutch," she urged. "It will not make a particle of difference to *me*, I assure you, and if it means that you will be more comfortable and safe, we must not let your vanity stand in the way."

But as the days went by, she found that she *did* mind the crutch. It seemed to distort his body, raising one shoulder above the other rather markedly, and she found that she did not like to watch him crossing a room. She found herself becoming a bit self-conscious when she was with him. Evidently there were others similarly affected, for the number of their invitations dwindled. Edwina began to feel edgy and cross, and her mother remarked that her usual serenity seemed to be deserting her.

One afternoon, when they had been invited to tea at the Milbankes', matters came to a climax. The Milbankes were mere acquaintances, but Edwina hoped that a strong friendship between the two families would develop. Hester Milbanke boasted two Dukes in her immediate family, and one of them was to attend the tea. Invitations to intimate gatherings with royalty were not at all to be despised, and Edwina had looked forward to the occasion with unusual eagerness. She dressed with the greatest care—a lovely, cream-colored "round gown" of the finest Alençon lace, with small, puffed sleeves and a deep flounce at the bottom. She would have been quite pleased with Henry's appearance, too, were it not for the crutch, for he wore an excellently cut coat of gray superfine, a striped satin waistcoat of the most subtle greens, and a pair of Hessians whose shine was unmarred by the slightest smudge or smear. With his white-streaked hair and his imposing height, he could have been the most handsome man in the room if he'd not had to carry the dreadful crutch under his arm.

It was with a blessed sense of relief that she saw him lean the crutch against an unoccupied chair beside him when they took their places around the tea table. While seated, Henry was the most imposing gentleman in the room. The conversation was very pleasant, and Edwina noted with pride that Henry had made three witty remarks which had caused the Duke to laugh uproariously. When Hester Milbanke leaned over to Henry and engaged his complete attention for more than a quarter of an hour, Edwina felt more than satisfied with Henry, with herself and with the success of the afternoon. Everything was going so well. Suddenly Henry, laughing at a quip Hester had whispered in his ear, leaned back; his arm pressed against the upper part of the crutch, swinging the lower end up into the air. As it flew up, it struck the edge of the silver tea tray and caused it to overturn. The silver tea pot slid to the floor, spilling its contents as it fell.

Edwina saw with horror a tea stain spreading down the front of her lovely gown. Cups and plates crashed to the floor with a horrid, smashing noise, splattering their contents over the clothing of everyone seated nearby. Edwina, her famous composure completely deserting her, screamed.

The Milbankes looked nonplussed for only a few seconds, but soon they laughed aside Lord Thorne's profuse apologies. The butler and two serving maids quickly swept away the debris. Another tray was hastily brought in, and a semblance of order was restored, but Edwina's color remained high and she was unable to say a single word. She sat unmoving, staring mutely at the shocking stain that marred the entire front of her dress, not even attempting to do her part to ease the tension in the room.

As soon as possible, Henry rose and offered her his arm. Stiffly, she acquiesced and the two bid their hosts good day. Mrs. Milbanke walked with them to the door, repeatedly assuring them that the accident had been a mere trifle and they were not to trouble themselves about it. Lord Thorne turned to thank her again, tripped on his crutch and fell flat on his face. Edwina, completely unnerved by this last horror, put her hand to her forehead and swooned.

To Edwina, the half-hour following had the atmosphere of a nightmare. Somehow they were helped into their carriage, somehow they arrived at her home, somehow she was led trembling to her bedroom. There, in the privacy of her room, and with only her mother and father to witness it, she gave way to the most hysterical outburst of her life.

In the library below, Henry waited to receive word of her condition. He had not expected his little plot to reap so dramatic a result. He paced the room guiltily, wondering if perhaps he'd gone too far. At last, Sir Edward and Lady Clara came in. "Sit down, my boy," Sir

Edward said nervously. "Do sit down."

"I hope you are not going to tell me that Edwina is ill!" Henry said worriedly.

"Oh, no, not at all," Lady Clara assured him. "She is merely a little overset. A mere nothing, but . . ."

"But?" Henry asked interestedly.

Lady Clara looked at her husband helplessly. "Don't look at *me*," Sir Edward said testily. "I want nothing to do with this. Female foolishness, I call it. Makes a man ashamed he has a daughter."

Lord Thorne looked from one to the other quizzically. "Is something wrong?"

Lady Clara, biting her underlip nervously, sat down on the sofa and tugged at Henry's arm. "Sit here beside me, Henry dear. I don't know quite how to tell you this . . ."

Henry obligingly sat beside her. She took his hand in both of hers. "Edwina is quite shaken by the events of this afternoon—" she began.

"As well she might be," Henry said humbly.

"Nonsense, boy!" Sir Edward barked. "Can't think where these women get their frippery notions. No one with a grain of sense could blame you for—" He shook his head, unable to go on.

"What is it you're trying to tell me?" Henry asked encouragingly.

"Edwina feels—although I'm certain it's only a momentary feeling—that she cannot go on with . . . with . . ." Lady Clara colored, stammered and looked miserably at the floor.

"With our wedding plans?" Henry prompted.

Lady Clara nodded. "She's been such an indulged child," she mumbled shamefacedly. "She always had everything just as she's wanted it—so easy, so perfect, so beautiful. She doesn't know how to cope with . . ."

"With imperfection," Henry supplied.

Lady Clara, her eyes spilling over with tears, looked at him gratefully. "Yes, that's it. I s-so d-dislike to give you p-pain . . ."

Henry stood up. "Don't cry, Lady Clara. I quite understand. Please assure Edwina that I wish her every happiness—"

"Listen, my boy," Sir Edward said affectionately, coming up to him and clapping him on the shoulder, "don't take this too badly. Chances are she'll come to her senses in a day or two. Bound to, you know. I've never before known the girl to behave so stupidly."

"Thank you, sir, but Edwina is quite right. She deserves perfection. I've known from the first that I'm not good enough for her."

He went quickly and unstumblingly to the door. Before he had closed it behind him, he heard Sir Edward mutter angrily, "Not good enough for her, *balderdash*! That fellow is *far* too good for your shatterbrained daughter, and so I intend to tell her before the day is out! The silly chit has tossed away her best chance!"

Chapter Twenty-one

SPRING IN CORNWALL can be a breathtaking surprise to someone who has seen it only in winter. Nell, who had fled to Thorndene to hide in her bedroom and weep, found herself drawn inexorably to the out-of-doors. At first it was a quality of the sunlight which drew her—it sparkled on the sea with glittering patches of gold which seemed to reflect themselves in the very air. She walked every morning along the cliffs, through air that seemed to glimmer with light. Merely to breathe was a joy. When her eyes became accustomed to the brightness of the sea-sparkled daylight, she began to notice how the landscape had lost its brooding, wintry grayness. Green seemed to be bursting forth everywhere. The woodlands along the estuary were vibrant with life. Dark-leaved rhododendrons of tremendous size had burst into blatantly brilliant bloom. Primroses and violets peeped out, waving their little flags of color in the breeze. She found her eyes drawn as often to the land as to the sea.

It was difficult to maintain her feeling of desolation in the midst of such joyous signs of rebirth and hope. Nature's annual miracle had a remarkably healing effect on her spirits, and she spent her days in almost cheerful tranquillity. She helped Mrs. Penloe and Gwinnys clean and freshen the rooms for the coming season. She set about, with the help of Will and Jemmy, to clear the gardens of their tangle of overgrowth and winter destruction. She rode the little mare along the path near the cliffs, with the spring breezes whipping her hair and brightening her cheeks. It was only late at night (when she couldn't control her thoughts) or during the cold evenings (when she sought the warmth of the kitchen fireplace and the company of the Penloes) that she permitted herself to think of Harry.

She had been welcomed by the Penloes with all the warmth that had been lacking when she'd arrived the first time. If they wondered at her pallor or her tendency to fall into pensive silences at unexpected times, they gave no sign of curiosity. But Mrs. Penloe was insatiable in her desire for news of "Master Harry," and Nell's tales of his London successes and his impending marriage filled her with delight. Nell's account of his triumphant entrance on the night of the Mannings' rout-party pleased Mrs. Penloe so much that she asked to hear the details over and over. Repeatedly Nell was asked to describe what he wore, how he'd looked, the fine folk to whom he'd spoken, how he'd crossed the entrance hall, how he'd gone up the stairs, how Miss Manning had greeted him, and how he'd become as admired and sought-after as he deserved to be.

Nell enjoyed relating the stories as much as the Penloes enjoyed hearing them, but as the days passed and June came near, her awareness of the swift approach of Harry's wedding day gave her increasing pain. Some nights, when sleep was slow in coming, she would remember the night in London when she'd gone to his room and they had clung together in despair. "If only I could tell you—" he whispered. Tell her what? That he loved her? She had believed it to be true, for a while. But if it were true, how could he permit himself to drift into a marriage with Edwina Manning? Roddy had spoken of honor, but even a gentleman of honor could find a way to cry off if he truly wished to.

She had not had the temerity to suggest to him that he could, if he chose, find a way out of his predicament. But she *had* sent him the key. It had been a foolish, impulsive act which now made her writhe in anguish and shame. He had not doubt found in it more evidence that she was brazen and vulgar. He didn't really love her. Those words he'd whispered into her ear probably had some other significance. She had been here for almost a month, and he'd not followed. He had sent no message to inquire about her whereabouts or her safety. Her dreams that he would come riding to her rescue were nothing but childish imaginings. She tried to school herself to push them aside.

June came in with a rainstorm as vehement and furious as any she'd experienced during the last autumn. The wind howled at the windows and down the chimneys as if it wanted to tear the building down. "Listen to *that* will 'ee?" Gwinnys muttered, adding a log to the fire in Nell's bedroom as Nell prepared for bed. "The wind's too angalish, I mind."

"Angalish?" Nell asked, having become attracted to the Cornish customs and language and eager to learn as much as she could. "Wait, don't tell me. Let me guess. Does it mean *angry*?"

"More like ... er ... cruel or vicious, I seem," Gwinnys said with puckered brow. She rose from the fire, brushed off her apron and turned to Nell with a possessive motherliness. "You'll be needin' a warmer nightdress, Miss Nell. Here, let me help 'ee."

After putting her mistress in a proper nightdress and

cap, and all but tucking her into bed like a babe, Gwinnys went to the door. "I be just down the hall, y'know, Miss Nell, if 'ee have need o' me."

Nell made a face at her. "Why would I have need of you, you goose?"

Gwinnys shrugged. "A wind like this'n is like to make one *nag-ridden*."

"Very well, if I'm troubled by nightmares, I'll be sure to call you," Nell promised, blowing out her candle.

Late that night, when the sound of thumping footsteps and the rattle of chains penetrated her dreams, Nell scolded herself in her sleep. "Gwinnys was right—I'm nag-ridden," she told herself. "I'm having nightmares, I suppose. He is *not* coming. There *is no ghost*. He is *not coming*!" But the sound persisted, and a sudden, loud crash caused her to sit up abruptly, her heart pounding so heavily in her chest that she could scarcely breathe. *"H-Harry?"* she whispered into the darkness, too wary of the pain of disappointment to permit herself to believe what she'd heard.

There was a moment of silence and she was almost convinced that it had been the wind that awakened her, when a flicker of light appeared behind the curtains and she distinctly heard a low, lugubrious moan. She pressed her trembling hands against her ears. "No, it *c-can't* be!" she told herself sternly. Another low moan reached her ears—she *couldn't* have mistaken it. "Harry, is it . . . *you*?" she asked urgently.

"I find that a most troublesome question," his voice responded. "Have you given keys to anyone *else*, you disreputable wench?"

She gave a gasping laugh. "Oh, Harry, you've *come*!" Choked with tears, she dropped her head in her hands. "I was so afraid—! I didn't dare *hope*—!"

"Madam!" Harry declared in mock severity. "Do you mean to imply that you doubted Harry D'Espry? That you imagined he would permit a trespasser to sleep *unmolested* in his bedroom?"

She lifted her head, her eyes shining, her cheeks sparkling with tears, and smiled tremulously. "Well, I did *hope* he would not leave me unmolested," she admitted.

He laughed joyously. "You *are* a shameless baggage, as half of London describes you."

"Do they, Harry?" she asked soberly.

"I'm afraid so. Four broken engagements! Shocking!"

"Were *you* shocked?"

"You *do* seem to be full of foolish questions tonight, girl. You know perfectly well that I prayed for nothing less. Your *last* jilt pleased me beyond words."

"I'm glad you were pleased." She paused and looked toward the glow beyond the curtains with her heart in her eyes. "And what is London saying of *you,* Harry?"

"They are extremely sorry for me. Miss Manning cried off, you see."

Her breath caught sharply in her throat. "*She* cried off? I don't believe it!"

"It's quite true, though. You see, my love, although society proved not quite as callous and superficial as *I* anticipated, it was a bit more so than *you* believed. Miss Manning, for example, came to realize that she could not live with my 'imperfection.'"

"I don't know what you're talking about, Harry. *What* imperfection?"

"Oh, my *sweet* Nell!" Harry sighed. "You are always a surprise and a delight to me. I was speaking of my missing leg, of course."

"But that's ridiculous! Edwina was not *at all* disturbed by it!"

"That was true only at first. But after you left, my dear, I began to stumble a great deal—"

"Stumble! Oh, Harry!" she cried in concern. She fumblingly struck a match and lit her bedside candle to take a look at him. But he was not visible.

"Don't be alarmed, my dear. It was only a pretense on my part."

"A pretense? I don't understand. Why?"

"Well, I realized that I'd been mistaken in putting my best foot forward, so to speak. I had done just what I'd accused society of doing—covering up and masking over all the illnesses, difficulties, deformities and problems. I'd hidden my crutch, mastered the use of a cane because it was less suggestive of infirmity, and kept my awkwardnesses, difficulties and pains well hidden. But my sham became a trap. I found myself imprisoned in a world of pretense and affectation, knotted to a woman who had no understanding of infirmity, and about to lose the one person with whom I could safely be myself."

"Oh, Harry, not *Roddy*?" Nell asked in surprise.

"Not Roddy, you goose!" Harry said disgustedly. *"You!"*

"Oh!" Nell whispered, overwhelmed.

"So I set about to bring my imperfection into prominence. I stumbled about a bit and I carried my crutch in public. And, in very little time, Edwina cried off."

"Just because you stumbled?"

"Well, once I fell on my face."

"Harry, what a cruel trick! Gwinnys would call it *angalish*! What did you expect to gain by *that*?"

"What I *did* gain—my freedom."

Nell sat for a moment in shocked silence. "Edwina is nothing but a top-lofty, addle-brained, overweening, calculating, odious *worm*!" Nell said wrathfully.

"Edwina is a refined, cultivated, very beautiful young lady—"

"Oh—?" Nell interjected challengingly.

"—who quickly became (especially after I'd been forced to compare her with another beautiful young lady of my acquaintance) the greatest bore I'd ever known."

Nell made a little, self-satisfied sound, very much like a purr, and smiled glowingly at the light behind the curtains. "Does that mean you...you...truly...?"

"Yes, you ninny, I do. Truly! I love you to distraction, and tomorrow morning, as soon as you come down to breakfast, I intend to take you in my arms and show you just how much!"

"But... I can't *wait* for tomorrow morning! Harry, don't you intend to show yourself *tonight*?"

"Show myself? Do you mean make an appearance? I can't. I threw away that ghost-shirt long ago."

"I mean *come out*, you gudgeon!"

"Come *out*?" he asked in horrified disapproval. "Out *there*? Have you no *shame*, girl? We are not yet even betrothed!"

She gurgled. "That is a mere formality. In my view, you have already committed yourself irrevocably into my clutches."

"You don't say! May I not even try to cry off?" he pleaded.

"Not a man of *honor*, sir! You told me you were a gentleman! Harry, will you *please* come out?"

"Good God, woman, it's the middle of the night! This is your *bedroom*! Why, oh why did I not pay greater heed when they told me what an outrageous little baggage you are?"

She thrust aside the bedclothes and swung her legs over the side of the bed. "If you don't come out, my lord, I shall dash across this room and behind those curtains, and I shall undoubtedly be knocked senseless for my pains," she warned.

"Very well, ma'am, I'll come out if you insist," he said grudgingly, "but remember that Harry Thorne in the *flesh* can be a great deal more dangerous than Harry D'Espry in *spirit*."

The curtains were pulled aside, and Harry swung into the room on his crutch. As soon as he caught sight of her, sitting on the edge of the bed in her nightdress, her chestnut curls tousled, her eyes misty, her feet bare and swinging above the floor like a child's, he stopped short. His heart seemed to swell within him in an agony of tenderness.

Nell stared at him for a moment to make sure she

wasn't dreaming. But he was too clearly *there* to be an illusion. The white streak in his hair, the crutch he leaned upon, the warm, almost embarrassed shyness in his eyes, the slight smile—all gave evidence of his authentic actuality. With a little cry, she leapt from the bed and ran across the room. His crutch clattered to the floor as he held out his arms and caught her to his chest.

This was no illusion, no dream. She knew it with certainty at last. His heart pounding against hers was no illusion. The broad shoulder on which her head was pressed was no illusion. The grasp which crushed the breath from her body was no illusion. Was this frightening, dizzying happiness the *danger* to which he'd referred? How foolish men were! She knew as clearly as if she could read the future that, as long as his very real arms remained tightly clasped about her, there was no danger she could not face...

Gwinnys had thought she heard voices and was sure Miss Nell must have cried out in her sleep. "I knowed it—she be nag-ridden," Gwinnys thought, "with the wind rampin' on so." She got out of bed and pattered across the hall. Quietly, she pushed open Nell's door. For a moment she stood gawking, scarcely trusting her own eyes. Then she silently closed the door again and ran barefooted down the hall, darted down the stairs, raced across the kitchen and out across the back hall to the Penloes' rooms. Pounding on the door, in complete disregard of the time of night, she shouted exuberantly, "Mrs. Penloe, Mrs. Penloe, wait till 'ee hear! Y' cain't *conceit* what I just seen! I'd *lay* 'ee won't b'lieve me, but, oh, Mrs. Penloe, 'tis truly *arear*!"